Brass Carriages and Glass Hearts

Other Proper Romances
by Nancy Campbell Allen

My Fair Gentleman
Beauty and the Clockwork Beast
The Secret of the India Orchid
Kiss of the Spindle
The Lady in the Coppergate Tower

Brass Carriages and Glass Hearts

NANCY CAMPBELL ALLEN

Visit us at ShadowMountain.com

Library of Congress Cataloging-in-Publication Data
Names: Allen, Nancy Campbell, 1969– author.
Title: Brass carriages and glass hearts / Nancy Campbell Allen.
Other titles: Proper romance.
Description: Salt Lake City : Shadow Mountain, [2020] | Series: Proper romance | Summary: "Detective-Inspector Oliver Reed is assigned to guard social activist Emme O'Shea on her trip to Scotland where she will speak at an important summit on shifter rights, but getting her there safely will be a challenge—especially when the two of them realize they might be falling in love with each other"—Provided by publisher.
Identifiers: LCCN 2020002212 | ISBN 9781629727370 (trade paperback)
Subjects: LCSH: Man-woman relationships—Fiction. | Shapeshifting—Fiction. | Political activists—Fiction. | Cinderella (Tale)—Adaptations. | Scotland, setting. | LCGFT: Vampire fiction. | Romance fiction. | Steampunk fiction. | Detective and mystery fiction.
Classification: LCC PS3551.L39644 B73 2020 | DDC 813/.54—dc23
LC record available at https://lccn.loc.gov/2020002212

Printed in the United States of America
LSC Communications, Crawfordsville, IN

10 9 8 7 6 5 4 3 2 1

To my cousin Roy,
who has the most loving and pure heart I know

The prince approached her,
took her by the hand and danced
with her. He would dance with
no other maiden, and never let
loose of her hand, and if anyone
else came to invite her, he said,
"This is my partner."

—"CINDERELLA,"
THE BROTHERS GRIMM, 1857

Chapter 1

Emmeline Castle O'Shea stood at a podium on the balcony of the Municipal Hall for Citizen Affairs and looked out with satisfaction at the murmuring crowd, feeling the energy build in the large room as she finished speaking.

"We worked tirelessly for the repeal of the Predatory Shifter Extermination Act, which was not only unethical and cruel but grossly illegal, yet factions within the Predatory Shifter Regulations Committee are meeting tonight with plans to see it slyly reinstated!"

The crowd, which had begun as a midsize gathering of Shifter Rights advocates, had grown in numbers as curious passersby peeked in to see what sort of ruckus they were missing. And ruckus it would inevitably become. Such was the nature of the business.

Emme was not an advocate of rioting, not *usually*, but when social justice was slow to evolve, certain consequences naturally followed. As president of the London chapter of the Shifter Rights Organization, she was firm in her admonition that violence was permitted only in cases of self-defense and that destruction of property not belonging to members of the hated Committee was neither advocated nor condoned.

Those parameters left plenty of room for movement and interpretation, of course, and Emme was aware that each successive gathering and protest had the potential to turn ugly. *Her* people were professional and knew their rights and responsibilities, but she couldn't be responsible for the unruly fringe elements that often joined whenever the SRO mounted a protest. Some people rioted for the sake of rioting.

People streamed in through the side doors and the back of the large hall, and a sense of foreboding snaked up her spine. The constabulary were already gathering, and she knew that a certain member of the Yard would not be far behind.

Tonight's cause, however, could not be ignored.

Months ago, she'd demanded the repeal of the Extermination Act—the sanctioned murder of law-abiding citizens who happened to shape-shift into predatory animals three days each month—which had drawn the attention of the International Shifter Rights Organization. With the international body's support, and through a few influential members of Parliament, the London chapter had brought about legislation that should have seen a permanent end to the barbaric practice.

So when Emme had received word that the PSRC intended to resurrect the horrifying Act, her blood had boiled and she'd nearly cried with anger.

"We must not allow this travesty to again rear its hideous head!" Her voice carried over the crowd, and the familiar sensation of exuding energy flowed from her as her frustration built. "The Committee finishes their clandestine meeting in ten minutes across the square, and we will greet them with voices raised in unity! The rights of the marginalized among us will be upheld!"

A loud cheer swelled through the room, building in intensity as several of her fellow SRO members whistled and called for the crowd to follow them outside. Emme wiped a trickle of sweat from her temple and impatiently removed her stylish, brown top hat. It was a new Castles' Boutique creation, and her mother had added it to Emme's burgeoning accessory collection.

"Emme!" Veronica, the London SRO's vice president, beckoned from the far end of the balcony. "There are hundreds already outside! Come quickly!"

Emme smiled grimly and tossed the hat on an empty chair. Bigger crowds meant better exposure. The Committee's attempt at the underhanded maneuver would not be tolerated; it was simply unacceptable! The SRO and its supporters would be heard, make no mistake.

She slung the long strap of her bag over her shoulder and across her body as she ran down the stairs, navigating her way through the crowd. People moved aside or patted her on the back or shouted words of encouragement. She wore breeches, boots, and a matching blouse and outer corset that her mother had demanded she treat carefully as the material was the boutique's newest addition from the Orient. Hester Castle O'Shea insisted that Emme be impeccably dressed, even when wearing trousers, but her fussing efforts were lost on her daughter. Emme was rarely still, and she ruined her clothing more often than not.

The evening air was cool, and night was quickly descending on the square where the Predatory Shifter Regulations Committee had concluded their "clandestine" meeting. People spilled out of the hall and crossed the short distance to a row of government buildings.

Veronica found her and grabbed her hand, pulling her forward at a run. "I worry we'll not be able to control this one," Veronica shouted. "I've spied at least two ne'er-do-well gangs spoiling for a fight."

Emme winced as the crowd's energy pushed at her from all sides. She forced herself to block it out. She couldn't afford to be overwhelmed by it now.

"Law enforcement are already watching," she shouted back to Veronica. "Let us hope they'll manage them." *And leave us alone.* Emme finished her thought as she pictured one very angry detective-inspector who always, *always*, was on hand to interfere with her duties as London SRO president. Oliver Reed was the bane of her existence, and she ran faster toward the wagon situated across the street from the committee buildings. She must hurry if she wanted to make herself seen or heard outside before he arrived.

She clambered up on the empty wagon bed, pulling Veronica along with her. They were joined by three other SRO members, who flanked Emme on all sides. She waved her arms at the crowd.

"Steady!" she shouted. "We do not accost individuals!"

She looked over the crowd as night continued to close in and gas lamps flickered to light. The sheer size of the gathering would make the morning headlines, and she hoped their efforts would be rewarded with success. Then she spied several buckets of rotten vegetables and mentally apologized to her mother for the inevitable ruination of her custom material.

Constables emerged through the crowd and began erecting a temporary barricade to keep the crowd under control. Emme watched their efforts with skepticism but knew that many of them identified with the population gathered and thus were unlikely to be hurt or accosted. If they hadn't been present for official duty, they might well have been part of the protesting crowd.

The crowd suddenly roared and booed, and she whipped her attention to the building entrance. Bryce Randolph, the Committee chairman, was only just visible as members of his security detail guided him quickly to one of two carriages that had pulled alongside the curb.

Other Committee members emerged, and the crowd roared. Emme flinched involuntarily as refuse began to fly, winging across the square and thunking against the carriages, the street, and the buildings.

"Not part of our plan!" Veronica yelled as they ducked down.

She was right—it hadn't been part of their plan *this time*. The fact that they'd done it before, at carefully chosen venues and functions, seemed to lend permission for people to hurl garbage each time they protested *anywhere*.

"If we are separated," Emme shouted to the others in the wagon, "meet back at the offices."

"Suppose we are arrested again?" one of the others yelled.

Emme laughed breathlessly, dodging to avoid a rotten tomato that flew past her head to splatter on one of the carriages.

"Sit comfortably while I secure bail money," she shouted back. "Never fear, we've endured worse!"

The wagon tipped, nudged forward by the encroaching crowd. "Jump down," Emme ordered the others. "Try to get clear of the mess!"

She looked over her shoulder at the constables, who barely kept the protesters back. In the distance, a familiar figure caught her eye, running at a full sprint into the mayhem.

No! Detective-Inspector Reed would not haul her away this time.

She made certain the others had jumped down from the wagon before climbing to the edge, looking for a spot to slip down and away into the crowd.

The wagon lurched as the crowd surged again, and Emme knew a moment of fear for the people close by who were in danger of being crushed. She shouted to them to clear the way, and as the contraption was roughly jolted again, she lost her balance and fell to the ground.

She scrambled up, dusting her stinging palms, and looked around desperately. She was petite, and being so small in such a large crowd was an extreme disadvantage. Dodging elbows, shouts, shoves, and one soggy, flying cabbage, she edged toward the carriages.

Bryce Randolph had climbed inside, followed by his security and two other Committee members. He made eye contact with her, and smiled.

She saw red and heard roaring in her ears that had nothing to do with the crowd. Her rage grew until she thought she might choke on it.

Climbing up on the carriage's running board, she slapped

her palm flat against the window. "You will not do this, do you hear me? I will never rest! I will see you finished, Randolph!" She continued pounding on the window, gratified when the glass cracked and his smirk slipped. "This is not over! The International Organization has been notified, and *I will see you finished*!"

Food and foul-smelling refuse flew about her on all sides, and she appreciated the effort people seemed to be making to avoid hitting her with it. The crowd cheered her on, but just as she drew back her fist again, hoping to smash the window entirely and truly make an impression on the vile people inside, an arm clamped around her waist from behind and hauled her away.

"Miss O'Shea!"

"No!" she shrieked as she struggled against his hold. "Let me go, Detective!" She clutched at the carriage, grasping and missing as his other arm wrapped around her shoulders, pulling her against his chest, which she knew from experience was unyielding as an oak tree. "You have no idea what that cretin is attempting!"

"I have every idea," his low voice growled in her ear, "and you are not helping your cause! Cease immediately!"

"No!" Her anger spilled over as she struggled against his arms, and she finally opened her mouth wide to sink her teeth in.

"Do not even think about it!" He jerked his arm away as he dragged her along.

"Unhand me!"

"Miss O'Shea, you are under arrest—blast, do *not* bite me!"

With dizzying speed, he spun her around and hauled her up and over his shoulder, clamping one arm behind her thighs like a sack of potatoes, a move that had served him well multiple times in the past. He gripped her right wrist in his other hand, bending her arm at an impossible angle. When she tried to straighten up or wriggle free, he simply pulled on her arm. He had her trapped, and she knew it.

She pounded ineffectually on his back with her free fist and cursed herself for neglecting to have her cousin, Isla, teach her defensive maneuvers against such a predicament. Her nose bounced uncomfortably into his back as he shoved through the crowd. The mayhem escalated to a fever pitch. She turned her head to protect her smarting nose, and her breath was expelled in grunts as he began to jog.

"Put . . . me . . . down . . ." she managed.

"Emmeline O'Shea, you are hereby under arrest for instigating a riot and assault on government property," he ground out as he continued dodging and twisting through the crowd.

"I am about . . . to lose . . . my dinner," she shouted in spurts.

"Lose your dinner!" he shouted back. "I have another suit of clothing in my office!"

"You *live* in your cursed office . . . I wager!" She grunted. "No decent neighborhood . . . would . . . have you!"

He shouted something in return, but his words were lost as the crowd shifted, jostling them violently from the side and nearly sending them sprawling. He barked an order to a constable, and Emme saw a blue blur in her periphery before Reed turned a corner and slowed marginally.

He whistled through his teeth, and Emme heard the hiss

of steam and crank of gears signaling the arrival of one of the Yard's horseless brass carriages. The brightly polished brass body with its black ornamental fixtures set the vehicles apart from others and were easily recognizable as police conveyances.

Reed slowed and finally bent down, shifting her from his shoulder. Before she could secure her footing, however, he tossed her into the carriage with what sounded suspiciously like a curse. She landed on the worn, black upholstered seat with an inelegant thump, and the little air she'd managed to suck into her lungs was expelled in an equally inelegant grunt.

She breathed heavily and put a hand to her midsection, truly wondering if she were about to cast up her accounts. She leaned forward and looked out the open door, considering her odds of successfully slipping past Reed and escaping down an alley before he could catch her.

His hand clamped on the door, and she sat up straight.

"—follow with anyone else accosting either government property or individuals," he directed his officers. "I shall be at the cells."

The detective gave orders to the driver and climbed inside, sitting across from her and slamming the door so hard the glass rattled.

Emme clenched her jaw shut to keep from screaming, but her breathing was still too labored to comfortably manage through her nose. It was just as well, because she had plenty to say. "Detective, you have *no idea—*"

"Stop!" He held up a hand and froze her with a look. "Not. A. Word."

Emme's mouth dropped open. "You cannot keep me from speaking."

"I can, and I shall. Unruly prisoners are often gagged."

She froze him with a look of her own before turning her eyes to the world outside. The crowd's noise faded as they drove away, and soon the only sounds were the mechanics of the carriage. Her anger had gone from a bubbling inferno to a slow burn. "You have no idea what that man is trying to do."

"I know that man a sight better than you do, so do not lecture me. Furthermore, regardless of what he is trying to do, you cannot accost him in his carriage or do damage to government property. I should think you would know that by now!" His shout echoed through the vehicle. "How were you even privy to details about a clandestine government meeting?"

"I have a confidential informant."

He gaped. "You have a confidential informant? On the *inside*?"

She lifted her chin, defensive. "*You* do! You have an entire network of informants all over the city."

"Lady, I am a *detective*!"

"You have no heart! You are . . . you are *heartless*, Detective. You are a heartless detective with no concept of the suffering—"

She gestured angrily, and his gaze narrowed on her hand. His nostrils flared as he reached into his pocket. He withdrew a handkerchief and thrust it at her. "Your hand is bleeding."

She paused in her tirade and looked at her hand, which was smeared red. She frowned. "Tomato?" No. Once she forced herself to take a breath, she felt the pain in her palm and along the side of her hand where she'd pounded on Bryce Randolph's carriage window. She wanted to refuse Reed's offer, but the blood steadily dripped, so she snatched the cloth from his fingers and wrapped her hand with it.

Something caught on the fabric, and she sucked in a breath as another sharp pain pierced her hand. Unwinding the cloth, she saw a shard of glass imbedded in her skin. She pulled it out with shaking fingers, her energy wearing down to numb shock as the carriage rolled along the streets.

She sniffed in satisfaction. "I did break the glass."

She didn't look at the detective but imagined she could hear his teeth grinding. The sound of a ringing bell came from the bag she still had slung across her body, but when she reached for the opening, the detective lunged forward.

"What are you doing?"

"My telescriber," she enunciated as though he were a child. "I am going to see who has sent me a message. Perhaps it is news of the fete from which we bolted."

He leaned back in his seat but watched her, unsmiling, unsympathetic.

She reached again for her bag and slowly withdrew the handheld messaging device, holding it up dramatically. "May I check for messages?"

He eyed her evenly and eventually looked out the window. She glanced down at the device, intending to skim the message, then put it away for later perusal in private, but one line caught her eye. Her breath stuck in her throat, and she stared.

Her hands shook as she opened the scriber and pushed a button to scroll to the message, which was brief:

Miss O'Shea, pursuant to your recent interview with Signore Giancarlo, the International Shifter Rights Organization is pleased to offer you the position of Spokeswoman. We look forward to further discussion. Signore Giancarlo will arrive in London next week and shall contact you then. Congratulations! Please respond to acknowledge receipt of message . . .

She lifted a trembling hand to her mouth. She had interviewed for the Spokeswoman position, hoping so much to be hired that she'd hardly allowed herself to think about it. Were it not for the night's events, she'd probably have been sitting at home, staring at the device, willing it to ding.

I did it. I did it! Her eyes filmed over, and she quickly blinked back tears she refused to shed in the presence of That Man. That she was receiving the most glorious news of her life whilst riding in a carriage with Detective-Inspector Reed on her way to a jail cell was a cruel twist of fate, but she refused to allow the moment to be tarnished.

"Is something wrong?" he asked.

She looked up at him, searching for signs of mockery. He did not look pleased, or even friendly, but neither did he seem flippant. The tone seemed genuine enough.

"Nothing is wrong." She cleared her throat. "I've received good news."

The silence stretched between them. He was not about to ask for details, and she was not about to offer them. Her problem, however, was that she was bursting with excitement, fairly bouncing in her seat with it. After a day of despair and worry about the Committee and Bryce Randolph's nefarious intentions, the message was like receiving first prize. Now that she had even more of a voice, she could bring shifter injustices immediately to the international body as a colleague and peer.

"I interviewed for a position with the ISRO."

He raised a brow, which always smacked of condescension to her, and she hated it. "And you have been hired for it?"

She nodded and lifted her chin. "Spokeswoman."

The silence stretched again. He slowly nodded. "Apropos."

She cleared her throat. "Quite. This means I shall resign as the London chapter president and turn over my duties to Veronica Stein. She will be much less . . . troublesome for you, I imagine."

He didn't agree or disagree. His expression turned speculative, and it raised her hackles.

"What?" she demanded.

"You've amassed your share of enemies. You should take precautions; I imagine the list will grow."

"You—chief among them."

He sighed and rubbed a hand along his head. "I am not your enemy, Miss O'Shea."

She disagreed, but for the sake of her improved mood, she said nothing.

"At any rate, congratulations." He didn't smile but nodded once and then looked out the window again. "With any luck, this will be the last time I arrest you."

A million snappy replies sprang to her lips, but she held them back, with effort. She looked down again at the message and smiled. Her life was about to change; she felt it to her core.

Chapter 2

Ten months later

Emme stood in the breakfast room of her family's lovely London townhome in Charrington Square and stared at two pieces of mail. Both letters referenced the upcoming multinational event—the "Summit for Shifter Relations and Rights"—in Edinburgh, Scotland, and both messages had caused her heart to pound, but for vastly different reasons. The energy she could feel emanating from them was a frenetic mix of positive and negative, and it caught her by surprise. She'd not felt the intense waves unsolicited for a very long time, and rarely from inanimate objects. She mentally titled the two messages "Good Letter" and "Bad Letter."

"Emme?" Her mother, Hester, glanced over her shoulder as she dished up a plate from the side buffet. "Will you please come to the shop today? Summit week looms large on the horizon, and if you persist in avoiding fittings, the dresses will not be ready in time."

The letters trembled in Emme's hand, and she clasped

the papers tightly to still them. She swallowed, and when spots appeared before her eyes, she realized she was holding her breath. "I . . . of course. I've a meeting with Isla and shall stop by the boutique before my luncheon with *Signore* Giancarlo . . ." Her voice trailed off, and she made a concerted effort to draw in a measured breath and exhale slowly.

Lady O'Shea's attention snapped to her. "What is it? What's happened?"

"Nothing . . . well, good news!" Emme managed a smile and placed the Good Letter atop the other. "I've been awarded the final time segment to speak before the international body votes on the proposed accord at the end of Summit week."

Mrs. O'Shea's mouth dropped open. "Emmeline! Dearest, that is wonderful news! Your comments will be the last they hear before they decide whether or not to sign. Your gift for emotional appeal will surely bring about good results."

Her mother rushed to hug her with one arm, her other hand balancing a plate of eggs and croissants. "I am so proud." Her eyes filmed over, and Emme felt a surge of warmth. Focused attention from her mother was a rarity.

"Thank you, Mama. I confess, I am relieved. I—"

"And the other letter?" Hester grinned and released Emme's shoulders as she grabbed the paper from beneath the Good Letter. "Another invitation to an important event? Your schedule has been so full with meetings and dinners lately that I can hardly remember them all!"

"Mama, wait, I'm certain it's—"

Hester's eyes scanned the Bad Letter, and they widened as she gasped a horrified breath. Her plate hit the ground and bounced, scattering food across the thick Persian rug. She put her hand to her midsection and swayed.

"Mama!" Emme grabbed Hester, whose face was dangerously pale. "I will get to the root of this. I'll . . . I'll have Isla help me find the sender. Please do not fret—"

"Do not . . . do not *fret*? Emmeline, you cannot go to the Summit meeting, not now. Not after this!" Hester held the letter up and shook it.

"No, Mama, do you not see? The sender is a coward, someone who thinks to scare me away from the most monumental event in history concerning shifter rights!"

"I forbid it! The meeting will occur with or without you. There are others who can speak on the organization's behalf."

Emme opened her mouth to snap back but paused and inhaled, trying to control her racing heart. "Mama. I am the *spokeswoman* for the International Shifter Rights Organization. I have clawed my way past every barrier my enemies have set before me, and I will *not* be bullied."

Hester looked at Emme, eyes flashing, and called out, "Barnesworth! Have the Horseless Traveler brought 'round front. Emmeline and I are going out."

Movement at the door caught Emme's eye, and she noted her stepsister, Lysette, entering the drawing room with her usual pause for dramatic effect. Lysette was Emme's junior by three years but stood several inches taller than Emme's own five feet and two inches. Her stepsister's hair was blonde perfection, every curl in place, and she wore a lovely pale-pink ensemble that included a satin corset trimmed in silver ribbon.

"Why, Mother, what has happened?" Lysette's large blue

eyes flicked from Emme to Hester, and Emme's nostrils flared of their own volition.

"Nothing." Emme turned to her mother and lowered her voice. "I shall see to it. Please, leave it be for now."

Lysette floated to Hester's side and placed a hand on her arm. "What could possibly be causing such an uproar?"

Emme snatched the paper from her mother's hand. "My personal correspondence. Please do not concern yourself with it."

Ignoring Lysette, Hester grasped Emme's arm, shoved her toward the door, and out into the hall with surprising strength.

"Mama—"

"Not a word," Hester enunciated through tight lips. "Barnesworth!"

The butler automaton, humanlike in appearance and movement, appeared from the cloak room with their wraps. "My lady. The Traveler is nearly ready."

"Mama," Emme tried again as Barnesworth helped her mother and then her into her wrap. "I want you to think for a moment. You are rushing to judgment—"

"A fine thing for you to say, young lady—you who rush into absolutely everything!"

Emme frowned as Hester nudged her out the front door and down the short walk to the street. "Not two minutes ago you were praising me!" She knew she should have enjoyed the moment while it lasted.

Hester Castle O'Shea had built a small empire with her sister, Bella Castle Cooper, and Castles' Boutique was one of London's premier clothiers. She'd done so with determination and focus, traits now directed full blast at Emme.

"Mother, where are we going?" Emme took the 'ton driver's hand and climbed into the vehicle, scooting over when her mother charged in behind her.

Hester smacked the switch that alerted the driver to proceed and then looked at Emme, her lips tight. "To the Yard."

"Wh . . . *where*? Why?" Emme's heart thumped. "That is the last place I want to go!"

Hester glared at her. "Is Detective-Inspector Reed looking for you again?"

"He is always looking for me. Mama, that man thinks I am responsible for every crime in London."

"Nonsense. Though you cannot deny your past acts of mischief have not painted you in an innocent light." Hester flipped the Talk switch and shouted to the driver, "Go faster!"

Emme briefly closed her eyes. She gripped her mother's hand and looked into her tense face. "I am fine. I shall be safe. I can protect myself; do you not remember who my cousin is?" She smiled and squeezed her mother's fingers. "Isla has taught me how to fight like an East End pugilist."

Hester's scowl deepened. "I told Bella we left you children alone too much. I just . . . It was necessary to build the business when we were both widowed, and we hoped we were doing the right and proper thing to support you all."

"Come now, don't be silly. We all survived childhood and are none the worse for wear."

To define Emme's upbringing as "unconventional" would be apt. Her mother and aunt had poured every moment and shilling into creating the shop, and although nannies had come and gone, Emme's cousin, Isla, had been the one to truly take the reins and care for both Emme and Isla's young sister, Melody. Their good friend, Hazel Hughes, now Mrs. MacInnes, had rounded out the small group, and they had experienced much more freedom than many other young ladies did.

Her mother sighed and sat back in the cushioned seat as the Traveler wound its way into the heart of London. She retained her hold of Emme's hand and looked out the window, though Emme could clearly feel her mother's sense of guilt. Emme felt a familiar pang of resentment that not only had her mother been largely absent for years building the business, but then she'd married an odious, oafish man with multiple daughters, changing their family forever. Even so, she did not like to see Hester's sadness.

Emme was a young woman of twenty-three who had pushed her way into circumstances and pursuits that a more attentive mother might have curtailed. Bittersweet though it was, her mother's inattention had provided benefits that far outweighed any negative consequence.

Of all the times for Hester to tighten the parental reins. Once they were actually at the Yard, Emme would have to diffuse her mother's panic, downplay the emergency, perhaps slip the threatening letter away from her mother and conveniently lose it. She wasn't stupid, however. The letter was a clear and graphic threat on her life, making sinister reference to the Ripper's handiwork and describing in detail exactly where Emme's bedroom was and what it looked like.

But Emmeline Castle O'Shea had been fighting her own battles for a long time; she was not in unfamiliar territory. She would simply make time for daily practice with the ray gun.

A neatly folded copy of the morning's largest newspaper

sat in the door compartment, and she opened it, hoping to find something that would distract Hester. Regrettably, the headline was not one inclined to aid Emme's cause.

Three Bodies Discovered in Edinburgh Alleyway Indicate Deliberate Attack

She scanned the article, but before she could refold the paper and set it aside, Hester grabbed it. Her lips thinned, small lines forming around her mouth, and Emme braced for another blast.

"That makes twelve murders over the last three Full Moon Phases, Emmeline, and all bear signs of a predatory shifter attack!" Hester glared at Emme as though she were the responsible party.

"Mama, they cannot possibly say for certain."

Hester rattled the paper in Emme's direction and read, "'Most certainly the work of human shifters, given clues left at the scene and autopsy findings.'"

Emme winced. The recent attacks on innocents over the last few months seemed to be the result of increased mayhem propagated by both predatory shifters and vampires. Emme thought it was all too coincidental and said as much. "Mother, do you not find it odd that we are witnessing an uptick in attacks just before the Summit meetings? It flies in the face of logic to assume a human shifter would oppose friendlier legislation. Why, if he were a murdering fiend, a broader acceptance of his kind might increase his opportunities."

"I know you are an advocate for the innocent, Emmeline, but perhaps we are putting ourselves in danger by—"

"Oh, Mother, not you too! We cannot deny people their rights simply because there may be a few bad members of their group who abuse them. We may as well lock ourselves up, then. Heaven knows there are plenty of bad humans—humans who do not Shift into animals but simply harbor an evil we might all potentially possess."

Hester's eyes were glossy with tears, and Emme realized she'd unleashed the whole of her emotion into the carriage with her appeal. The air felt thick with it, and Emme had no desire to make her mother cry. She gently took Hester's hand into her own. "We mustn't be ruled by fear. Much of this is hysteria concocted by the few who wish to control the many."

"Emmeline."

"Mama?"

"Do not attempt to control my emotions when I am simply looking after your safety."

"I wasn't trying to control anything, I—"

The Traveler lurched to a stop by the tall building alongside the Thames, and before Emme could draw a decent breath, Hester yanked her from the vehicle and marched her up the wide steps and inside the building.

"We require an immediate audience with Chief-Inspector Conley," Hester told the young officer at a desk.

The constable looked at her in surprise. He was young, and his uniform looked new and crisp. The name on his badge read "Brinley."

You poor, poor boy, Emme wanted to say.

"I regret the Chief-Inspector is occupied at the moment." Brinley's open face showed regret. "May I take your name, madam? Perhaps later—"

"We will see him now. Either you interrupt him, or I shall."

"But . . . but, madam—"

"You may tell him Lady Ronald O'Shea requires an immediate audience. He will recognize my name, as Castles' recently donated a generous sum of money to the Metropolitan Police's uniform fund."

Emme closed her eyes and quietly exhaled. "Mother."

"Emmeline."

Emme smiled tightly at the young man. "We shall schedule an appointment for next week." That might buy her enough time to insure her mother forgot the matter entirely.

It was not to be. "We shall meet with the Chief-Inspector *now*."

Brinley cleared his throat, his cheeks red, and hurried to the door behind his desk. He knocked quietly, keeping one eye on Emme's mother. A muffled command came from within, and he opened the door and murmured something inside.

Almost immediately, two gentlemen in suits left the Chief-Inspector's office looking befuddled, followed by a taller man impeccably dressed in dark attire that matched his black hair and dark eyes.

Emme sucked in a breath. Nigel Crowe? If she had a nemesis other than Detective-Inspector Reed, it was Mr. Crowe, former member of the Predatory Shifter Regulations Committee. She had come up against him and his cold disregard for the shifter community time and again during her crusade, though she'd not seen him for months, not since he'd returned from Port Lucy with Isla and Daniel. He'd been in

London for a short time and now, regrettably, appeared to be back.

Isla insisted Nigel was a changed man, but when he saw Emme now, he blinked in surprise before his face settled into its customary judgmental perusal. He stopped before Emme and her mother and offered a short bow.

"Lady O'Shea, Miss O'Shea, a delight." His tone indicated otherwise.

"Likewise, Mr. . . ." Hester searched for his name.

"Crowe," Emme supplied. "You've returned. A short visit, I hope?" She caught her mother's glance from her peripheral vision. "I presume," she amended.

Mr. Crowe's lips twitched so slightly she might have missed it had she blinked, but it was the closest thing she'd ever seen to humor in the man. "I plan to remain for a time. I have work to finish here."

"What sort of work is that, Mr. Crowe?" Hester asked.

He flicked his attention to Emme's mother. "I am resuming my former position on a government committee."

Emme felt heat rise from her middle and feared it would explode out of her ears. He was returning to the PSRC? So much for Isla's claims about his change of heart. "Your timing is impeccable, Mr. Crowe. You're just in time for the Summit in Edinburgh."

"Indeed. It promises to be extraordinary. Might I assume you will be in attendance for the activities?"

"Yes, the entire week," Emme snapped, just as her mother answered, "Not if I have anything to say about it."

Emme stared at Hester. "Mother, enough." She grasped

her elbow. "Let us please return home where we can discuss the matter privately. This visit is rash and unnecessary."

Hester planted her feet and refused to move.

Chief-Inspector Conley appeared in the doorway of his office. He managed a strained smile for Hester, and Emme fought the urge to bolt like a hunted fox. The Yard was the last place on earth she wanted to be. While she'd not done anything technically illegal in some time, her instinct to avoid the place had become so ingrained it was now second nature. That she'd also encountered Nigel Crowe was a scenario she imagined the fates would congratulate themselves for concocting for some time.

"Ladies." Mr. Crowe inclined his head and left.

"Lady O'Shea, has something happened?" The Chief-Inspector was a stocky man who held his own quite well in street altercations—Emme had witnessed it firsthand—but he also possessed diplomatic skills necessary in dealing with the public, specifically the overwrought public. He extended an arm. "Please, do come in."

"Thank you, Chief-Inspector," Hester said. "I am—I mean, we have . . . Something has indeed happened." Hester's lip trembled, and for the first time since reading the Bad Letter, some of her fury had faded, leaving only fear in its place. "Emmeline is to address the international body at the Summit, and someone is threatening her most horribly about it. I've told her she absolutely cannot attend, and furthermore, you must find the miscreant who wrote this thing and bring him to justice!"

CI Conley's brow lifted, and he tilted his head as he indicated two chairs, and then pulled his chair out from behind his desk to sit with them. His entire demeanor was suddenly alert, focused. "Tell me about the threat. It is written?"

Emme sighed, irritated that her heart began to thump as Hester handed over the Bad Letter. It was real now. The threat was now a tangible *thing* she couldn't dismiss or laugh away. The crude, horrible words on the page, the vile threats to her health and well-being, filled her thoughts as Conley quietly read the paper, his jaw tightening. Her knee bounced, just the tiniest bit, and a shudder spread from it until she shook as though she were outside in the cold. Her mother looked at her, eyes liquid, now aware that Emme wasn't unaffected. Emme stood, unable to remain in the chair, shivering for no good reason. The office was plenty warm.

CI Conley quietly went to the door and murmured something to Brinley. Emme heard the name "Reed."

She snapped her attention to Conley. "What was that?"

He glanced at her in surprise but did not offer a response, nor was she in a position to demand one. He resumed his seat next to Hester.

Emme paced to the window and folded her arms across her middle, rubbing them briskly. *For goodness' sake, pull yourself together.* She gritted her teeth and looked down onto the busy autumn day below. She could not afford to show the slightest weakness in front of her mother, or Conley either. Anyone with the power to hinder or halt her efforts to attend the Summit must not see an ounce of falter in her resolve. It was too important, and she had worked too diligently, sacrificed too much.

The room was quiet. She breathed softly and then turned around. "Mother, Chief-Inspector, while I agree this letter is vile in the extreme, I will not allow it to prevent me from attending the Summit. I have appointments to meet personally with diplomats from several key states, and I have just received word I will address the assembly directly before the culminating midnight votes." She looked at Hester. "Mama, you know I will go. I will do whatever I must, but I would rather not be forced to sneak away on foot under the cover of darkness. Please do not make this difficult for me."

Conley smiled and covered it partially with his finger as he rubbed his lip and sat back in his chair. "Miss O'Shea, I believe you would do just that. I cannot pretend to approve of everything you've organized through the years—the protests disrupting traffic, whipping crowds into a frenzy outside government offices, chaining yourself to wheels of certain PSRC members' carriages to draw attention to the cause, orchestrating the tampering with government vehicles—"

Hester gasped. "Government vehicles? Emme! Why was I not aware—"

Conley glanced at Hester and shook his head. "No harm done, and no evidence directly connecting your daughter to the incident—"

"That's right," Emme interrupted but stopped when Conley shot her a dark look.

"My point is, I understand the concern, and given your level of involvement at the Summit, I do not take this threat idly. Is it the only one you've received?"

Emme hesitated. "It's the most *recent* one."

"What?" Hester's eyes popped.

"I've received rude mail on occasion, but not like this. This is the only one of such magnitude." Emme chewed the inside of her lip. She ought not to have said anything about the other letters. "Mama, I believe we've taken enough of the Chief-Inspector's time. He is aware of the issue, and we shall all be vigilant."

"Absolutely not," her mother spat out. "This morning has become more horrifying as time has passed. I am not leaving here without guaranteed protection for you."

"Mother, that is—"

A quiet knock sounded on the door before it cracked open. Detective-Inspector Reed stood at the threshold, his eyes widening in surprise.

Conley beckoned Reed inside, and Emme's heart tripped over itself in mortified consternation. Of all people to witness the current spectacle!

"Detective," Conley said, standing and handing him the Bad Letter. "An issue of concern has arisen, and I would have your involvement in the matter."

"Surely not—" Emme began.

"Emmeline!" Hester's sharp command surprised her into silence.

Reed looked at Hester and then at Emme as he took the Bad Letter. He gave the paper his attention, and despite herself, Emme watched his face as he read. His features tightened as his eyes scanned the letter, and a muscle worked in his jaw.

"When was this delivered?" he asked Emme, giving her his full regard.

She cleared her throat, intensely uncomfortable. "Less than an hour ago."

"By special messenger or regular post?"

"Regular post." She fought to keep the worry she felt

from showing on her face, but hiding her feelings was not her strong suit. She looked out the window again at the city below, aware that the three others in the room held immense power to keep her from the Summit. Perhaps that had been the letter writer's plan all along.

"Lady O'Shea," Conley said, "with your approval, Detective-Inspector Reed and I will confer as to the best course of action. Will you be available this evening at home for further consultation?"

Hester nodded. "Chief-Inspector, you have my eternal gratitude. And my apologies about the government vehicles and sabotage. I'd no idea her behavior—" Hester glanced over her shoulder and lowered her voice. "I was not nearly attentive enough when she was young, regrettably, and although now Emme is a woman of twenty-three, she hasn't a husband to keep her in check, or a father, really, as my husband has never been the sort to be, well, *fatherly* to her—"

"I am standing right here," Emme muttered and turned from the window. It had been some time since her mother had explained away Emme's behavior to another, and she'd forgotten how it made the tips of her ears burn. Detective-Inspector Reed glanced at her with a hint of pity, which only added to the deep sense of shame she was surprised she still felt after all these years.

"Mama, I have a full schedule today. I shall hail a cab and meet you at home. Chief-Inspector, Detective-Inspector, thank you both for your time." She inclined her head and made her way to the door.

"Wait, Emmeline, we shall ride together." Hester stood

suddenly and would have toppled back into her seat if Conley had not caught her arm.

Emme left the office and the thick air of concern filling it, taking a deep breath and fighting the urge to exit the building at a run.

The outer area was a hive of industry where typewriters clacked, 'tons filed paperwork, and detectives and constables went about their work, talking, laughing, and conferring. She dimly registered her mother bidding Conley farewell, but as they approached the stairs to descend, Conley called out to her.

She turned and waited, noting Detective-Inspector Reed standing at Conley's door. His hands were in his pockets, and he watched her, expression speculative, assessing, giving nothing away. As usual.

Conley reached her and extended his hand. She took it, and he said, "Miss O'Shea, I understand your desire to shrug aside this threat, but I would urge caution." He placed his hand atop hers and gave a gentle squeeze. "Be circumspect and vigilant, but rest assured I shall do all in my power to see you safely and successfully through the Summit."

She was touched by the sincerity in his voice and dared to hope he might convince Hester to step aside and allow Emme's activities to proceed.

"Many thanks, Chief-Inspector." She smiled, trying to appear calm but knowing her cold hand was likely betraying her anxiety. "I look forward to your visit this evening," she lied, choking out the words and worrying her smile was becoming a grimace. She stopped just short of suggesting he make the visit alone, glancing again at Reed, who now stood at Brinley's desk, still holding the Bad Letter.

He said something to Brinley, who nodded and fished in his desk drawer for what looked like a sheet of vellum. It proved to be two sheets, as Reed slipped the letter between them. Emme swallowed. They would send it to fingermark experts who would undoubtedly try to discern any prints in addition to hers, Hester's, Conley's, or Reed's. They would eliminate hers readily enough, as she'd had her fingermarks printed and filed on more than one occasion. Hester would need to offer a sample, but Emme wasn't about to suggest it. She suddenly felt that if she didn't escape the building immediately, she would scream and run up and down the halls like a madwoman.

Conley released her hand and nodded to Hester before turning away. Hester took Emme's elbow with a hand that trembled, but firmed her grip and marched the both of them down the stairs.

Emme made a concerted effort to not look over her shoulder at the men who were about to determine her fate and her future for the coming days. That one of those men was her greatest foe caused her almost as much concern as the threatening letter he held in his hand. Uncertainty settled into her stomach as Hester ushered her outside and into their waiting coach.

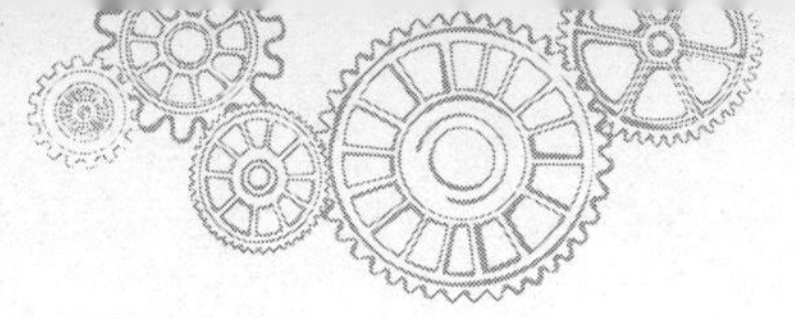

Chapter 3

As evening approached, Oliver Reed joined Chief-Inspector Conley outside the front steps of the Yard. Conley had asked him to take on the role of Miss O'Shea's bodyguard, and Oliver had agreed—reluctantly. He'd turned his excuses around in his mind all day but consistently returned to the initial conclusion: she would shake off anyone else at the first suggestion of something she'd prefer not to do. He was likely the only man in all of London with a will iron enough to match hers.

Perhaps his internal disquiet was due to the suddenness of the change, the urgency of the situation. He and Conley made their way outside to one of the Yard's sturdy and functional carriage-and-'ton-driver combinations. Brinley and another young officer, Constable Tyler, joined them, and the four men climbed inside.

"I've not had time to formulate even a rudimentary plan," Oliver told Conley as the carriage pulled away from the curb and bumped its way down the street. Autumn was upon the city, and while the summer had been quite warm, the wind had turned crisp. Rain fell more frequently, and rain gear was essential.

Conley nodded. "We'll solidify it in the next few days after we have more details about Miss O'Shea's scheduled appearances and responsibilities. We'll also need to include you in her travel itinerary and lodging arrangements. She'll have a maid with her, I presume, but, Oliver, you must remain near her at all times. I hesitate to mention it, but she's eluded you on more than one occasion. Perhaps she has no reason to do so now, but—"

"Perhaps she'll be afraid enough for life and limb now that it will not be an issue," Oliver interrupted.

Conley closed his mouth. Brinley and Tyler exchanged glances and looked anywhere but at Oliver, who took a quiet breath and muttered an apology. He looked out the small window at the gas lamps flickering to life. A light rain began to fall, clouding the images and turning the world to distorted shadows. He would be well-advised to visit Gentleman Maxwell's and put his agitation to good use in a boxing match.

The carriage wound its way through the streets, eventually pulling to a stop outside the O'Shea home. Stately and tall, it matched the others in Charrington Square, an area familiar to Oliver. One of his best friends, Dr. Samuel MacInnes, lived several doors down with his wife, Hazel. Oliver's parents were deceased, his sister lived on the coast, and his brother had become a sore spot, so Oliver's friends—Sam, Daniel Pickett, and Miles Blake—had become his family. The four of them had originally met when they served together in the military in India, under Oliver as their captain, and had remained close ever since.

Sam's recent marriage to Hazel meant that Oliver was now the only single man in their group, but he didn't care to see that status change anytime soon. Life was complicated, and was about to become even more so.

Oliver and the three other men stepped out of the carriage, through the rain, and into the O'Shea home, where a 'ton butler took their hats and overcoats. Voices drifted into the cavernous front hall from a room to the right, and the butler inclined his head.

"If you would, gentlemen, the drawing room." As he led them to the room, the noise grew in volume, and the voices distinguished themselves from one another.

"—concerns all of us, Mother, and to think that we would be excluded from any discussion on the matter is absurd and, frankly, insulting—"

A male voice chimed in, then an older female, but as Oliver listened to the din, he frowned. None of them was Emmeline herself, and having heard plenty of her voice, he would know it anywhere.

The butler breached the threshold and announced them to the family, and all conversation abruptly ceased.

Oliver entered behind Conley, noting the thick tension in the room. Sir Ronald O'Shea, Baron Tallywind, and Lady O'Shea were seated near the hearth with Sir Ronald's twin daughters—Lysette and Madeline. Apart from the group, standing near the double doors leading out to the garden, was Emmeline, her expression unreadable. That was odd; she was usually as easily read as a book. Her bearing was straight, arms folded back as though clasping her hands casually behind her. In the window's reflection, however, Oliver noted her tightly clenched fists.

Her eyes flicked to his, and she immediately dropped her arms to her sides and flexed her fingers. She cleared her throat and seemed to shake herself loose from the drama that swirled around the room. She stepped forward and folded her hands demurely before her, inclining her head. "Chief-Inspector Conley, Detective-Inspector Reed, good of you to visit. I believe, however, that the course of action concerning your involvement here has yet to be decided."

"My sister is sadly misrepresenting the facts." Lysette joined them in the middle of the room. Hers was a traditional beauty, and Oliver doubted there was a man alive who would deny it. She smiled at him, as she always did when he'd had occasion to visit the home looking for Emmeline only to find she had escaped his inquiry yet again. Lysette was always more than amenable to the prospect of playing hostess for him until her "errant, unruly sister" found her way back home.

He had seen enough of Lysette's practiced behavior to know she wielded it like a weapon. She was overt, as opposed to her twin, Madeline, who remained in the shadows, almost as if she would rather be invisible. Madeline's appearance was different; she was shorter, her hair darker. Her eyes, though, were a brilliant aqua. She shrank back into the sofa pillows even as Lysette demanded the room's attention.

Lysette glanced at Lady O'Shea and then focused her attention on Conley first, then settled on Oliver. "My mother seems to have forgotten she has several daughters, not one.

The youngest are safe at school, but the rest of us will be attending the festivities in Edinburgh, and we all require protection from this horrible person who wishes us harm."

"I imagine you will be safe, Lysette, as long as you distance yourself from any meetings of true substance," Emmeline said.

"I would hardly expect a bluestocking activist to understand that the truest threat will be to the family's most valuable asset." Lysette's blue eyes narrowed a fraction.

Oliver felt as though he were at a polo match. He ticked his glance back to Emmeline, whose lips twitched up on one side but otherwise remained impassive.

"Enough." Lady O'Shea made her way over to the two women and stood between them.

Sir Ronald followed her but stood awkwardly to the side. "Cease your bickering, girls," he said, and from the blank expressions pointed at him in response, it was clear he was attempting to present an authoritative image for the sake of their visitors.

Lady O'Shea cleared her throat. "Chief-Inspector, my initial request for Emmeline still remains, though I was remiss in considering the potential danger to the rest of the family."

"You see, of course," Lysette interrupted, looking at Oliver, "how an otherwise loving parent might appear to show favoritism by entrusting the safety of one daughter to the protection of the Yard's finest talent and leaving the others vulnerable."

Emmeline swept a hand toward Oliver without taking her eyes from Lysette. "They're all yours, dearest. I do not require round-the-clock nannies." She looked at her mother. "I appreciate your concern, Mama, but I have had the day to consider the matter, and I am convinced this morning's rush to judgment and mad flight to the Yard were an overreaction."

Lady O'Shea's eyes widened, and her mouth dropped open. "Emmeline, do you not remember that letter?" She moved to her daughter and grasped her arm. "I do. I remember every word." Her lips tightened, and she lowered her voice. Her profile was to him, but Oliver saw the sheen of tears gathering, and from Emmeline's uncomfortable expression, he assumed it was a rarity. "I will enlist the help of Daniel Pickett, then, and Isla."

Emmeline's eyes closed briefly, and she whispered, "Mama, *please*, let us discuss this later." She glanced around the room at the faces watching the drama continue. Constables Brinley and Tyler hovered behind Conley, quiet but riveted.

Conley cleared his throat. "Sir Ronald, with your permission, I should like to instruct my two constables to speak with your staff concerning one line in the message Miss Emmeline received, the one intimating that the sender is aware of your home's interior."

Sir Ronald frowned. "That is rubbish, surely."

"Nevertheless, several people work here at the house throughout the course of a day and are frequently in and out?"

O'Shea nodded. "Yes, but surely—"

"Papa," Lysette interrupted, "I believe the Chief-Inspector's suggestion is sound. Families of our stature do bear the burden of multiple servants. Why, on any given day, there are several I'm sure I don't know."

"True enough, Lyssie. Very well, Chief-Inspector, your men may question the staff."

"Barnesworth." Lady O'Shea motioned to the butler, who stood at the doorway. "Show the constables to the kitchen and introduce them to Mrs. Stanway. She will direct them further."

Brinley and Tyler awaited a nod from Conley, then followed the butler from the room.

Lysette looked at Emmeline. "The sender may be one of your associates. They are unseemly, and he could be one of hundreds. It really is beyond the pale of you, Emmeline, to carry on to the point that you endanger us all."

Emmeline looked at her sister flatly. "To my knowledge, any threats sent to this house have been addressed to me, Lysette, so you needn't worry about your own safety."

Lysette's eyes widened. "Emmeline, someone is aware of the layout of this house! How can you possibly be so selfish?" She turned to Conley and Oliver. "Surely you understand my perspective." Her pretty blue eyes clouded, and Oliver felt a flash of irritation. He did not appreciate emotional manipulation.

He had seen enough. He looked at Conley with a nod and spoke for them. "Sir Ronald, Lady O'Shea, I would ask your permission for a word alone with your daughter." He pointedly looked at Emmeline. "This one."

Lady O'Shea swallowed and blinked at him. She finally nodded and released her death grip on Emmeline's arm.

"Detective-Inspector Reed." Lysette moved closer. "I hope you'll not dismiss my earlier comments. My safety must also be considered. And Madeline's."

Oliver nodded amiably. “Of course, of course.” He clapped his hand on Conley’s shoulder. “I’ll leave you in the capable hands of my superior to discuss it while I have a word with your sister.”

Conley turned his head toward Oliver, and Oliver gave his shoulder a squeeze before releasing it with a friendly slap.

“Mr. Reed,” Emmeline said, picking up his cue, “perhaps you’ll join me in the library. We’ll leave the Chief-Inspector here to discuss the matter with the others. My itinerary in Scotland will be different from theirs, and we will seldom cross paths.” Without waiting to see if he followed her, she left the room.

Oliver, his back to the others, winked at Conley before following Emmeline across the hall into a richly appointed library with warm tones, leather-bound books, and furniture. Globes and maps covered the tables and walls, and sconces lit each corner. A fire blazed warmly in the hearth, and it was blissfully, peacefully quiet.

Emmeline took a deep breath and blew it out softly. She seemed to appreciate the peace, too, but she wasn’t still. She paced silently across the hearth, hands on her hips, for a long time without looking at him. She was dressed in a dark skirt and emerald-green corset that defined a trim torso. Long white sleeves came to a lacy point on the back of her hands, her fingers splayed across her waist.

Oliver studied her carefully, taking advantage of the unguarded moment. What he knew of Emmeline O’Shea stemmed from things he’d gleaned observing her in social settings, usually while she was marching for her cause, which was protecting and advocating for the rights of the shape-shifting population. She was a tireless champion for those unjustly persecuted—especially predatory shifters—and he didn't fault her for that in the least. As a matter of point, he agreed with her. Where they differed was in approach. Tactics.

She disturbed the peace. She broke in, broke out, picketed, marched, yelled, chained herself to buildings, littered leaflets, and disrupted official meetings and gatherings. She was underfoot, in the way, either leading the charge or lending support.

His job was to maintain order. She disrupted it. She could whip a crowd into a well-meaning frenzy faster than anyone else, and he did not know how she did it.

The majority of his exchanges with her involved screaming, slapping, dragging, pulling, or shoving—actions mostly taken against him. Those pretty hands resting on her pretty hips usually came at him shaped like claws. This pensive woman who currently paced in the quiet room was not someone he'd met.

"I read your editorial piece in *The Times* last week." He approached slowly, hands in pockets the way he would when trying to disarm a skittish felon.

She stopped moving and looked at him, eyes wary.

He almost smiled. "It was very good."

She remained in one spot, still staring.

He took pity on her and returned them to familiar footing. "Will wonders never cease?" he murmured. "I have rendered Emmeline O'Shea speechless."

She scowled at him. "Thank you for the compliment of my editorial. I wasn't aware you approved of such ideas."

"I wholeheartedly support equality and decency for one and all. We differ on how best to achieve it."

She opened her mouth, then closed it and shook her head. "That is a discussion for another day. Detective, let us be honest with one another. You do not want this assignment, nor do I want you, or anyone, assigned to me. I have weapons—legal, as you are aware—and can defend myself if necessary. My mother overreacted, and I regret that this whole affair has become such an . . . affair."

He reached her side, and she did not retreat, which he grudgingly respected. He stood several inches taller than she, so she was forced to look up at him. She regarded him evenly, probably assuming he would jump at the chance to be absolved of the responsibility to see to her safety.

"You forget that I have read the letter," he said.

She swallowed, parted her lips as if to speak, but then stepped aside and sank into one of two chairs flanking the hearth. The firelight reflected on her face as she stared into the flames, chewing thoughtfully on the inside of her lip. "You were correct, of course, in your observation months ago in the police carriage. I am amassing an entire stable of enemies."

Oliver sat opposite and leaned toward her, bracing his elbows on his knees. "I've no doubt you can defend yourself. You and I have engaged in more tussles than I care to remember, and I've suffered my share of bruises; even then, I imagine you were using restraint. If not, it is a lie I'll choose to believe."

She laughed quietly, reluctantly, and closed her eyes.

"But, Emmeline—may I call you Emmeline?—I daresay

I've touched you with more familiarity than any other man in your life—"

Finally, a decent laugh, and even a blush. He ought to have known that little short of shocking her would disarm her.

"My friends call me Emme."

"You prefer I call you Emmeline, then, very well."

She rolled her eyes at him, but a corner of her mouth lifted.

"Regrettably, I have seen ugly things over the course of my career. The malice in the letter you received is . . . extreme."

She exhaled, and her knee bounced restlessly. She looked deflated, and for all that she usually drove him mad with frustration, he did not like seeing her that way. "It is sobering to realize someone hates me so very much."

"Someone hates your *cause* very much, hates the shifter community, and likely realizes your voice has grown powerful. I doubt you would have received such a threat otherwise."

"But why, after all this time? I have been so involved, devoted, for years." She looked at him in bafflement, green eyes wide and fringed with dark lashes that matched the midnight blackness of her hair.

"Perhaps they read your editorial as well, Spokeswoman O'Shea. Your voice is a powerful one, and you are about to address the world. Chief-Inspector Conley has asked that I fill the role of bodyguard for you."

Chapter 4

Emme tried not to stare at the man sitting across from her. Detective-Inspector Reed was to be her *bodyguard*? He was treating her nicely, which meant he'd already begun the role. And that could mean only one thing: the threatening letter was truly as awful as she'd feared, though she'd tried to convince herself otherwise.

If only Reed would simply return to his usual, horrible self, her life could resume its normal rhythm and flow. Certain things should be predictable, constant. She should be able to count on the reliability of the detective's rotten timing and interference in every meaningful event she planned.

Emme was nothing if not honest. "You're treating me kindly, and I find it quite off-putting."

He raised a brow. "Do you doubt my sincerity?"

Emme sighed. "No, I believe you are sincere. If you would behave toward me as you customarily do, then I could dismiss the severity of that blasted letter and be on my merry way."

He was quiet, and she glanced at him. His lips twitched in a smile. "How do I customarily behave toward you?"

"With complete and utter contempt."

Something quickly crossed his features but was gone before she could identify it. "I have certainly never felt contempt for you. My apologies."

She nodded stiffly, knowing the polite thing would be to also apologize for any discomfort she may have caused. "I . . . apologize for bruising you—your person—in any past . . . altercations."

"Accepted."

Silence stretched between them, and Emme stilled her bouncing knee with effort. If there was one trait she appreciated about the detective, it was that he was skilled at holding his emotions in check. All indications as to his frame of mind she gleaned from the emotions he allowed to cross his face. On rare occasion, she'd seen his eyes blaze so hotly at her in frustration she would not have been surprised had flames shot from his eye sockets. There had been occasions when his frustration had spilled over and rushed at her, but for the most part, he kept himself pulled together. Professional.

As a child, she'd realized she felt people's emotions as energy, occasionally seeing visual auras, and the sensations were overwhelming. When nobody seemed to understand what she was talking about, she'd figured out a solution on her own. She'd learned to turn the phenomenon off, rather like flipping a Tesla lamp switch or closing a door.

She'd practiced controlling it and usually managed to keep the emotional assaults at bay. On the odd occasion when faced with a person she found difficult to assess, someone like the detective, she cracked open the door slightly for a glimpse of intuition, but never more than a glimpse. The risk of the door swinging wide open and leaving her overwhelmed and panicked was significant enough that she avoided it as a rule.

Since her appointment as the International Shifter Rights Organization spokeswoman, the onslaught of intense emotion had begun seeping from under the closed door; the Bad Letter had only made it worse. She suspected the reason was connected to her stress levels, but there was much at stake, and she couldn't afford the lapse.

She was tired and wanted to retreat to her bedroom, where she could remove her shoes and sprawl across her bed while scribbling lists in her journal. She was mostly prepared for her journey north but still had a few details to attend to, and she was extremely displeased that forces outside her control were dictating her actions. Because of the Bad Letter, Detective-Inspector Reed had landed directly, literally, in her path, and now the most exciting event of her life would be marred by his presence *the entire time.* At least, she consoled herself, she had the next few days to herself.

"I'm curious about the date selection for the week of the meetings," he said, interrupting her thoughts. "The fact that the full moon hits toward the end—it is symbolic or happenstance?"

She nodded. "Many people have wondered. Initially, it was happenstance, but once the organizers realized it, they embraced it. Many lodging houses and hotels have added features to accommodate shifters for those needing it. The hope is that the cause's point will be proven—that even in the midst of a huge festival during the full moon, shifters are not to be feared." She paused. "While every eventuality has been addressed and readdressed, I confess unease at the thought of what others might do to exploit the timing."

"Are you imagining anything specific?"

She frowned. "No, I suppose I have become jaded the past few years. I've met many who are not to be trusted."

He nodded, pursing his lips. "In certain circles, caution is never wasted. I should think it unwise to be oblivious to potential trouble."

"Security forces will be present everywhere, at all times, and we have the comfort of knowing safety is paramount." She shook her head. "So many countries represented, all gathered in one place—sometimes it seems like a recipe for disaster."

Silence hung heavy for a moment, then Detective-Inspector Reed shifted in his seat. "I will require a copy of your travel itinerary and schedule of activities during the Summit."

She swallowed. She would be civil, and she would be grateful. Perhaps he would blend into whatever woodwork they found themselves near and she wouldn't even be aware of his constant, looming, disapproving, judgmental presence. "Of course. I'll have a packet of information ready for you tomorrow."

"Excellent." He withdrew a small notebook and pen from his pocket. "And your schedule for tomorrow?"

She blinked. "I shall have the information delivered to you at the Yard, or to any address you prefer, Detective-Inspector. You needn't bother retrieving it here."

He smiled, pen poised. "I require your schedule for security purposes. I've cleared my calendaring to accommodate yours."

"You've . . . but . . . already?" She made an effort not to raise her voice. "We do not leave for a few days. I fear you have inconvenienced yourself unnecessarily." She smiled, feeling patient and amiable. "Do not bother yourself one moment before you must."

His smile remained, and she imagined he was also feeling quite patient and amiable. "I fear I am already several moments behind. You received the letter this morning."

"Sir." She clasped her hands in her lap. "Am I to understand you believe your duties extend to home care?"

"As it happens, Chief-Inspector Conley has arranged for round-the-clock surveillance of uniformed officers on the property, though I alone will accompany you whenever you leave the house." He paused and tapped his pen against the notebook. "Where will you be tomorrow, and when?"

"Mr. Reed, I do *not* require your presence at my mother's boutique for dress alterations."

"Time?"

She let out a frustrated sigh. "I cannot have you following me around all day."

"Why is that, Miss O'Shea? Do your plans include illegal activity?" He leaned forward again, notebook and pen hanging between his knees. She'd seen those intense brown eyes before in close quarters—usually while he was pulling her from illegally rigged scaffolding as she yelled into a megaphone. They were alone, now, in the quiet of her library, discussing his efforts to keep her safe. She was much more comfortable confronting him in a crowd.

She sat up straight and scowled. "Detective-Inspector, heaven knows that letter was a horrifying shock. Though I still believe my mother's reaction to it was premature, I am not an idiot. I certainly see the benefit of protection while I am in Scotland. Here, though? As I shop and dine with friends and attend meetings?"

"Can't imagine what I was thinking. Crimes are never committed in the city while one is shopping and dining with friends and attending meetings. Especially against one who has been specifically targeted and warned away from an event that *one is still obviously planning to attend.*" He maintained an even expression, but his jaw had tightened and his words became increasingly clipped.

She studied him openly. His face was an honest one, and—if *she* were being honest—a handsome one. Everything about him was efficient and lean: clean-shaven, strong cheekbones, well-defined jaw, straight nose, firm brow, and an air of quiet speculation around him that gave little indication of the nature of his thoughts.

He was principled and driven, and she knew from Daniel Pickett that Oliver Reed was one of few men he would trust with his life, and Isla's. Phrases from the Bad Letter floated through her thoughts, snippets of horrible words and threats, and despite herself, her shoulders slumped. She was suddenly weary. "Detective-Inspector Reed—"

"Oliver," he said quietly.

Her breath caught in her throat, and she paused. She scratched her temple with her fingertip, befuddled and painfully aware of it. She cleared her throat. "The odds of something happening to me before I arrive at the Summit are quite slim, and I believe you agree. Your superior has tasked you with an assignment, and you are duty bound to a fault.

In this instance, however, please know I genuinely do not wish to waste your valuable time. We can meet in Edinburgh in a few days. If the Chief-Inspector insists, you might turn your attention to Lysette. She seems quite eager for your attention." She paused, thinking. It was true, and she'd only tonight realized it. Lysette had seemed unusually interested in the detective.

He studied her for a prolonged moment and finally set his notebook and pen on the side table by his elbow. "Indulge me." He sat back in the chair. "Reflect on each instance our paths have crossed over the last two years."

She took a breath and pulled her brows together in thought. "Too numerous to count," she finally admitted. "Dozens, certainly."

Her nostrils flared as she reviewed moments in her memories when she'd been in the city, knee-deep in a cause-worthy scuffle, only to see him closing in upon her like one of the Four Horsemen of the Apocalypse. Without fail, she knew her time was up when she saw his face or felt his hands grabbing her from behind just as a surging crowd was about to truly stir up some mayhem. He constantly interfered, until she found herself—sometimes literally—screaming in frustration.

"With few exceptions," he said quietly, "I have been to nearly every public gathering and demonstration the local Shifter Rights Organization has sponsored because I agree with the foundational premise of the gatherings. I have only interfered when my duties as a detective have demanded it. What is the constant, Emme, at the end of every gathering? When chaos erupts, arrests are made, mobs dispersed, who is always there?"

She chewed on her lip, unwilling to answer his question but determined to keep her attention on his face when she would rather have looked safely away.

He leaned forward again, and, perched as she was on the edge of her seat, he suddenly felt very close. "*I* am the constant. I am always there. I never quit. Because I am there, because my men are there, you are able to say the things that must be said and then live to do so again another day."

The intensity of his voice vibrated through her. She swallowed, searching for a response, but found herself at a loss. They were not in a crowded street among throngs of activists and constables. When had they ever conversed for an extended amount of time with this level of calm civility?

"I am resolute in the execution of my responsibilities, Emmeline, and your interactions with me have proven that to be true. You cannot deny that."

She finally found her voice, but it was thready and lacked her usual energy. "I do not deny it."

"Then you'll not find yourself surprised when I arrive on your doorstep tomorrow morning. For you, not your sister."

She regarded him, brows drawn, before finally releasing a small sigh. "I sleep late."

"No, you do not."

"Of course I do."

"Your meetings with shifter advocacy groups usually occur well before the midday meal."

"How are you privy to such details?"

"I am a detective. I detect."

"Mercy," she muttered. She shook her head and planted her hands on the arms of the chair. "Very well." She stood, and he followed suit, which was to her detriment because her eyes were at his chest level. Rather than crane her neck upward, she stepped to the side, literally giving up ground, and resenting it. "I shall leave the house tomorrow morning at nine to go to Castles' Boutique for final alterations on some dresses. I personally do not see the need for so many, but my mother is insistent."

"Morning dresses, luncheon attire, evening dresses, and the like?"

"Why, Mr. Reed, how well-informed you are." She moved slowly to the door, and he fell in step beside her. "I had planned to travel with one trunk and one portmanteau. I fear I shall be laden with much more than that as Mother insists I also bring additional changes of clothing for each event I attend. I do not often bother worrying over such details, so I am certain she is correct."

"Your mother takes pride in your appearance and her shop as well. Her dedication certainly speaks to the success of the place."

Emme thought of her mother and Aunt Bella building Castles' from nothing and smiled. "She has worked diligently my whole life. I am proud of her efforts."

The detective matched his stride to her slow one, and as they neared the door, she slowed further still. Voices still drifted across the hall from the drawing room, and she was reluctant to return. Lysette's voice, and then her stepfather's, lifted above the rest, and Emme's shoulders tightened.

"I imagine dressing the family in clothing from the boutique provides for excellent advertising."

Emme blinked, distracted and tired, and pulled her

attention back to the detective. "The best advertising is accomplished with Lysette. She has the perfect form, after all. She is tall, so the clothing drapes well on her, shows it to its best advantage."

"Is that your sister's personal opinion, or fact?"

His dry comment caught her by surprise, and she laughed. "Much as I would love to claim otherwise, she is not wrong. She does wear clothing well."

They stood at the library threshold, and Emme knew she couldn't avoid rejoining the family. She spent as little time as possible with them, and at the end of an emotionally tiring day, she didn't possess the mental energy to spar with Lysette.

The detective stood just behind her shoulder and waited. "Shall we join the rest in the drawing room?" His voice was low and pleasant in her ear. Relaxing, even. That would never do. Heaven help her if she actually began to *not* hate the man. It would mean the world had stopped spinning and Hades's environs had truly frozen over.

As they crossed the hall, she heard her stepfather's voice—the jovial one he used with his friends—raised in conversation. They entered the drawing room to see Mr. Jenkins, one of Sir Ronald's hunting cronies, taking a seat with the family and Chief-Inspector Conley.

Emme tensed, wondering if Detective-Inspector Reed noted the slight pause in her step. She was often uneasy when her stepfather hosted his friends, and tonight the air around them swirled with an unusually charged emotion that stood her hair on end.

Chapter 5

Emme kept an eye on the two big-game hunters as they shook hands and exchanged greetings.

Oliver stepped close. "Does Mr. Jenkins visit your father often?" he murmured to Emme.

"Do you know him?"

"Crossed paths occasionally through the years. Old money, but not much in the way of social graces."

Emme crossed her arms over her chest, one hand gripping her bicep. She lifted a shoulder. "You *are* an observant detective. He has called occasionally, but I admit I do not know the date or time of his last visit. I am frequently away from home."

"Do join us, Detective, Emmeline," her mother said, motioning toward the seating arrangement around the hearth.

"No need, really," Lysette said pleasantly from her seat beside Hester. "Emmeline will not be at the house party, so the details do not concern her." She addressed Emme. "This conversation will be a bore for you, sister. I wonder if the detective might appreciate a cup of tea back in the library."

The entire group focused on them, and her gift for reading people's emotions wasn't necessary to feel the discomfort in the room. Emme raised her eyebrows at Lysette, who was not usually so gauche in the presence of others. Even her stepfather glanced at Lysette and cleared his throat.

"Of course, you may join us if you wish." He chuckled, but it sounded forced. "Jenkins, perhaps you would even prefer it. Our Emmeline has the spirit of a tigress and the cunning to match. Lead a potential suitor on a merry chase, she would, but as you're an expert hunter, she might have met her match!"

Jenkins looked at Emmeline as if seeing her for the first time, then joined in Sir Ronald's laughter.

Emme's face warmed, and she glanced at her mother, who frowned, and Lysette, who looked at her father with a wince, perhaps a flash of dismay, before covering it with a laugh. Madeline's brow creased, and she regarded Emme in sympathy. Emme couldn't bring herself to look at Chief-Inspector Conley.

She waited a beat, then another, for her mother to say something, but aside from an expression of censure clearly aimed at Sir Ronald, which he missed entirely, she remained silent. Emme's heart sank.

Detective-Inspector Reed stirred. "Tea actually would be just the thing," he said. "Miss O'Shea, do you mind?"

"Not in the least." She managed a smile.

As she turned to lead the detective from the room, her stepfather continued in an aside to Jenkins, "Could certainly do worse than have a pretty young woman at your side, eh, my friend?"

Emme quickened her step. She heard her mother's voice as she left the room but didn't stop to listen.

She crossed the hall to the library again, when the detective stopped her with a hand on her elbow. "You needn't entertain me," he said, and to her relief, she didn't read pity in his face. "Honestly, I am glad for the escape. The thought of sitting with Jenkins for any length of time brings on head pain."

Emme shook her head with a quiet, humorless laugh. "He's a perfect match for Sir Ronald."

"Did I hear him say that Jenkins is a hunter?"

She nodded. "Sir Ronald's family hunting lodge is a few miles outside Edinburgh, and he is hosting a gathering there during Summit week. Lysette has been sending invitations for weeks to his big-game hunting friends."

The detective looked across the hall, speculation on his face. "I wonder what sort of big game they are hoping to track near Edinburgh."

Emme lifted her shoulder, tension knotted in her neck. "Who can say? They travel to Africa twice yearly, sometimes more, but perhaps the thirst for the hunt is difficult to quench." She winced, remembering Sir Ronald's clumsy comment that Mr. Jenkins consider courting her. In an attempt to smooth over a bad situation, he had made it infinitely worse.

"Perhaps instead of tea," the detective said, "you might answer a question? Do you have any other threatening messages or notes in your possession that you've received in recent days?"

Emme put a hand to the back of her neck, absently massaging her tense muscles, and wondered if she should admit she had a small boxful. "I do, but they are not nearly as severe as the one I received today. I hardly think they matter."

"I should be the judge of that."

She sighed, wishing she could escape to somewhere far away. Would this day never end?

"Emmeline, our past exchanges have been contentious, without a doubt, but I would have you know of my true admiration for the intentions of your heart. The . . . the *rightness* of your motivation is something I have always understood and agreed with." He paused. "It is important to me that you know this."

She looked away, chewing on her lip. "Why is that? My opinion of your convictions does not signify."

"It does signify. To me, it does."

She looked up at him. "You must stop. You mustn't—" She turned her face away and pressed her lips together.

"Mustn't what?"

"You must stop being nice!" She had the presence of mind to keep her voice down, though she wanted to shout. "There are certain things in life I hope to see changed. There are other things I depend on to remain the same. If you continue with this kindness nonsense, I shall lose my focus entirely."

"You would prefer I throw you over my shoulder instead?"

Her eyes widened. "No!"

He frowned. "Emmeline, I jest. I will not hurt you."

"I know you will not."

"I—I do not understand. You've never been afraid of me. You know I've not ever meant you any ill will—"

She breathed out and stepped closer, gesturing as though explaining a complicated concept to a child. "I am not afraid of you. I know you mean me no harm. I am . . . I am . . ." She placed her hand on her forehead. "I am fatigued. My thoughts will be clear in the morning. Come with me, then, and I'll give you the blasted letters." She made for the stairs, assuming he would follow her.

He did, though with a frown. "Where are we going? Would you prefer I wait in the library?"

"No. We are going to my sitting room, so you needn't worry for my reputation."

They reached the second-floor landing, and she led him along a corridor to the right.

"I hardly think these other notes are worth examination, but do what you will." She opened a set of double doors to reveal her moderately sized sitting room with an open door to the adjoining bedchamber.

"This is the family wing?" he asked.

"No, the family wing is on the other side. Once the twins decided they needed separate bedrooms, someone had to move to the guest wing."

He raised a brow. "I should think one of *them* would move to the guest wing, as your room was already established."

She picked up an envelope packet from a side table and kept her reaction carefully neutral. "Lysette expressed absolute dismay at the prospect of being so far from Madeline. By that time, I was happy to have some distance from everyone."

He accepted the packet from her with a light frown. "This feels like more than a few notes."

She shrugged. "Please do not make it more of an issue

than is necessary. Isla discovered them during a recent visit and insisted I keep them. She even conducted some preliminary investigations into their origins, but they resulted in nothing."

"I certainly hope they are still nothing of consequence. You must understand the necessity of pursuing all clues." He half smiled. "Forewarned is forearmed."

"Yes, well, then." She made a motion with her hands, feeling tears of exhaustion threatening, and that would never do. "Off you go. Tomorrow will arrive before we know it."

Irritation finally showed on his face. "Miss O'Shea, I am not a flea or a child or a 'ton. We needn't be friendly if you do not wish it, but I expect a measure of professional courtesy. I apologize if you do not care for my methods, but I will not shirk my responsibility simply because you either find it an inconvenience or do not wish to face the severity of the facts."

She released a quiet sigh and closed her eyes. "Detective-Inspector . . . Oliver . . . apologies. You are absolutely right. I appreciate your kind thoughts and apologize for my"—she twirled a hand meant to encompass everything that had happened that day—"rudeness. You are performing a task required of your position as a detective, and tonight I am feeling very much the self-absorbed person you initially thought me to be."

He looked at her for a moment. "Thank you," he said. "I'll endeavor to respect your customary sense of independence and try to stay out of your way."

She shook her head, feeling herself blush. "You have behaved as one would hope or expect you to in this situation.

You have not offended me, and I shall adapt to my circumstances as would a responsible adult. This state of affairs is certainly not of your doing." She took a deep breath and tried to find a sense of lightness. "There is a silver lining to the day. Because we'll be in Edinburgh, I'll not be forced to fabricate excuses for missing the house party at the hunting lodge."

Oliver tucked the packet beneath his arm and slowly made his way to the door with her. "Is that a common problem?"

She grimaced. "I abhor hunting, and they are gleeful with it. They do not hunt to provide food; they do it for sport, and I cannot understand that. Even with all the additional activities that accompany a house party, things I enjoy, when we are at the hunting lodge, I am unable to fully relax."

"Silver lining, indeed. I am useless at any house party. I am unable to fully relax regardless of the location."

"You are not one for holidays, then." She stopped at the door and leaned against the frame, folding her arms, but loosely this time. Comfortably. She would never have admitted it aloud, but something about his solidity, his calmness, was soothing.

"I am not. Much to my sister's frustration. I have an open invitation to visit with her husband and two children in their home on the coast. They are all delightful, but while I am there, I always feel a sense of urgency to return to work. I am certain such an attitude is unhealthy."

"We have that in common," Emme said with a wry smile. "Besides, people's auras are always muddled during the holidays. Too much stress, I suppose."

He paused. "People's . . . auras?"

She sighed and muttered, "Never mind."

"No, no. Are you telling me, Emmeline, that you read auras?"

She frowned, her brows creasing. "And if I do? It is not unheard of, I'll have you know, nor does it make a freak of me."

He shook his head. "I am suggesting no such thing. My mother read auras, so I've a healthy respect for it. I am . . . surprised. I think I understand the workings of your brain only to realize I do not. You are an enigma."

She studied him for a moment, chewing on her lip. Soft light from the Tesla torches lining the hallway glinted off his thick, dark hair. His brown eyes were warm, and for a fanciful moment, she imagined he could see through her.

"How does an ability to see auras conflict with whatever interpretation of me you had formed?" she asked.

"You are practical, logical, efficient. Such personalities are often removed from outbursts of emotion." He paused.

"Continue."

He tilted his head. "Seeing you protesting at events, leading activities for the organization, one might assume you are a creative sort, very much an emotional sort. But in casual conversation, in the general ebb and flow of daily activities, you are structured, well-ordered. Efficient, tidy. Little use for fluff."

He paused as if waiting for her response. She looked at him for a long moment, weighing her words and trying to decide what to tell him. She finally sighed.

"I am, by nature, efficient and well-ordered. I prefer a day free from chaos. But I have inside me"—she paused, her voice low, and gestured with her hand—"so many feelings. Some of them are my own. Many of them come from others. As a child, I was bombarded by it, and I saw auras everywhere. By the time I realized it was abnormal, I was old enough to realize I would have to find a solution on my own."

She took a breath and continued. "I can control the bombardment. Usually. I do not often let it in. People are quite easily read without it. You, however, are not. Well," she amended dryly, "our usual exchanges are easily enough understood. I am not burdened by you, however, in the manner I experience with others. For that I am grateful."

Silence fell in the hall for a moment. She finally quietly added, "I do not share that part of myself. With anyone, Oliver. Ever."

He swallowed, looking intensely uncomfortable. He shoved his hands into his trouser pockets and met her eyes.

"You would appreciate an intimate admission in kind. Very well." He paused. "My younger brother, Lawrence, is a vampire," he admitted quietly. "He lives in Scotland, and last I knew, he was part of a rather nefarious group." He paused. "I am well-placed professionally to have reached out to law enforcement across the border for more information, but my attempts have been . . . lackluster." His voice was low, and he fell silent.

She nodded slowly. "You avoid it. I would do the same." One corner of her mouth tilted up, but she felt a deep stab of sadness for him. "Families are quite the complicated lot. You've seen mine."

He returned her almost-smile. "Complicated. Indeed." He stepped farther into the hallway. "The day has been . . . eventful. You should rest. Brinley and Tyler will be on patrol outside, on rotation with another pair of constables, around the clock. Should anything untoward occur, alert them at once, and they will contact me."

"I imagine we shall be fine." She frowned. "You should rest as well, detective. You seem ready to drop on the spot." Her mouth turned up then—fully, smugly. "Perhaps you are not accustomed to such a long day's work."

He laughed and shook his head as he made his way down the hallway. "That must be the reason," he said over his shoulder. "My usual day involves a steady diet of bonbons and the theatre." He paused at the end of the corridor and looked back with a polite nod. Then he rounded the corner and was gone.

Chapter 6

"No, Miss O'Shea, I will not wait outside the boutique. I will be both outside and inside, observing." Oliver didn't know why he'd assumed the day would be a smooth one with few conflicts. They had yet to leave O'Shea property and already the woman was questioning his methods.

The carriage had settled at the curb, and the driver held the door open for them, but Emmeline merely regarded Oliver with a raised brow that, if he'd been a lesser man, might have made him feel like a fool.

"Mr. Reed." She motioned to the driver to wait and walked over to Oliver. "I appreciate your zeal. We must establish boundaries at the outset, however. I am not accustomed to anyone dogging my heels all day, and I should think you would enjoy a respite from my admittedly exhausting company. I truly cannot imagine danger befalling me while I shop in a building full of people."

He eyed her evenly. "Two months ago, in Wilson's Haberdashery, a clerk was stabbed five times in the supply room at the back of the store, arm's length from oblivious shoppers on the other side of the curtain. The suspect was in and out of the establishment before anyone was the wiser."

"Oh. Well." She tapped her foot and looked at the waiting carriage. "Did you apprehend the suspect?"

"Of course."

She looked at him, lips twitching in a smile. "Of course," she repeated. She turned her attention to the house with a small shake of her head, and her expression changed, then stilled.

He followed her gaze to see her stepsisters exiting the house.

Lysette O'Shea was bedecked in an ensemble of dark blue and gray, while Madeline O'Shea, truly pretty in her own right, wore a similar style but in muted pastels. Lysette paused and looked Emme up and down, taking in the snug, light-colored breeches and boots, blouse and trim corset that, Oliver had to admit, rested quite nicely on her small frame. A small top hat perched at an angle atop her glossy black hair, which was fashioned into a simple braid hanging forward over her left shoulder.

Emme's ensemble was typical for her, from what Oliver had witnessed, when she went about her daily business and activities, and sometimes to events she knew might require quick flight or escape. He knew whether an event might require extra manpower to oversee whenever one of his constables reported that "Miss O'Shea's wearin' breeches today."

Emme met Lysette's rude perusal with narrowed eyes and a smile. "Sisters," she said. "You're up and about early this morning."

"We knew you planned to visit the boutique this morning, and since we also have finalizations on dress fittings," Lysette told her, "we thought to join you." She smiled at Oliver.

"The boutique is merely one of many stops on my agenda for the day. If you're thinking to keep the carriage for your disposal, we should travel separately."

"Nonsense. We'll make arrangements when we're finished at the shop. You may use the carriage as you will."

Oliver watched the scene play out, learning the dynamics and undercurrents that shifted between the sisters. There was no love lost, that was painfully clear, and he'd realized the extent of Lysette's penchant for troublemaking the night before when she'd slighted Emme in public.

Madeline, whom he had yet to hear utter a word, finally said, "We can take another carriage, Emmeline." A faint smile played around her mouth, but at Lysette's annoyed glance, she fell silent, her brows drawing together over her aqua-colored eyes before she smoothed her forehead into a neutral expression.

"Think nothing of it, Madeline," Emme said to her with a quick smile. "Dover will help you into the carriage while I grab a wrap. The air is a touch colder than I expected." She stepped to one side as the 'ton driver helped the other women into the carriage.

"Wait here," Emme said under her breath to Oliver, then dashed inside. She returned moments later with a light pelisse draped over one arm. Dover stood at the carriage, ready to assist Emme, but she waved him off. "Settle yourself at the controls, Dover. The detective can assist me."

Oliver approached slowly, amused in spite of himself, and watched for his cues. He would wager his pension that he and Emmeline were not getting inside the carriage.

Emme made a show of putting her foot on the bottom step and then paused, looking behind the carriage at the empty street. "Oh, Detective-Inspector, I believe I see Isla's carriage approaching. I must wait just a moment to be sure. Ladies, I'll see you at the shop; I'll ride with my cousin."

Lysette responded, but her words were lost as Emme flipped up the steps, slammed the door shut, and pointed Dover forward.

The servant tipped his hat to her with a wink and set the carriage in motion. The carriage wobbled as someone moved erratically from inside, and Lysette opened a window. Her hand could be seen, and she yelled, "No! Detective, wait!"

Emme watched the vehicle disappear down the street before turning to Oliver with a sigh. "One irritant vanquished. For the moment."

"Will the driver stop?"

"No. We have an understanding."

"Might I assume Lysette doesn't usually ask to accompany you around town?"

"You might, and you would be correct. She wants to weasel information from me or from you, or perhaps she seeks your company. Unfortunately for her, she doesn't know the things I do."

"Oh?" He put his hands in his pockets, affecting a casual stance even as his eyes flicked up and down the street, registering two nannies strolling with perambulators, four gardeners tending to roses in front gardens, and a delivery man circling around the house across the way with a wire crate of milk bottles. "What do you know that your sister doesn't?" He had to admit curiosity. For all that he'd studied Emmeline O'Shea's movements and general habits, knew of her deeply held convictions, there were aspects of the woman he suspected nobody knew.

"I know you play your cards close to your vest. After last night, you'll have recognized her as one who manipulates, and so you'll keep information from her—even the inconsequential—if only to prevent potential drama." She looked up at him.

He tilted his head. "Astute. Guesswork, though? This charade over the carriage just now was of no import, but you gambled I would follow your lead. Our past interactions would have given you no indication I might."

Her lips twitched. "Because our past interactions show a decided example of your desire for complete control over everything?"

He lifted a shoulder, and the corner of his mouth turned up, catching him by surprise. He was not one who smiled often.

She shrugged. "As much as you assume you have learned of me in the past few years, I have learned the same of you. Words cannot express the level of disappointment I would experience if a person of your integrity and intellect fell victim to my stepsister's machinations."

She paused. "She is mean, Detective. Cruel. If you were to fall under the spell she weaves, as so many unsuspecting men do, I would lose hope for your gender entirely." She looked at him and then away, and he was surprised to see a light flush on her cheeks. She'd undoubtedly given him much more than she'd intended. "Wait here. I'll instruct Barnesworth to have another carriage brought 'round."

Oliver watched as she went back to the door and poked her head inside. She gave instructions to the butler as she shrugged into her pelisse, her movements precise and efficient. She was physically strong and quicker than he'd ever imagined possible, especially the first time he'd been forced to give chase. She'd been caught spying on a PSRC meeting from the grounds outside the building. He'd torn his trousers climbing over a gate she'd vaulted with seemingly little effort, and watched her vanish into the trees. That had been two years ago and had marked the beginning of a steep uptick in his attendance at Gentleman Maxwell's Gymnasium.

She rejoined him at the curb and pulled a notebook and pen from a reticule hanging from her wrist. "Today's itinerary, as you've requested. First, Castles' Boutique for a torture session I hope will last less than one hour. I trust you will clear the storage rooms of any potential assassins."

He withdrew his own notebook, glad they were finally getting to the business of her schedule. He shot her a flat look at her reference to the murder. "Continue."

"I plan to dine with Isla and Daniel Pickett for an early luncheon at the Tea Room. Fortuitous for you, is it not?"

"Indeed. Odd that our social circles seem to overlap."

She looked up at him, finger poised on her notebook. "Of course they overlap. My blood is not blue but for my mother's marriage, Detective, and while you enjoy a reputation of certain renown, it is not from birthright either but from impressive military service." She paused, her gaze turning speculative. "Which you left."

"True enough."

"Could have climbed through the ranks, they say." She tapped her pen against her lip and narrowed her eyes. "Already well on your way . . ."

He nodded at her notebook. "Next item on the schedule."

She regarded him for another long moment through narrowed eyes but finally turned back to her schedule. His military service and reasons for leaving were nothing he cared to discuss with anyone.

"Yesterday descended into mayhem, what with the Bad Letter and all, so I was forced to reschedule a meeting with the International Shifter Rights Organization president. Thankfully, he was willing to accommodate me. He hasn't much time but is available today for twenty minutes at three o'clock."

Oliver nodded. "Giuseppe Giancarlo?"

"Yes. His London office is in the International Relations Building, not far from the Tea Room, should our schedule run late."

The International Relations Building housed organizations and committees from various countries, and security was tight. It was one of a few buildings where she ought to be safe. "Will I require official clearance to sit in the meeting?"

She frowned. "We'll not be discussing state secrets. Not that I'm privy to those, Detective-Inspector. I daresay your clearance for all things secretive exceeds mine every day of the week."

"Perhaps not so much now. I wonder if you realize the

significance of your position. As the spokeswoman for the organization, you ought to have had personal security options in place long before now."

"We discussed it briefly, but there didn't seem to be a reason—until now." She chewed on her lower lip for a moment and released it with a small sigh. "I shall see how matters stand once the Summit meetings conclude."

An automated carriage sounded in the distance, and Oliver lifted his head to see it was a rented hack farther down the street and not one belonging to the family. Emme was jotting something in her notebook, and he glanced down at her schedule to see the next calendared item.

The carriage engine sounded louder as it approached, and the hair on Oliver's neck stood up as he realized it was gaining speed at an alarming rate. He whipped his head up in time to see it barreling down upon them, swerving toward where he stood with Emme.

He threw his arms around her and hauled her back, stumbling. He tried to shield her as they fell to the pavement, but they came down hard on his arm and her shoulder. Wincing, he cradled her head with his hand as they rolled, and as they came to a painful stop, he lifted his eyes. The carriage was fast disappearing down the street, and he squinted to see any distinguishing marks on it.

"Sir!" Footsteps sounded beside them as the two uniformed constables assigned to the house that morning came running from the side yard. "Sir, are you hurt?"

Oliver grunted as he rolled slightly and looked at Emme. One of her arms was wrapped around his back, and her other hand clutched a fistful of his shirt. Her breath was quick, and her large green eyes searched his, confused. They also held an element he'd never seen in her: fear.

"Are you hurt?" he managed. He tried to loosen his hold but felt as though his arms had locked in place. His hand still gripped the back of her head, and he forced his fingers to relax. The constables hovered nearby, apparently uncertain which limb to grab in assistance.

She inhaled shallowly and licked her lips, her expressive brow drawing in a frown. "Nothing broken, no. What on earth . . . I couldn't see . . ."

"Carriage nearly ran us down." He finally was able to loosen his arms, feeling the scrapes and bruises in full as he moved.

She pulled her arm from around his back and winced. She looked at his face. "Oh! You're bleeding." She looked up at the constables, who still gaped. "Give me a handkerchief."

She shoved at Oliver's chest, and he shifted to take his weight off her, involuntarily grunting when she caught him in the stomach with her elbow.

She winced again as they sat up, favoring her side, and he was reluctant to release her entirely. Dirt smudged her cheek, and her hat and notebook lay on the walk next to his. He looked down the street, but other than catching the attention of the gardeners and nannies, nobody else was about, and all was as it had been moments before.

"No, turn your head back this way." Emme placed her hand on Oliver's cheek and reached around his other shoulder, effectively embracing his head.

"I've got to see if there are other threats—"

"If you see a carriage, we'll move."

He was trying to see around her arm, which was reaching up to the constable who'd now moved behind him, probably in an effort to help them stand. Oliver turned his head toward her, and the tip of his nose brushed against her neck. He smelled the light floral scent he'd come to associate with her. He'd never experienced it in a situation that didn't also involve one of them antagonizing the other, and he was suddenly very much aware of his arm still holding her, his hand splayed across her back.

"Thank you," she said to the constable, but the words landed in Oliver's ear. She pulled her arm back, holding a white cloth. She placed it against his cheek and held it for a moment, frowning at him, and then bit her lip as she examined the side of his face, lifting the edge of the cloth.

He was too stunned to move, completely at sea, entirely out of his element. The day before, when Oliver had expressed frustration over his role as Miss O'Shea's bodyguard, Conley had said, "You'll allow she's extraordinarily pretty." He swallowed. *Pretty* did not begin to describe Emmeline Castle O'Shea. The woman was a force of nature, and he was holding her intimately.

"Your face," she muttered. "Perhaps we should visit Sam and Hazel."

"I am fine," he managed. He cleared his throat, trying to make sense of their tangled limbs. She still held the cloth pressed to his face, and when he moved his hand to his cheek, she shook her head.

"Wait." She lifted the cloth and examined his face. Her eyes narrowed as she dabbed at his skin, gently at first, and then firmly.

He winced. "It will be fine."

"Be still. You've rocks in your face." Her eyes flicked to his, and she gave him a wry smile. "Surely a big, strong man can withstand a few scrapes."

His mouth went slack. "Miss O'Shea, are you attempting to soothe my fears?"

"Well, forgive me, Detective, but you do seem a mite flustered. There." She flicked away a pebble and dusted off his shoulder. "No more embedded rubble." She flashed another smile, and he blinked. She folded the cloth and pressed it to his jaw. "Hold it here for a moment—there's one spot that still wants to bleed."

Oliver was so rarely caught off guard that he momentarily lost his objectivity. He placed his hand against the cloth and felt her flingers slip from beneath his. He took close note of her face; she was extremely pale. As she dropped her arm, she flinched in pain and put her hand to her shoulder.

"I knew you landed hard," he murmured and wiped firmly at his jaw before dropping the handkerchief and gently probing her shoulder. "I am sorry. There was so little time. I tried to take most of the hit, but—"

"Don't be silly. You saved my life." She bit the inside of her lip, which he was coming to recognize as one of her nervous habits. She tilted her chin up, though, and put on a brave face. "Dare I hope that was an accident?"

"I do not know."

"Do not ever shield me from the truth. I would have your word that you will always inform me when you learn something that concerns me." She paused. "Please."

"My primary objective is to keep you safe. As such, there may be instances where judgment must be mine to make."

Her jaw tightened. "Will you compromise?"

"Not as it concerns your safety."

She shook her head impatiently. "No. I mean, will you reach an agreement with me? If you will be honest, forthcoming at all times regardless of circumstance, I will follow your directive without question."

One of the constables cleared his throat, and Emme held up a finger at him while still looking at Oliver. "I cannot bear remaining in the dark, Detective. Ignorance is the worst vulnerability of all."

He nodded. "You have my word."

Relief flickered in her eyes. "Thank you."

"Sir?"

"Yes, Constable." Oliver shifted his weight and looked down at himself, realizing Emme's leg was bent at the knee and sprawled over one of his, which was extended. He raised a brow, glad there were few people about.

"Emme!" The cry carrying down the street pulled his attention, and he turned to see Sam and his wife, Hazel, running toward them.

"Oh, dear." Emme sighed and moved, kicking Oliver in the process and offering a mumbled, "Apologies," before shoving herself upright.

Oliver also stood, dusting his clothing, his actions and occasional grunt of discomfort mirroring Emme's.

"Well, we are a sight, aren't we," she muttered. She pulled at the side of her coat and twisted around, trying ineffectually to wipe dirt from her back.

Oliver awkwardly brushed her shoulder, dropping his hand when she subtly winced. Instead, he took stock of his own clothing, noting a small tear near the jacket hem. He removed his coat and shook it as Hazel skidded to a stop next to them, grasping Emme's shoulders.

"Eugene said you were nearly run down by a carriage!" Hazel held Emme at arm's length and looked her up and down. "He witnessed the whole incident from the front window!"

Emme's face brightened, and Oliver watched her transform into the devil-may-care woman he so often encountered in times of trouble. She rolled her eyes and, with a small laugh, hugged her friend. "I am completely fine, as you can see. It was an odd accident and nothing more."

She met Oliver's gaze over Hazel's shoulder and widened her eyes at him with a subtle shake of her head. Her attention flitted briefly to Sam, and then she pulled back from Hazel with another smile.

"Accident?" Sam murmured to Oliver. "And why are you here?"

One of the constables handed Oliver his notebook and pencil, which had gone flying in the chaos. He pocketed them as he regarded Sam. "Protective detail."

Sam pursed his lips and nodded. "So, not an accident."

Emme interrupted, motioning to Oliver's face. "Dr. MacInnes, perhaps you'll offer your professional opinion regarding the detective's wound. Will he require bandaging?" She looked at Oliver. "I'm happy to continue to Castles' alone. I can meet you there later, if you'd like." She brushed a hand over her coat again as the family carriage finally approached.

Oliver narrowed his eyes. Such a plan would fit beautifully with Emme's clear preference to go about her day independently. Her acceptance of the situation was tenuous; he'd not be surprised to learn that a corner of her brain still believed her life wasn't truly in danger.

"My face is fine," he told her drily and wiped at his bloodied cheek again with the constable's donated handkerchief.

Sam frowned and moved closer as if to take a look, but Oliver brushed his hand aside. He spied Emme's notebook on the ground and retrieved it and her hat. "Your notes. We'd best be off in order to maintain your schedule for the day." He motioned to the constables and quietly said, "One of you remain here. The other go around to these homes and talk to witnesses. Take down every detail, no matter how small."

"Yes, sir." The constables nodded.

By now, the ruckus had alerted the butler and two other servants from inside. Emme huffed out a breath. She shrugged out of her dirtied coat and handed it to the butler, saying, "Wouldn't you know, the weather has warmed considerably! Barnesworth, please give the pelisse to my maid for immediate laundering." A brisk gust of wind rushed over the group, nullifying her statement.

"Here." Hazel removed her own light-colored coat and placed it around Emme's shoulders.

"Nonsense, Hazel, I—"

Hazel's lips firmed, and she looked in Emme's eyes as she reached for Emme's wrist and shoved it into the sleeve. "Something is amiss, but I'll not insist on explanations now."

Emme closed her mouth and obediently threaded her other arm through the other sleeve. Hazel straightened the collar and tucked a few stray curls back into Emme's braid. "We'll visit later, make no mistake." She took Emme's hat from Oliver and placed it carefully back on Emme's head.

Oliver still held Emme's notebook and pen, which he now handed to her. "Yes, we'll chat later," he told the MacInneses, who looked at them with a combination of concern and suspicion. "As it stands, we are late for a dress fitting."

Sam's eyebrow shot up, and Hazel squinted, first at him, then Emme.

"Miss O'Shea," Oliver said and gestured to the carriage, where a footman held open the door.

Emme planted a quick kiss on Hazel's cheek. "I am well. I promise." She turned and accepted the driver's hand, climbing into the carriage.

Oliver followed closely on her heels, suspicious she might give the driver instructions to leave him behind. With a quick wave to their friends, who were still frozen in place, Oliver settled into the seat across from Emme.

Emme blew a kiss to Hazel through the window, giving her a quick smile as the carriage pulled away from the curb. The smile slowly faded as the carriage moved down the street, and Emme settled back, resting her head against the seat.

She closed her eyes and said, "It may have been only an accident. A novice driver, perhaps."

"Perhaps." He felt the opposite to be true, and he suspected she did, also. He reached into his pocket and retrieved his own unsoiled handkerchief and handed it across to her. "You've a smudge of dirt, just there." He motioned to her jawline.

"Oh," she said, and taking it from him, rubbed her face, somehow managing to wipe every part of her skin except the dirty segment. "Thank you. Wouldn't do to arrive at the boutique looking as though I've been playing games at the park."

He frowned and gestured impatiently to the handkerchief, which she returned with a smirk.

"I wasn't going to keep it, Detective."

He scoffed and shook his head, moving toward her with a beckoning motion. "You've missed the spot entirely."

She scooted forward warily, turning her head as he took her chin in one hand and wiped at the dirt with the cloth.

What had begun perfunctorily enough merged into a moment altogether more intimate. He'd never had occasion to *gently* hold her face, and he was disconcerted to note the softness of her skin beneath his fingertips. She swallowed, and the subtle movement of her throat drew his attention to the lines of her neck and the evidence of a rapid pulse just beneath her skin.

He cleared his throat and pulled back slightly, dismayed to see the stubborn dirt clinging to her face. "Doesn't want to come clean," he murmured, for the first time feeling awkward in her presence.

The corner of her mouth turned up. "Please do not spit on the cloth. It will bring to mind my mother's relentless scrubbing and scolding when I played as a child."

"There," he said, relieved to have most of the spot cleared, and pocketed the cloth. "Unfortunately, the rest seems to be a small bruise." He settled back into his seat and considered flipping through his notebook to give his hands something to do.

"Thank you." She nodded once, completely composed, and had he not seen the evidence of her rapidly beating heart, he'd have believed she was unaffected by the awkward moment. Of course, she might still be feeling the aftereffects of nearly being run down by a carriage.

"You'll want to glance in a mirror." He gestured to her cheek. "To be sure the spot is gone."

"No, I mean, thank you, Detective, for saving my life. Accident or no, I might be in very different circumstances right now if not for your quick action." A light flush stained her cheeks, and she looked down at her hands.

"You're welcome." He smiled in spite of himself when her right knee began bouncing. It was her tell. Agitation, nervousness, discomfort—that bounce signaled her state of mind while seated. He'd have to observe her while standing; she was rarely still, so he had no notion of her idiosyncrasies then. Of course, it could be that her constant movement was another tell.

She was complicated—most people were—and he rarely made the mistake of analyzing a person in only one dimension. Defining Emmeline O'Shea as "a nuisance" had been tidy and convenient for him but would no longer suffice. If he were to truly keep her safe, he figured he'd better start digging.

Chapter 7

Emme forced herself to be still. She stood on a stool in one of Castles' Boutique's three plush fitting rooms as two seamstresses pinned her dress. It was the eighth dress her mother insisted she'd needed, and with an inwardly resigned sigh, she mentally readjusted the size of traveling trunk she'd need.

A quick knock sounded before the door opened a crack to reveal Hester and Lysette, who slipped into the room and took stock of the progress, both examining Emme with hands on hips.

"Lovely," Hester announced with a satisfied nod. "The ice-blue is perfect, just as I knew it would be." She smiled at Emme. "You'll wear this when you address the international representatives the last night of the Summit."

Emme's heart thumped at the pride in Hester's expression. She smiled, absurdly wishing she and her mother could spend the day together alone, just the two of them.

"Have you been falling out of trees again, Emmeline? You've an enormous bruise on your shoulder blade and elbow!" Lysette's voice carried from behind and grew as the young woman circled around Emme to stand beside Hester.

Hester frowned and moved around Emme. "Oh, Emmeline!"

Lysette's mouth ticked up slightly. It was inevitable. Lysette smelled blood and circled like a shark.

Emme gritted her teeth. "A minor skirmish with a runaway carriage, Mother. It was not intentional, I assure you."

There was a beat of silence, and then Hester appeared in front of Emme. Even the seamstresses pinning the dress paused as though fearful of her reaction. "Runaway carriage?"

"Yes. An accident, nothing more."

Hester pursed her lips, spots of color appearing high on her cheeks. "I'll speak to Detective-Inspector Reed. Why was he not protecting you?"

"He was. His quick thinking is the reason I was spared." Emme flicked a glance at Lysette, exasperated when her stepsister arched a brow and lifted one corner of her mouth. Why? Why did Lysette find it necessary to bring attention to Emme's flaws? Was she looking to cause problems with Hester?

Hester grasped Emme's hand. "Perhaps it wasn't an accident. It might have been an attempt on your life!"

"It was an accident," Emme told her evenly.

"You ought to have ridden with us after all," Lysette said, studying a cuticle.

"Where is the detective now?" Hester clutched Emme's fingers.

"Searching for nefarious perpetrators amongst the garters

and ribbons." Emme motioned to the store floor with her thumb.

"Shall I express our thanks for you, Mother? For saving Emmeline's life?" Lysette asked.

"She doesn't need you to speak for her," Emme snapped.

"Girls, please, no quarreling." Hester put her hand to her head and made her way to the door. "I'll find the detective myself." She left the room, Lysette close on her heels.

The seamstresses finished quickly and helped Emme out of the dress full of pins and needles and into a fresh dress; her breeches needed to be mended after the morning's adventure. She was braiding her hair, thinking of how nice the detective had smelled when her nose had been pressed against his neck as he'd shielded her from danger—she frowned; finding him the least bit attractive was not part of her plan—when a knock sounded at the door.

A shopgirl stood there, with the detective himself hovering close behind.

"Miss O'Shea? The detective wonders if you are finished." She glanced over her shoulder and then back to Emme.

"I can see that." She nodded at Mr. Reed. "We must escape before my mother decides I need yet another dress. This fitting has thrown off my schedule."

She looked around the store's main level at the newest available fashions on display, matching accessories, glittering crystal chandeliers, and trays of small, sugared treats. The shop invoked feelings of warmth, and Emme had spent much of her life within its walls. It was only later as conflicts increased with Lysette that Emme's relationship with the store had become complicated.

She waved to her mother, who was consulting with a customer. Hester held up a finger and mouthed, "One moment!"

Emme shook her head and mouthed back, "I'll be home tonight." She made a beeline for the door, gritting her teeth with a smile as she stood aside for an influx of customers. A few women greeted her by name, which she answered with a small wave on her way out the door.

She pulled out her pocket watch, prepared to give the detective instructions, when she felt Oliver's light touch on her back.

"This way," he said, gesturing to a horseless carriage cab waiting in the street. "We should be on time for lunch."

She blinked. "Oh. Well, excellent." Emme held tight control over the operational details of her life, and she couldn't decide if she was irritated he had taken the proverbial reins or grateful for the help.

The driver moved to climb down from the front seat of the carriage, but Oliver waved him back. "I'll see to it," he told the man. He flipped down the steps for Emme and offered his hand.

She stood for a moment, her mouth quirked at the irony of how their situation had changed. "Look at how well we play nicely together!" She took his hand, realizing she'd forgotten to put on her gloves—not a rare occurrence—and noted he didn't wear any either. His hand was lean and strong, and she suddenly felt warmer than the air warranted. She settled into the seat, refusing to blush. Emmeline O'Shea was not the blushing kind.

The detective sat next to her, rather than across, and

rapped the ceiling to signal the driver. The conveyance pulled into traffic with a clink of gears and a hiss of steam.

"There would never be occasion for us to behave with anything other than perfect cordiality if *one* of us would remember the rule of law and behave accordingly." He tilted his head with a bland expression.

"Ha ha. Perhaps the *other* one of us should endeavor to remember the *first* is doing nothing but exercising her rights to protest unjust governmental tyranny and buffoonery."

His lips twitched. "Hmm. I suppose we must content ourselves with a friendly disagreement over the reality of the matter."

"Yes, I suppose we must. Now, tell me, did you find anyone suspicious in the boutique? I was most relieved at the lack of assassins in the dressing rooms."

He glanced at her and braced one arm along the back of the seat, his hand near her shoulder. He seemed casual enough, but she knew everything he did was calculated. His eyes took in the streets and the people outside the carriage even as they conversed, and the casual posture he affected allowed him a more natural view of the area through the side and back windows.

"I noted three assassins and dispatched them posthaste to Newgate. Realizing there is little that is more important than a woman being fitted for her wardrobe, I took extra care to be efficient and quick." He tipped his head deferentially toward her.

"I do not know if I should be amused that you are willing to engage in silly wordplay or irritated that you would so roundly insult me and my entire gender."

"You'll forgive the assumption, but a man of modest means and little exposure to polite society must rely on conjecture and limited observation."

She scoffed. "Detective-Inspector Reed, you see the entire world at a glance, and nothing escapes your notice. You do not rely on conjecture or limited observation to form an opinion."

He was quiet for a moment, and she wondered what he was thinking, as his face gave nothing away.

A shout near some shops caught his attention, and her heart thumped despite her resolve to pretend she hadn't a death threat looming over her head. He took it in as he did everything else—with a few seconds of analysis, a barely discernable twitch of tension in his muscles, and then relaxation as the shout proved to be nothing more than a friendly argument. He turned his head and studied her with that same analytical expression.

"Emmeline, I owe you an apology."

Her heart stuttered. Usually, hearing her name in its entirety meant nothing good, but on his lips, it was somehow . . . well, it was something. She cleared her throat. "And why would that be, *Oliver*?" She tested his given name, thinking she would sound playful. Instead, she sounded rather breathless, and it made her scowl.

"I am perhaps proving you wrong, to some extent. You suggest I do not form opinions based on limited observation, and yet I have formed erroneous opinions about you based on observations obtained mostly in—well, contentious circumstances." He paused. "I had assumed you to be a person of extreme self-preoccupation."

His comment stung, and she stared at him for a moment before looking away and biting the inside of her lip. She opened her mouth, but the words caught. She cleared her throat and swallowed. “My entire preoccupation, my entire world these last few years has focused on righting the wrongs to the shifter community. It has given me a sense of purpose, I suppose, but no small amount of trial as well.” Her lips tightened. She didn’t know why she felt the need to explain herself to him. His opinion of her meant nothing, and furthermore, he’d been one of those trials that had made her life difficult.

“Emmeline.”

She didn’t trust herself to look at him. Her eyes felt suspiciously hot.

He placed his fingertips on her shoulder and gave it a little squeeze. “Emme.”

She huffed a small sigh and looked at him, narrowing her eyes and forcing back the mere thought of self-conscious tears. Why on earth would she allow his opinion of her to carry such weight?

“I have never doubted your devotion to the cause, never once considered you selfish. In my mind, your life and your activism have been one, and it was my erroneous assumption that your perception allowed analysis of only those things. I ought to have realized you’d figured me out as well. I’ve never doubted your intelligence, merely the scope of your observation.” He paused. “If I have wounded your sensibilities, I apologize.”

“Wounded my sensibilities,” she muttered and looked away again. “Detective, if my sensibilities weren’t wounded the first time you carried me over your shoulder out of the PSRC meeting gallery, they certainly aren't now."

"Ah yes. That was the second time I'd had occasion to make your acquaintance. I don't think I ever formally apologized for knocking the breath out of your lungs so abruptly."

Emme cast him a side glance, her bruised feelings easing. "You've performed that maneuver more than once. It would be good of you to apologize now."

He inclined his head. "You have my apology. It would also be good of you to say, 'Detective-Inspector Reed, I apologize for the yelling and repeated beating of the cowbell that disrupted the meeting and necessitated your presence in the first place.'"

She sighed. "Ah, but that would be an insincere apology."

He smiled before turning his attention back to the street. "As would mine."

Finally, her lips twitched into a reluctant smile. His glib admission had garnered him more respect from her than anything else he could have said.

They continued in comfortable silence for a time, and her thoughts turned to the amount of time she had at her disposal before leaving town. She pulled her notebook from her reticule and flipped through pages of notes, lists, and a multitude of tasks that ordinarily wouldn't have overwhelmed her. She wasn't ordinarily concerned for life and limb, however, and was finding it bothersome.

"The visit with Carlo this afternoon will not be long," she told him as she added a note to one of the lists.

"Carlo?"

"Oh," she shook her head, distracted. "*Signore* Giancarlo. 'Carlo' is his address of preference casually."

"I've never met the man, only heard he is of a noble Italian family and galvanized the shifter relations community into a strong, international voice."

She smiled. "That he has. I was intimidated at our first meeting, but he is charming and humble, disarming."

Oliver's attention vacillated between their conversation and the street around them. "He must be personable to establish such familiarity with colleagues so quickly. Not common in elder generations."

Emme looked up in surprise. "Oh, he is not elderly; perhaps that accounts for it. Plus, he is Italian, you know, and very warm."

Oliver looked at her, brows raised in equal surprise. "I had assumed . . . That is, I supposed one who had made such accomplishments on an international stage would be of a . . . mature nature."

"One might assume as much, but as a matter of fact, he and I are the youngest of the entire organization. Most of our members and representatives have known several years of experience in the field."

Oliver studied her, his expression inscrutable. "It is certainly to your credit that you've accomplished so much at a young age."

Emme shook her head and waved her hand. "I do not fool myself entirely. As the face of the organization, it has not escaped my attention that my literal *face* may have played a significant role in securing the position more than my merit. I do hope I'm proving myself as more than just a pleasant image, however. I've been told by the representative from Austria-Hungary that I compensate for my lack of experience with enthusiasm." She smiled and turned again to her notes.

Oliver was silent for a moment and then said, "Not only have I misjudged you, I was completely wrong."

Emme frowned. "How so?" She added a note to the margin of her packing list to insist her mother track down the larger trunk as the necessity of it was her fault.

"You're not self-absorbed. I do believe you're entirely self-ignorant."

She jerked her head up and squinted at him. "I do not even know what that means."

"The attention you brought to the Extermination Act culminated in its *dismissal.* Do you not suppose that such an accomplishment would warrant a person a fairly significant role in any related organization?"

"I was one of many voices, and I would never delude myself into believing otherwise."

He shifted in his seat, brows drawn together as he looked at her. "Yours is the loudest, by far, Miss Emmeline, and you may trust my authority on the matter."

She rolled her eyes and folded her hands over her notebook, giving him her full regard. "Detective, I have a pleasant, young face and a healthy inheritance. I am an idealist but also a realist. Due to absolutely no effort of my own, I am a woman of privilege, and it would be irresponsible of me to ever forget it. As lovely as it would be to think I have achieved some measure of status due to my merits, I must be honest."

"Why would you not allow it to be both?"

"Privilege and merit?"

"Certainly."

She tipped her head, pensive. "Perhaps the privilege allows for quicker development of merit." She paused, concerned she presented a false sense of humility. "I—"

She fumbled for the words, unsure she could define her emotions even to herself. Always, the emotions. "I have seen children lose mothers or fathers to either the Committee's unholy zealotry or need to hide from the Committee's unholy zealotry." She paused again, frowning. "I do not understand why some people are dropped at fortune's doorstep and others must fight daily, *continually*, for the opportunity to simply live. To be treated with fairness and decency. Or to be left alone, if desired."

Her throat closed, and she cleared it. "To be teased or insulted for another's entertainment is unpleasant enough. To be *persecuted*—hunted? That is unthinkable, and if others with the means and the time can speak on behalf of those marginalized . . . Well, then, they should do it."

Silence filled the carriage, and she looked out the window, uncomfortable. "I do not mean to sound didactic. You will think I am preaching, no doubt. A bored young woman of means who champions a cause that has nothing to do with her."

She heard his quiet inhale and exhale. "I am thinking I have no doubt as to the reasons for your appointment as the spokeswoman for the International SRO."

She turned to look at him, unsure if she ought to brace for sarcasm or perhaps some sort of censure. She'd always expected it from him, even as she never understood how he maintained a brotherly friendship with a predatory shifter while simultaneously working to thwart her efforts.

"I've never heard Emmeline O'Shea speak to the crowd before the riot. I've not taken the opportunity, and I should have."

The tension in her shoulders eased, but only slightly. "Would you have supported my work rather than stymied it?"

His lips twitched. "No."

She frowned and thumped her hands on her notebook. "Whyever not? Lord Blackwell is your best friend."

"As long as your work includes a decent into social mayhem, *my* work necessitates a return to order." A ghost of a smile played on his lips, but his focus was direct, and she felt pinned to her seat. "You should not assume you are alone in your attempts to affect change. Many of us approach the same issue but from different vantage points. Different methods. One doesn't necessarily negate the other, and probably all are necessary in their own way."

She scrutinized him, wishing he would speak with less nuance and more detail. "Dare I hope you've committed legally questionable acts in the name of the greater good?"

"Even if I had, I would not admit such to you."

She frowned. "That does not stand to reason. If ever there was a person who would appreciate such activity, it is I."

"Be that as it may, I do not feel the need for a confidante."

"Pity," she grumbled, more to herself than him.

He gave her a sidelong glance, clearly amused. "The horror of my personal matters falling into your hands is quite enough to keep me awake at night."

She huffed and turned back to her notebook. "As if

sharing secrets with me would put them at risk of exposure. Quite the opposite, you should know."

She sniffed, piqued. She wasn't sure why—she'd never cared to know Detective-Inspector Reed's secrets before. He was an intriguing puzzle, and the more time she spent with him, the more evident that became. She would never have guessed that he attempted in any way to affect societal change. In her mind, he'd been stuffy, unyielding, and entirely unsympathetic to any entity other than his precious law.

"I shall bear that in mind," he said. There was humor in his voice, but when she glanced at him, he was as impassive and impossible to read as ever.

It shouldn't matter one way or the other whether she could read him. They were not friends, and they could be considered colleagues only in the loosest of terms. No, understanding the inner workings of Oliver Reed's mind was so low on the list of her priorities as to be nonexistent. She would tolerate his company for the next two weeks, and when their time together ended, she might not know him any better than she did now, an idea she was entirely comfortable with. Fine, in fact. Better than fine. They were oil and water, the two of them, naturally repelling each other. She was grateful for the professionalism he possessed because it would keep her safe, but such was the extent of their connection.

The carriage swayed and bumped lightly as they traveled to the Tea Room, and the length of Oliver's leg brushed up against hers. She glanced down in irritation, her frown deepening when the detective made no move to shift away. What was it about the male species that they seemed to expect, as their due, the right to space? Acreage. Even the most proper of her male acquaintances, who sat with legs crossed and elbows in, seemed to occupy excess space around them with an extreme sense of entitlement.

She kept an irritated huff from escaping her lips but couldn't stop the eye roll as she flipped absently through her notebook. Her attention was scattered, her focus far-flung and unlikely to return until she was no longer in such close confines with the detective. She wondered absently if the heating mechanism inside the carriage had been activated.

She subtly checked the instrument switch panel on the side of the vehicle, noting the heat indicator was in the neutral position. She scowled.

"What is it?" Oliver asked, his voice a pleasantly low rumble that entered her ear and traveled insidiously through to her extremities.

"Nothing," she snapped. "It grows warm, and I do not care for it."

"Perhaps you carry a fan?"

"Perhaps *you* carry a fan!" Even as the phrase left her lips, she drew her own brows together in befuddlement. As arguments went, her statement was ridiculous. Why would he carry a fan?

His lips twitched. "I do not," he said, appearing to deeply consider the topic, "but I suppose I could from this point forward as a service to you."

She took a measured breath. "Kind of you to offer, Detective, but that is unnecessary. I do indeed have a fan of my own—several, in fact. One for each ensemble."

"Shall I retrieve it for you? From your reticule?"

Emme was certain heat in the form of steam was escaping

her ears. What a ridiculously inane conversation. The notion that this man who was her nemesis—she mustn't forget—was teasing her flitted on the edges of her thoughts, and she brushed it away angrily. They had no business discussing fans or any other sort of accessory.

She opened her reticule with more force than necessary and shoved her hand in, her fingers closing around her fan. She pulled it out and flipped it open with a flair worthy of a French courtesan. She waved it in her face and glanced at him, only to see his familiar, assessing regard.

"Better?" he asked.

"Yes," she ground out. "But perhaps matters might be improved upon if you were to move your person over on the bench. This carriage is ridiculously small."

He raised a brow in surprise. "Oh, you ought to have said so earlier. I was unaware you were feeling cramped. Here." He put his hand on the seat between them and then moved to the bench opposite her. "There. Much more room."

She nodded stiffly, still fanning herself and relishing the light breeze. The problem now, however, was that he was positioned directly in her line of sight, and his long legs stretched forward until he was nearly into her personal space yet again. He'd braced his feet on either side of hers, and she was irritated that he didn't turn to the side slightly and cross one leg atop the other. It would have been the polite thing to do. It was highly suspicious, because she knew he possessed impeccable manners.

She drew in a deep breath, briefly closing her eyes and counting to ten. For the rest of the brief ride, she scribbled notes in the margins of her lists, which kept her brain and hand partially occupied, though she was altogether too aware of the man sitting across from her, apparently not suffering ill effects from having spent the entire morning and early afternoon together. Or if he was, he hid it well. Of course, why should *he* be the irritated one? *She* wasn't encroaching upon his space, his schedule, his entire life.

That wasn't completely true, she conceded, knowing he'd set his own life aside for hers, but she was happier wallowing in her own sense of victimhood and frustration. Perhaps it was better. If she was too busy being irritated with him, she was less likely to allow in the unsettling fears that stemmed from the Bad Letter and had continued through the accident that morning. Far better to find something—or someone—to be irritated with than to be afraid.

Chapter 8

The days leading to the Summit were filled with planning meetings with the International SRO and Signore Giancarlo, last-minute shopping, one additional dress fitting, and dinner with Daniel and Isla. Oliver was her shadow for the entirety, and, to her surprise, Emme found herself growing accustomed to his company. She even began asking for his opinion on a variety of issues that arose during the day, at first because he was often the only one at hand when she was mulling something over, and later because she realized his judgment was sound and she was of a similar mind with him more often than not.

There were no further threats on her life, although one luncheon was canceled because arsenic had been found in three of the teapots. A quick investigation proved the culprit to be an employee who was protesting the restaurant's use of manufactured spices. The target had been the restaurant, and the poison was not intended for any one person.

Miles and Lucy Blake had arrived in Town, and together with Daniel and Isla, and Sam and Hazel, Emme and Oliver had attended the theatre and enjoyed dinner at the Blake townhome. It was not lost on Emme that she and Oliver rounded out the group as the last "couple," but nothing could have been further from the truth. They were only just learning how to be civilized with each other.

In preparation for one of Emme's presentations about shifter history, Lucy had loaned Emme two small, old journals containing some of the Blake family history. Emme kept them, along with her personal notes, observations she'd made over the last three years, a small ray gun, a knife, a tin of fresh biscuits, and a military canteen, in a medium-sized portmanteau that resembled a carpetbag. It was heavy, but Emme couldn't bring herself to put the priceless journals in a trunk that would leave her side during travel. She couldn't afford to lose them, if even for a moment.

The evening of departure finally arrived. The nighttime flight would allow Emme to accomplish more the first day of the gathering instead of spending time traveling. She made a final sweep of her bedroom, satisfied she had packed everything she might need for her trip.

She paused before her vanity and examined her appearance. She wore a stylish new outfit in burgundy and black, designed by her mother with the shop's latest acquisitions. Hester had also upgraded Rosie, Emme's 'ton maid, to include programming for the latest in hairstyling. Emme's hair was an impressive coiffure with braids, twists, and a thin strand of pearls.

She smoothed her corset and ran her hands along the beautiful fabric of her trousers, which were tucked neatly into her new black boots. She exhaled, nervous, and then told herself to smile. She was embarking on the adventure of a lifetime, and she would enjoy every moment of it. She would be with friends and colleagues who cared for her and whom she enjoyed in return, and her family would be busy with activities of their own. Lysette's barbed tongue and her stepfather's oafish attitude would be far away from her.

Rosie entered the room and tipped her head. "Your mother sends for you, Miss Emmeline."

Emme had requested basic programming for Rosie as she wanted little fuss and interference from her maid, and although her mother and Lysette were uncomprehending of her wishes, she found Rosie to be a perfect match for her busy life.

"Thank you, Rosie." Emme retrieved her newest top hat from the vanity and placed it on her head, tilting it at the perfect angle. The hat was also burgundy, decorated with small flowers and feathers that matched her ensemble. A small pair of goggles rested on the brim, completing the look. Emme had to admit she did look rather fetching in the new clothing.

She picked up her carpetbag and, with one last look at her bedroom, made her way to the door. "If I haven't thought of it by now, it's too late," she muttered.

She stepped into the hallway only to stumble into Madeline, who jumped back with a hand over her heart.

"Oh! Apologies, Emmeline."

"No need, Madeline, none at all." Emme shook her head but had to admit some confusion. Hester was usually the only family who ventured into the guest wing.

Madeline twisted her fingers, and then, as if realizing what she was doing, clasped her hands firmly together and stilled the movement. She took a deep breath and smiled. "I do not know how much access we shall have with each other in Edinburgh, and I want to wish you well." She nodded once and firmed her chin. "I . . . You must be so glad. You have worked diligently . . . I cannot imagine . . ."

Emme tried not to stare, confused not only by the oddity of the conversation but that it was occurring at all. She raised her brows in what she hoped was encouragement as Madeline floundered for words.

"I only . . . I wish you well, Emme. I have every confidence you will say amazing things and people will be moved. You possess such an incredible gift." Madeline's eyes were suddenly bright, and she firmed her lips, smiling and lifting her chin again.

"Madeline, I hardly know what to say," Emme admitted, shocked but touched. "Thank you." She carefully reached forward and embraced her awkwardly, and they both shared a nervous laugh.

Emme drew back and looked at her stepsister. Madeline had rich, brown hair shot through with stunning strands of gold and deep red. She usually styled it as simply as possible, though, and Emme had long suspected it was a maneuver meant to keep Lysette at bay.

While Lysette was the quintessential English Rose, Madeline was exotic. Her features held an understated beauty, her eyes a captivating aqua color, but she often wore clothing that washed out her complexion and did little to flatter her frame. Hester remarked occasionally, quietly, that she would love to "fuss just a bit" over Madeline's appearance, but she was always politely refused.

"Madeline," Emme said impulsively, "perhaps when we return home, you and I could take tea somewhere . . . away from here."

Madeline nodded, but her eyes flickered away for the briefest of moments. She smiled again but looked as though it took effort. She cleared her throat, eyes glossy. "That would be lovely."

"Well, I had best be off. Perhaps we shall see one another in Edinburgh." Emme walked toward the stairs, and Madeline hesitated but then fell into step with her.

"Perhaps." Her gaze darted again, and when they reached the landing, she looked toward the family wing. Nobody was there, and Madeline visibly relaxed, if only a fraction.

Something was off, like one flat note in a chord. Emme glanced at her stepsister, more curious than ever. The energy emanating from Madeline was subtly chaotic, as though she was upset but tamping it down. Emme wished she had a moment to investigate. It would have to wait until the Summit was over, sadly.

Voices echoed through the front hall, and Emme heard Oliver's baritone. Her heart beat faster, and she cursed the wretched organ for its betrayal. As she descended the stairs with Madeline, she decided that, of course, she could be professional with the detective, and, of course, there was no reason to object to his presence. She was professional and friendly with Carlo, and she saw him rarely. She was cordial and pleasant with her colleagues in the Shifter Rights Organization, and there were some among that number who irritated her to no end.

Deciding to behave professionally toward her *former*

nemesis was no reason for her heart to thump in anticipation of seeing him. Perhaps her subconscious simply reacted to him as it had in earlier days when his presence signaled an imminent visit to a jail cell. That must be it. Satisfied she'd reached a logical conclusion, she stepped onto the main level with a clearer head. She smiled at Madeline, who nodded and scurried off.

Hester and Barnesworth stood at the door with the detective. Hester glanced at Madeline's disappearing form, and then at Emme, who shrugged. Hester's brow creased, and Emme was struck with the notion that she probably had inherited her insatiable curiosity about people and their conundrums from her mother.

Hester motioned toward Emme. "Come along. I sent Rosie up for you ages ago."

"Ages, Mother? I would hardly say that—" Emme stumbled over her words as Oliver subtly removed her valise from her hand and cupped her elbow.

"We must make haste," he said, and she looked up at him in surprise.

Blast it all to heaven and back, when had the man gotten so handsome? He wasn't smiling, didn't look at all charming, but as she looked at his face her treacherous heart thumped again.

He wore a fine hat and a simply styled but impeccably made suit. That accounted for his sudden appeal. Her mother was the queen of style, which made Emme a lady-in-waiting, at the least. She knew good clothing when she saw it, and oh, how it could do wonders for a person. Mystery solved, she turned and grasped Hester in a quick embrace.

Hester squeezed her tightly. "Darling," she said, and Emme heard the tears in her voice.

Emme closed her eyes against the sudden sting of emotion she felt.

"Please," Hester continued, "please, please do not do anything foolish."

Emme's eyes snapped open as Hester still held her tightly. "I know you will behave. Please remember everything you've ever learned about decorum and poise."

Emme ground her teeth together and pushed free from the bone-crushing embrace. She forced her mouth into what she hoped resembled a smile. "I will not embarrass you, Mother. Never fear."

Hester sighed and placed her hand alongside Emme's face. "It isn't only that. Be safe, dearest. Do not take unnecessary risks. Are you certain you do not want to take Rosie with you? Rented maids are not always reliable."

"I will be fine." She kissed her mother's cheek and paused, thinking. "Watch for Madeline, though. There is something—"

Oliver quietly cleared his throat from his place by the door. Emme didn't need to read his emotions to know he was impatient. Well, he could wait one more moment.

"Perhaps choose a special dress for Madeline." Emme said. "Something that flatters her coloring. And make her wear it in Edinburgh. Telescribe a message when you've arrived there."

Hester's surprise was visible on her face, but she nodded and quickly kissed Emme's cheek.

Oliver ushered her out to the carriage, which was weighed

down with trunks. He—rather aggressively, she thought—assisted her into the vehicle and gave the driver quick commands in an undertone. When he joined her in the carriage, he sat opposite her, and she knew a moment's odd disappointment that he wasn't sitting beside her. It was just as well because now she could continue to admire his suit, which was absolutely the reason her heart thumped hard again.

"Apologies for the rush," he said as the carriage moved forward and then gained speed. "Friendship with Daniel Pickett will not buy a delay in departure."

Emme rolled her eyes but then checked the timepiece pinned to her bodice. "Why were you not at the house earlier?"

"I arrived in plenty of time but was unaware of the effort required to load all of your"—he waved a hand at the back of the carriage—"accoutrements. Lady O'Shea was most particular about the trunk placement. Made me memorize the order and instructions for each."

"Welcome to a glimpse of my world, sir. Misery does love company, so naturally I now find myself giddy." She sighed. "This portmanteau is the only piece of vital import to me. The rest is my mother's doing."

"Your bag—what is in it?"

"Notes and references for my presentations at the meetings. A few books." She leaned back. "I would be quite at sea without them. There is so much information . . ." She shook her head and sighed. "I wish I had Hazel's brain. That woman never forgets a thing."

"You have steeped yourself in this world for some time, Emmeline. I imagine you would succeed without even one note."

She tipped her head at him. "Why, thank you, Detective. Untrue, but flattering all the same."

He shot her a flat look. "I do not bother with flattery."

"Ah, noted. I shall beat my inflated ego back down to size." Her knee bounced, and she looked out the window at the autumn evening. The sky was overcast and would soon be dark.

"Are you apprehensive about traveling? The endeavor as a whole?"

She turned her attention back to him. "Why do you ask?"

He pointed to her knee, which bounced quite independently of her will. She clamped her hand on it, which only furthered the image in her head that her nervous habits stemmed from some external force she must literally stop.

She sighed. "I do not mind travel. I am unsure of my abilities to do justice to my duties this week."

He settled back into the seat and exhaled quietly. She realized that if he'd been inclined to bounce a knee as a sign of nerves, he'd have been doing it.

"*You're* apprehensive," she stated.

He nodded slowly. His attention was drawn to the city beyond the carriage windows and then finally settled on her. "We are behind schedule, and I do not wish to miss the flight. Additionally, the Chief-Inspector and I are no closer to ascertaining the sender of your Bad Letter, and I'd hoped for some clues by now. It is frustratingly free of fingerprints or other identifying features."

"You must have some suspicions. You're familiar enough with London's nefarious characters at all levels of social strata."

He inclined his head in assent but paused as if deciding whether or not to share his thoughts.

"You promised, no secrets," she said.

"I promised no secrets regarding credible information. I made no promise to divulge to you my every thought."

"That is just as well, because I do not want your every thought. Only those relevant to me."

One corner of his mouth twitched, and she thought for a moment he might smile. "Very well. I have asked myself which group among our society has the most to lose at the prospect of a successful Summit gathering."

"The Committee," she said without hesitation. That they both knew exactly which committee she meant was telling. The government was full of committees at every level; the PSRC warranted a category of its own.

He nodded again. "It certainly isn't a new thought. From the moment I read the letter, I suspected someone in that circle. Randolph has amassed his share of powerful supporters—whether through self-interest on their part or coercion on his, I'm not certain. Fact remains, I cannot simply launch an investigation into his life, or anyone else on the PSRC, without just cause. Even then, it would be politically . . . complicated."

She swallowed past a lump of unease. Hearing it verbalized in such terms threw her situation into rather stark relief. It could well be that her enemies were connected well enough politically that injury to her—or worse—might be conveniently swept away. If the carriage incident the other morning was any indication, damage done to her person under the guise of "accident" was most likely her enemy's preferred scenario. Take her down with an assassin's bullet, and she would become a martyr. An accident, however, was simply one of life's tragedies.

Oliver leaned forward, dipping his head to catch her eye. "This is why I am here. I will not let anything happen to you."

"Oh, I know," she said, trying to sound light and unconcerned.

He looked pointedly at her knee, which was bouncing again.

She huffed a sigh and leaned forward, bracing her elbows on her knees and put her fingertips to her temples. "I haven't time for this, nor energy," she admitted quietly but then added, "I don't suppose anybody ever does."

"I do."

She looked at him. "You've been obliged to set aside your entire workload for this assignment." When he didn't respond, she flushed. "The Yard's top detective has been tasked with playing my nanny."

"I am not playing nanny."

"All because my mother made so much noise." She was hit with a wave of uncomfortable guilt. The man was truly a professional, one of the best to be had, and her situation had effectively rolled over his career. She'd noted it before, but then he had irritated her so much she hadn't cared.

She sat up, feeling mortified but tamping it down. "Detective, I realize we are late in the proverbial game, but I am willing to be nannied by a lesser officer of the law. Or I shall task my mother with hiring a private security entity, someone who can join me in Edinburgh. I am loath to admit

I've not been attentive of the toll this assignment takes on your professional, not to mention personal, life." She meant every word, but the thought of another man sitting across from her in the carriage was distasteful in the extreme.

He shook his head, this time his mouth quirking into a half smile. "The Chief-Inspector and I briefly discussed that notion, Miss O'Shea, and just as quickly set it aside. You would run roughshod"—he held out a hand—"unintentionally, over anyone else. I am familiar not only with your circumstances but with your proclivities for escape and evasion."

She scowled, fairly certain she should feel offense. "I'll not evade my own bodyguard. I can put on my best behavior when I wish it."

He'd been studying the windows again, but he turned his attention to her fully, unblinking. "There will be no changing of the guard, and we needn't discuss it again."

She was stunned into silence, which was a rarity. His tone brooked no argument, and she suspected if she tried, he'd either ignore her or, more likely, tie a gag around her mouth. He held her gaze as though anticipating her contradiction. His attitude was rather high-handed, she thought, almost paternal. Well, no, she amended, *not* paternal. Fraternal? Not that, either. There was nothing familial in the least about the energy that swirled in the confines of the small carriage.

She drew in a quiet breath and slowly released it. "Very well."

He studied her a fraction longer and then turned his attention back to the outside world.

"You should know, however, that I—"

His flat gaze pinned her to the seat, and she decided, for now, she would allow him the final word. Or scowl, rather.

She looked out the other window and fanned her face with her hand. "Grows warm again," she murmured. "What is happening in these carriages?"

His movement in her periphery drew her attention back to him as he reached into an inner pocket and withdrew a small, simple fan. It was completely without adornment and nearly child-sized, and he handed it to her wordlessly without removing his gaze from the window.

She stared at the thing in her hand and opened her mouth, but then closed it again and simply flicked the fan open instead. Truth was indeed stranger than fiction. She felt a laugh bubbling up inside, but as her companion didn't seem inclined to share in her mirth at the moment, she swallowed it back and fanned herself.

She saw out her window that they were nearing the airfield. She ought to have been relieved, but oddly enough, the tight energy that remained in the carriage was intriguing, the warmth less intrusive.

The vehicle rolled to a stop with a hiss of steam, and Oliver exited first, then took her hand as she climbed down. With a small, awkward nod, she folded the fan and returned it to him. He raised one brow and put it back in his inner jacket pocket. She pursed her lips to hold back her smile. His expression didn't change, but he winked at her and moved around to the back of the carriage to give instructions to the gathering airstrip attendants.

Her heart thumped hard in her chest, and she wordlessly reached back into the carriage for her portmanteau. She saw his hat on the seat and picked it up, noting the smooth sensation of the fabric beneath her fingertips. She examined it, taking in the clean lines and absence of frippery or adornment. It suited the man quite well, she decided as she looked at him directing the transfer of her multitudinous trunks. Two of them were to be shipped directly to the ISRO building in Edinburgh, but before she could comment on it, he had already delivered the information to the attendants, along with the accompanying paperwork.

His glance flicked to her, as though to assure himself of her whereabouts, as he explained the last of the instructions for the remainder of the luggage. She made her way closer to him, figuring if she stayed by his side, his attention wouldn't be fractured as though looking after an errant child. She was struck by the utter insanity of the moment; a month before, she would have laid down on a train track before lifting so much as a finger to make Oliver Reed's life easier.

She stood next to him as he tested the locks on the trunks before allowing the 'tons to take them away. The other pile of luggage was gathered into a wagon to take to their airship, which was a hive of activity with airfield workers loading trunks and cases into the cargo hold. One of the boxes slipped and nearly fell from the wagon, and Oliver barked a sharp command at the attendant as he grasped Emme's elbow and ushered her toward the passenger stairs.

His eyes swept the area as he absently took the hat Emme handed him. The airship loomed large above them, the Pickett logo prominent, and Oliver looked up at the enormous balloon.

Emme watched him for a moment before asking, "Have you not flown much?"

He frowned. "I fly frequently." His free hand gripped the rail as they began climbing the stairs.

"You do not seem comfortable with it," she observed, wondering if she would upset his masculine sensibilities by pointing it out.

"I said I fly frequently. I do not claim to enjoy it."

"Excellent," she said brightly. They drew near the hull but were forced to wait as the line slowed. "Finally, circumstances in which I have the upper hand."

He shook his head as he positioned her ahead of him and reached his arms around her to grip the handrails on either side. She realized that rather than doing so out of fear, he had caged himself around her like a shield. She gripped her portmanteau with both hands, struck by the solemnity of the moment, by the lengths to which he was willing to go to protect her life. Much to her surprise, it worried her. The thought of him injured or worse while keeping her safe caused a lump to form in her throat, and she swallowed past it.

"You finally have the upper hand?" he murmured close to her ear because she stood one step above him. "What you don't seem to realize, Miss O'Shea, is that you always do."

His nearness provided a combination of comfort and disquiet. "Given that you're a military man, discomfort with heights must have been a nuisance. Did your training involve air-jumping?"

He nodded, a telltale tightening of his jaw betraying his thoughts on the matter. "We trained in both traditional parachute and Jump Wings."

Her brow lifted in surprise. "My goodness, the thought of leaping from anything using Jump Wings frightens even me." Jump Wings were mechanical contraptions that strapped onto the arms and around the torso and, when unfurled, allowed the wearer to float to the ground. They were notoriously heavy, however, and difficult to maneuver without a fair amount of strength.

He nodded and glanced at her askance. His lips twitched, just short of a smile. "Even you," he echoed. "I suppose I should be grateful. If I never use Jump Wings again, it would be too soon."

Standing on the airship steps, his arms enclosing her in a safe cocoon, she felt content. She looked at him, noting the smoothly shaved skin along his jaw and the contrast between his skin and the crisp white collar of his shirt. He was a distressed damsel's dream come true, and if she were the distressed sort, her heart might flutter at the close proximity. She noted the subtle smell of his shaving soap, the warmth of his body as it protected her from a light breeze, the arms that were nearly closed around her in an embrace.

Fortunate she was that her feelings for the man were professional. The fact that she was so aware of him spoke volumes about her biological state of affairs. Perhaps when the Summit was finished, she would consider suitors. Clearly, it was time.

Chapter 9

Oliver settled next to Emme in the upper passenger section of the comfortable, classically appointed Pickett airship leaving for Edinburgh. The cabin was sparsely occupied, the bulk of the passengers seated one deck below in equally well-appointed, if not slightly smaller seating. A mild weather disturbance was predicted, but as Emme had planned from the beginning to arrive at the Summit's festivities early, a small delay was not an issue for concern.

He sat in the aisle seat, she in the middle, and the seat next to the windows held her portmanteau containing all of her papers and the two old Blackwell diaries that discussed the "family condition." His smaller travel case sat beside hers, looking inconsequential.

Her knee bounced restlessly, occasionally bumping against his, and he finally clamped his hand down on her leg, which was encased in formfitting breeches. He'd acted instinctively, casually, to calm her or at least keep her from jostling his leg, but as his fingers closed around her knee, he felt an unexpected, dangerous urge to leave his hand there. If he shifted closer to her, she could nestle beneath his arm, perhaps even rest against his shoulder.

He deliberately moved his hand. No sense in complicating their current situation even further by completely destroying all professional decorum and risking her wrath. Their time spent together the last few days—time spent companionably and without hostility—had led them both to unsteady ground where, against all earthly odds, they'd begun to find each other attractive. She was single-minded, however, and determined to execute her planned course. An attraction to him might be diverting for her, but he knew better than anyone that if something stood in her way, she'd crush it.

Therefore, no knee-holding, no comfortable snuggling while en route to her destiny, no impossible—and highly inconvenient, if he were honest—flirtation could take place in their odd relationship. Additionally, he forced himself to remember she was his to protect, and he could little afford the distraction. She was his assignment, and her enemies were desperate to keep her away from the Summit. Feelings that reached beyond the bounds of strict professionalism could undermine his efforts to keep her from harm.

She was scowling at him, and he lifted a brow. "I apologize if my overwrought nerves are bothersome." She began bouncing her knee again.

He fought a smile and forced himself not to pat her knee again. "Do try to rest. The security team at the airfield conducted an additional sweep of the ship before we lifted off, and I'm confident we are safe. Aside from some possible bad weather, we should enjoy an uneventful flight."

Her brow furrowed, and he easily read her stress, but she nodded and leaned back, resting her head against the seat. She'd set her hat on the shelf above them, and he appreciated it. There was no denying she was a beautiful woman, but hats hampered his view of her hair, and sometimes the mesh veil that extended from the brim covered her eyes. It was light material and entirely ornamental, but he didn't like having to peer around an annoying scrap of fabric to read her expression.

She sighed and squeezed her eyes closed. His mouth twitched in a smile as he watched her dramatic attempts to relax, and when she opened her eyes with another sigh, he shook his head. "That was pathetic, Miss O'Shea. Perhaps your cousin might be prevailed upon to instruct you in meditation techniques."

She made a face at him. "She's instructed me more than once, I'll have you know. I just . . . I'm restless."

"I am guessing you didn't sleep well last night—another reason why it would be to your benefit to rest now."

"You didn't sleep well either."

"Why do you draw that conclusion?"

"Your eyes."

"What about them?"

"They're tired."

He smiled. "My mother made that observation when I was young. She frequently told me I had tired eyes."

Her mouth quirked up. "I imagine you were a serious child. Probably lost sleep while envisioning your future as a law-enforcing tyrant."

He laughed softly. "Believe it or not, my dream as a child was not to be a detective. I wanted to be a train conductor."

She tilted her head. "How adorably normal! I'm not certain I believe you."

He put a hand to his heart. "My mother would attest to it."

She relaxed against the seat, angling her body toward him. "If I should, by some miracle, actually sleep, please tell the flight attendant to leave a tin of crackers and soda water."

"You do not want an entire meal?"

"No. But I suspect I'll be ready for the snack in a few hours." She took a deep breath and slowly released it, allowing her eyelids to drift softly closed.

They sat in comfortable silence, and as Oliver relaxed, he wondered if he might be on the verge of sleep himself. As long as they were safe in the cabin, high in the air, he could afford a few hours of rest. The Stirling Engine that powered the ship's propellers hummed quietly in the night, and the ship rose and descended as it navigated the reported stormy weather.

They had been in the air for a few hours when a slow sense of unease washed over him. He'd dozed in and out of sleep, but something felt wrong. He frowned, listening carefully, and took a quick look around the cabin's interior. The lights were low, and the handful of passengers were sleeping.

Emme stirred and stretched, but stilled midmovement and her eyes shot to his. "We're turning."

He nodded noncommittally. "Another maneuver around the storm most likely." No, something was wrong, and his stomach tightened.

Emme straightened and reached for the window shade, lifting the curtain and peering out. She looked down, and then up, and her fingers tightened into a fist. "Oliver," she murmured, "the sky is clear, and we are turning east."

He didn't waste time arguing but rose and crossed the aisle to the empty row of seats adjacent theirs. His heart quickened. There might be a dozen explanations—perhaps weather instrumentation showed evidence of a worsening storm ahead and the captain thought to skirt it.

He looked back at Emme, whose eyes were wide. "We must speak with the captain," she told him. "Something feels . . ."

He understood completely but didn't want to escalate her anxiety. "I'll speak with him. You wait here."

"No." She stood and exited their row, stepping ahead of him down the aisle. She stopped a 'ton who was preparing to deliver tea. "Why has the captain diverted our course?"

Oliver caught up to Emme as the 'ton regarded her silently, cogs whirring. "I am unware of course alteration," he answered finally.

"Step aside." Oliver propelled Emme toward the door leading to the outer deck and stairs up to the wheelhouse. The outer deck was enclosed but felt significantly cooler than the interior cabin. Emme held her arms tightly against her chest as they climbed the stairs, but whether from cold or worry he didn't know.

"Do not fret unless we find reason." He raised his brows and waited for a response. She looked at him, her lips tightened. When they reached the top step, she passed a shaking hand across her forehead.

He knocked firmly on the wheelhouse door, then spied movement through the window. The polished wood and shining brass handles matched the rest of the tastefully decorated craft, the hallmark of Pickett Airfleet. The door opened, revealing a man Oliver recognized.

"Ensign Barclay?" He'd known the man in India but hadn't formed a favorable opinion of him. He was cagey, always giving Oliver the impression of untrustworthiness. He was slight and possessed a shrewd air. He reminded Oliver of a weasel.

The man grinned. "It's 'Captain' now, Reed. 'Inspector' Reed, I hear."

"How long have you been piloting?" Oliver studied the man, alarm bells sounding in his head. "Mr. Pickett hired you?"

"Of course. Pickett hires all his captains." Barclay smiled. "A new assignment, it is."

"We're flying off course," Emme interjected. "Why?"

Barclay turned his attention to Emme, studying her with beady eyes.

Oliver felt her tense, but she waited for the man to answer her question.

"Miss O'Shea, we are not flying off course but merely avoiding the storm. We are a short hour outside Edinburgh as we speak."

"I wish to see your weather charts."

His eyes narrowed at her, and he didn't bother with a smile. "And I'll be askin' you to return to the cabin."

"Let me see the charts, Barclay," Oliver said, "and we'll

return to the cabin. If we're truly still headed for Edinburgh, you've no reason not to prove it."

"This is my domain, Reed, and you'll return immediately to your seats or I'll have you detained in the brig by security 'tons."

Emme shook her head, her lips thinned and tight with anger. "Daniel Pickett is my cousin's husband, and your days as a pilot for this airline are numbered. If you truly are in his employ."

She stormed down the stairs, and Oliver looked at Barclay, whose expression was thunderous as he watched Emme's descent. A sickening feeling settled into his gut. "Where are you taking this ship, Barclay?"

Barclay turned his attention back to Oliver. "You'll know when we arrive."

Oliver grabbed the man by his lapels and pulled him close. "You'll tell me now."

Vindictive satisfaction crossed Barclay's features. "Portugal."

Oliver's mouth slackened. "Por . . . Portugal?" He shook the smaller man. "Who is paying you to take us there?"

"I follow orders of some powerful people, Reed. Release me immediately."

"I am placing you under arrest, Barclay, and demand you immediately set course for Edinburgh." Oliver's temperature rose, and he felt a vein throb in his temple.

Barclay broke Oliver's grip and stepped back with a sneer, holding a ray gun—the kind Oliver saw only on the black market.

Oliver inched his hand slowly toward the holster at his

side but stopped when Barclay's eyes widened and he lunged forward, his hand steady on his gun.

"Get back to the cabin," Barclay ground out through his teeth. "And don't even think about parachuting. I had them removed. The only thing on board are Jump Wings, and I doubt your pretty friend knows how to maneuver them."

Oliver stared at the man, breathing hard. "I suggest you enjoy your final days of freedom, you fool. You've no idea what you've done."

Barclay grinned. "Wish I could see Pickett's face when he realizes one of his fleet disappeared right from under his nose, and with his best friend aboard. Pity you won't be there to see his face, either."

"Who hired you?"

Barclay's grin faded. "Get out of my wheelhouse." He put the gun in Oliver's ribs and shoved. "Now."

Oliver stared at him for a long moment before heading back down the stairs to the passenger cabin. He pulled his scriber from his pocket only to realize he had no signal. They were beyond the Tesla coils' reach, even if he could plug into a stationary charger. He would have to devise a plan on his own to disarm Barclay and take control of the ship.

He ran a hand through his hair, a sense of urgency filling him, along with a heavy dose of hopelessness. Emme was going to be beside herself, and strangling Barclay would be first on her list of things to do.

He entered the cabin and made his way to their row only to find it empty. He clutched the back of his seat, staring. His travel case was still by the window, but Emme's portmanteau was gone. Where on earth would she go? They were hundreds of feet in the air.

The lavatory. That must be it. He hurried to the small compartment at the end of the cabin, relieved to find it locked. She must be inside. He stood for a few awkward minutes until the door finally opened, but an older man exited, frowning as Oliver gaped at him.

Surely, surely she wouldn't . . .

He told himself not to panic as he jogged the length of the cabin aisle to the exit. He took the stairs to the lower decks and began searching. Emme didn't know there weren't any parachutes aboard, and by her own admission, she'd never used Jump Wings. He passed a small infirmary and the cargo-hold doors, rounding the corner. His stomach lurched as he felt the ship jolt, and the hum of the Stirling Engine lowered in pitch.

He ran for the engine room, frowning at the lack of light within. Someone had switched off the lamps, and he tripped over one inert 'ton who lay near the Stirling Engine oil drum. Swearing, he pulled a small torch from his pocket. The 'ton's back panel had been pried open, as evidenced by the bent metal, and the function tins had been pulled free, tossed on the floor beside the robot.

A noise across the room caught his attention, and he moved quickly to the controls, which had been shoved into a slower function. It was a crude maneuver, used in times of emergency, and he gritted his teeth as he flashed the light around the room. Of course, Emmeline O'Shea would have the wherewithal to engage the emergency procedures on an airship. The engines had been placed into a neutral position, still holding the ship aloft but hovering in a relatively small area.

"Emme!" His shout rang out as he flicked the light back and forth. Another disabled 'ton lay near the door, and he shook his head as he made his way across the room. He admitted a reluctant sense of admiration for Emme's quick thinking but had to wonder how many 'tons she'd disabled in her life to render them useless so quickly.

What would she do now? Confront Barclay, most likely. His foot was on the bottom stair when he remembered her empty seat in the cabin, specifically the seat next to the window that now held only his travel case.

The few precious minutes he'd wasted outside the lavatory door had given her time to stay ahead of him. His heart picked up its rhythm as he turned and broke into a run to the small room near the cargo hold. He tried the handle, which should have been locked but turned in his hand. It opened an inch but then held fast. Something was wedged underneath it on the other side. The shining brass handle bore telltale scratches from whatever implement Emme had used to unlock it.

He pounded on the door, his fury and fear rising in tandem. "Emmeline! Open this door!" Jump Wings were military grade, hard to maneuver, and specifically fitted to an individual. She couldn't simply throw on a pair of wings and jump out of a passenger airship.

She wouldn't.

His heart lodged in his throat.

She would. Of course she would.

He backed up a step and kicked the door hard, satisfied

when the hinges gave away enough that he could shove the door open a few more inches. An alarmingly cold blast of air hit his face, and he realized his worst fears were coming to fruition. She was going to jump from the airship. If she hadn't already.

He shoved with strength borne from fear and dislodged the pole she'd wedged against the door. The room contained rope, tools, and sundry supplies anchored to the walls, and an area that should have held enough tightly folded, compact parachutes for each passenger aboard. Those shelves were empty—Barclay hadn't lied—but in three specialized compartments were black Jump Wings. The fourth compartment was empty and missing its set of wings.

Chapter 10

He rushed to the open door. The world was dark, and he shined the feeble light from his Tesla torch down toward the earth, catching the faintest glint of shiny black Jump Wings as they spiraled down. She was falling fast, much too fast, and he shouted helplessly at her, heart pounding out of his chest. He turned back toward the remaining Jump Wings, shrugged into a set, and fastened its buckles across his chest, abdomen, and around each arm as quickly as he could.

Shouts sounded from out in the hall, and he slammed the ruined door closed before going back to the exit, searching desperately in the black night for a sign of Emme. Feeling faint, desperate, and terrified on every possible level, he rolled from the aircraft, found his bearings in the free fall, and threw open the wings with a loud snap as the segments opened and slid into place.

He'd Wing Jumped enough to be familiar with the process, had even done training exercises with his men at night, but they'd known what they were jumping into. The terrain below was a dark mass of nothingness.

Emme.

He kept searching the area below, confident in his abilities to slow and guide his descent but knowing she was completely, literally untrained. He pulled the wings in and angled for a forward dive, increasing his speed in hopes of catching up to her. He had a rough idea of how far from the ground they'd been flying and adjusted accordingly, counting off several seconds before fully opening the wings again to slow his rapid fall.

Over his shoulder, the moon mercifully inched from behind a cloud, throwing a silver glow to the ground. He noted several things simultaneously. The first was that they were out over the water. The second was the beach; he adjusted the wings to aim for it. The third was Emme, who, to his immense relief, had managed the wings well enough to slow her descent and was also shifting toward the sand and rocks at the water's edge.

His eyes streamed against the cold wind—they'd not had time to don goggles or proper head gear or gloves—and he squinted, keeping Emme in sight. She pulled on the wings and angled her body toward solid ground. He maintained position directly over her, torn between grim satisfaction that she seemed to be maneuvering the wings, and increasing worry at her erratic movement.

Her wings tipped from one side to the other, violently, and he knew her arms would be straining against the heavy contraption. She was dangerously off-balance, and he couldn't divine the reason as the winds were steady with relatively little gusting. He saw a dark shape fall as though she'd dropped something, and he realized it was her portmanteau. As he executed a tight spiral and dove again to pick up speed, he saw the luggage hit the rocky beach.

Emme was clear of the water, but his heart lodged in his throat as he watched her try to steady the wings and unfurl them to their fullest as she pulled against the wind and angled her body to make contact feetfirst.

He'd never felt so helpless. He circled and dove, snapping his own wings open wide and pulling so hard his shoulders and chest ached, wondering if he would reach her only to witness her death. At the least, she could have broken bones, untold injuries. And he had no idea where they were.

She finally hit the ground, and he clenched his jaw at her involuntary cry of pain. Cursing and praying simultaneously, he made the rest of his own rapid descent, pulled hard against a gust of wind, and landed thirty feet from her.

His arms and legs were leaden as he fumbled with the fastenings. His fingers were cold and numb, and he stumbled forward across the rocky shoreline, wings dragging and scraping, until he finally released the buckles. He fell to one knee and picked himself up again. He couldn't reach her quickly enough, couldn't help her, couldn't save her . . . His breath came in harsh, desperate gasps, and his lungs burned.

"Emme!" He skidded the last several feet, finally scrambling on hands and knees to her side. She was sitting up, gasping for breath, unable to pull her wrists free of the contraption and unfasten the bindings.

He lunged at her, pulling at the fastenings, his words a hoarse torrent of frustration and bone-deep fear. He knew in the back of his mind that he was ranting, cursing, and not making any sense. He was furious, terrified, and not giving her even a fraction of a second to respond. He finally freed the last of the harness and pulled her arms through, shoving the heavy accessory away, where it clattered against the rocks.

He put his hands on her shoulders, ran them down her arms, her torso, her legs. Her frantic gasps for air began to even out. She moved carefully, which suggested no spinal injury, although he couldn't be sure. If there were broken bones, though, they would be in her legs. She stayed relatively stationary, placing a hand on his shoulder for balance, until he reached her left ankle and she cried out in pain.

"I'm sorry," she gasped. "Oliver, Oliver, I am so sorry! I couldn't . . . I didn't know where he was taking us . . . I just acted so quickly . . ." Her words came in a torrent, and she sounded much as he had, as though there were a million things to say and no way to express them coherently.

He took a deep breath and sat on the ground next to her, energy stores depleted.

"I am so dreadfully sorry, Oliver. Why on earth did you follow me? I hoped to be gone before you realized . . . You are terrified of heights, and you followed me—Oliver, blast you to Hades, why did you follow me?" She cried hoarsely, her hand clutching his shoulder. "I knew you could handle the captain, and I don't have time to be abducted," she babbled. "You were safe. I knew you could manage . . ."

He closed his eyes wearily and wrapped his arms around her middle, pulling her onto his lap. Her tears continued in earnest, and she put her arms tightly around his neck, sobbing.

"Who hates me so much?" she cried. "Why is someone

working so hard to destroy one simple visit to a gathering? I am—" Her voice broke. "I am kind. I am a kind person. Who would be so hateful to someone who wants the best of life for everyone?"

His heart cracked, and his own eyes burned. He held her close to his chest and grasped the back of her head and neck, placing a kiss on her tangled hair. "Hush," he finally managed. "There, now, you'll make yourself sick." He rocked slightly and continued to murmur in quiet tones, tapping into a well of patience he didn't know he possessed. His own feelings were still a mass of anger and fear, but some of the frustration dissipated as he realized she was in agony over the fact he'd followed her out of the airship.

"As if I would let you jump to your death alone," he said quietly. He rested his cheek against her forehead as she sniffed and her breath hitched. "You should know by now that nothing would stop me from following you." He paused and closed his eyes. "Emmeline, tonight exceeds even what I've come to expect from you."

Her breathing slowed, but her tears continued to fall onto his neck and roll into the hollow of his throat. "Oh, Oliver. I am so sorry. I will never be able to apologize enough. I just—I was so angry. I knew in my bones that if I didn't get off that ship, I would never arrive in Edinburgh.

"It is my life—" Her voice broke again. "I have given all that I am to this thing, and that someone wishes to sabotage such a good purpose . . . I do not understand the evil of the hearts of some. It baffles me. It makes no sense. I will die defying somebody's despicable attempts to destroy me and what I aim to do, but—" She took a deep, shuddering breath. "I did not intend for you to make that same choice."

She sniffled. "Job responsibilities or no, you are not obligated to risk yourself for me." She lifted her head. "Truly. It is enough. Everything about my life is a jumbled mass of craziness, and if your life is forfeit because of it, because of me . . . I cannot have that."

He shook his head and placed his hands on either side of her face. "I will not stand aside as the most vibrant, passionate person I know is in danger from those who are not worthy to spend time in her company. Whoever is behind this is foul, and I'll not see you destroyed at their hands. I will not allow it to happen."

Her brow wrinkled, and her eyes were glossy with tears. "You need not maintain such fierce devotion to a job."

He shook his head again. "You cannot possibly believe I'm sitting here with you right now simply because of fealty to my work."

She grasped his wrist and closed her eyes, causing tears to spill over. "I'm sorry," she whispered again. She opened her eyes, wide and vulnerable, as though begging him to understand her reasons for her desperate behavior. "I had to do it. I didn't have time to negotiate with the captain because we were nearly over the water."

"I know."

She turned her lips into his palm and kissed it softly, closing her eyes. "I'm so sorry," she whispered against his skin.

"Emme, I understand why you did it. Don't apologize anymore. I forgive you." He meant the last as an attempt at levity, hoping for a smile.

She opened her eyes, and the sad regret there gave him pause. She was so different from the woman he thought he'd known. Far from the entitled person he'd decided she was, her passion for others ruled her head and her heart. Her biggest regret from her insane airship bail was for him.

He wiped her tears with his thumbs, reluctant to lower his hands. Her eyes flickered from his to his mouth, and she inhaled deeply, slowly. It was going to happen, inevitable, really, he decided. Perhaps on some level he figured he'd known from the very first time he'd thrown her over his shoulder that someday he would kiss Emme O'Shea.

She leaned into him, her arms tightening, and he needed no further encouragement. He met her lips with his, fitting them together perfectly, like two parts of a now-completed whole. He carefully pulled her closer, wrapping his arm around her and slanting his lips across hers while shoving his hand into the glorious mass of her unbound hair, her pins having been lost several hundred feet in the air.

He had wanted to kiss her forever. Her response was equally passionate and unrestrained but somehow even better than he could have imagined. Perhaps they were giddy to simply be alive, but he allowed himself to enjoy the fact that she met his ardor completely.

She pulled back and eventually opened her eyes. She exhaled softly against his lips and again brushed her mouth against his in the lightest of caresses. "You're very good at that," she whispered.

He smiled against her mouth. "So are you."

"I don't suppose we can just stay here for a while."

"Here? On the rocky beach?"

"Yes."

"No," he sighed, "we should move. If we can remain hidden, this may be a better strategy for avoiding your enemies. I highly doubt they would have predicted such a turn of events."

She shifted in his arms, one hand cupping the back of his neck. She rested her head against his shoulder, and her whole body seemed more languid, as if all of her energy had drained from her in one moment.

He smiled. "Now she wants to rest," he murmured, rubbing his hand along her side, amazed she had come through the fall relatively unscathed. "Does your ankle hurt still?"

"Yes." She nodded as strands of her hair lifted in the wind and snagged on his stubble. "Most abominably." She lifted her head. "Not to worry, however. I shall find a walking stick, and we'll be on our way."

He raised one brow, which she regarded with a scowl. It was a pattern he was beginning to recognize. "A walking stick will solve the problem?"

"Yes."

"You're indignant."

"You're insulting my plan."

"No, no, it's a perfectly sound plan. But, Miss O'Shea, I suspect you have a broken bone inside that stylish riding boot. We may require something more substantial than a walking stick. For now, I'll carry you on my back until we can locate civilization."

She bit her lip. "I'd rather you carry my portmanteau, if you don't mind."

He remembered her mad tumble from the sky, off-balance

from that blasted piece of luggage. "How were you carrying that?"

"I'd fashioned a length of rope around the handles and tied it to my waist and balanced it between my knees. The knot began slipping, and I finally had to let it fall."

"Thankfully," he muttered. "If you'd tried to land while still maneuvering that thing—"

"I couldn't leave it behind. It contains the Blackwell family diaries and all of my documentation for my address to the international assembly."

He managed a smile. "Priorities."

"You may find it ridiculous, but I should be quite lost without that bag. It would negate all of this effort, which would be a shame."

He inclined his head. "We are in total agreement on that score. To waste the efforts of this night would be a tragedy."

"So you'll carry the portmanteau?"

"No. I'll carry you."

Her lips twitched in a smile. "As you said—priorities."

Chapter 11

Emme's ankle throbbed until she thought she'd be sick. The crushing pain added to the terror still racing through her because she'd jumped from an airship, making her dizzy and miserable.

Oliver had told her to stop apologizing, but she'd known he had an aversion to heights and Wing Jumping. She'd had no other options. She had hoped he wouldn't follow her, that by the time he realized what she'd done, the ship would be too far out over open water to even allow him the option.

He carried her on his back for nearly a mile, with her carrying the portmanteau and having him pause so she could switch it between her hands, until he began to stagger and she finally insisted they stop.

The world was still dark, and rolling meadows stretched into the distance. Using her scriber, they'd been able to determine a rough idea of their location, but it was far from precise. Oliver estimated their walking distance from the nearest city at one hour and had fashioned a walking stick for her from a gnarled tree limb.

"My ankle is not broken," she repeated as they stood at the side of the road.

He studied her with his hands on his hips. "You cannot move it an inch without screaming in pain."

She frowned. "I wouldn't say I've been screaming in pain—"

He looked at her flatly. "You've been screaming in pain." He'd insisted earlier that she keep her boot on, knowing once she removed it, her ankle would swell.

She bent down and placed a tentative hold on her ankle, testing it from every angle with her fingertips and biting her lip against the pain. She straightened and said, "Nothing grinds together, and there are no protruding bones. It is merely a sprain."

"Also no small thing."

He massaged the back of his neck, and if she weren't so distracted by her own discomfort, she'd have offered to do it for him. The kiss had been beyond description, and quite likely the only thing that could have distracted her from the pain not only in her ankle but in her shoulders and back as well. She'd decided she could fashion a career out of kissing Oliver Reed and be forever content.

He looked into the distance and then behind them. A light rain had begun to fall, and he motioned toward a nearby copse of trees. "We'll hunker down there until either an opportunity presents itself or I'm struck with a sudden flash of brilliance."

Only yesterday, she'd have teased about the concept of brilliance paying him even a passing visit. Now, she felt a sudden surge of awkwardness. She'd had a very literal taste of him and was in entirely new territory. She nodded and began hobbling with her walking stick as he picked up the portmanteau.

His patience had clearly run thin by the time they were several yards from the trees. The rain had increased its efforts, and he put his arm around her waist. "Relax against me," he told her brusquely, then lifted her against his side.

Her breath left her lungs in a grunt as her feet dangled a few inches off the ground. He maneuvered both her and her luggage into the trees, setting her down when unruly branches and twigs hit them in the face. She managed to avoid "screaming in pain" but couldn't stop the gasp that escaped when she bumped her foot against a rock.

She hopped on her right foot, teetering and balancing her weight, and belatedly remembered she held a walking stick to aid in the effort. While she worked at keeping herself upright, Oliver moved farther into the trees.

"We'll sit here for a time, at least until the rain stops." He appeared again at her side and repeated the awkward half lift to carry her to a dry spot under the entwined trees and branches.

"My portman—"

"I'll get it," he snapped.

He disappeared through the trees to retrieve the bag that had become a source of contention over the last few hours. She chewed on her lip, wondering if he would be restored to good humor if she kissed him again. It wasn't in her nature to manipulate people for whom she genuinely cared, but desperate times and all that. Now that she'd been the recipient of

Detective-Inspector Reed's charming side, she found she liked it better over there.

She examined the small area of ground at the center of four tree trunks and gingerly sat down. She clenched her teeth to keep from crying, knowing she was fully responsible for her current state of affairs. She was not one to place blame on another when it rested firmly on her own shoulders, and she was still trying to forgive herself for Oliver's involvement.

It had been his choice, her rational brain pointed out. But he would never have made such a choice if not for her actions. She couldn't regret it, when all was said and done, because she'd known to her bones that the smarmy captain had no intention of releasing them. She'd felt his malevolence without reading his aura or examining his feelings. According to Oliver, they'd been headed for Portugal. Portugal!

She rotated her head and put a hand to her neck as Oliver returned with the portmanteau. He dropped it on one side of her and sat down on the other. He sighed and leaned against a tree trunk, his hip aligned companionably against hers, and put his arm around her shoulders. He gently pulled her closer and closed his eyes.

"Get some sleep if you can," he murmured. "Rest your ankle, and in a few hours, we'll move again. Someone is bound to come along the road eventually, and we'll beg for a ride to the nearest inn."

She tipped her head against his shoulder and sighed quietly. "Are you hungry?"

He cracked one eye open and gave her a side glance. "I fear I neglected to bring the soda water and cracker tin you requested from the flight 'ton."

"I have food in the portmanteau."

He opened both eyes. "You said it contained only documents."

"I didn't say it contained *only* documents. I make a habit of keeping portable food bits on hand."

"You do? Why?"

"One never knows how long any given activity will take. Protest rallies tend to last several hours, especially if we encounter interference of any kind."

He half smiled. "The law-enforcement kind?"

"Exactly. So you see, you've yourself to thank for the fact that I am prepared." She sat up and pulled the bag to her, opening the top clasp with fingers that still felt sore from the intense cold of her impromptu airship departure. She reached inside and located a biscuit tin and small canteen of water, pulling them out and showing Oliver.

"Miss O'Shea, you've impressed me yet again with your resourcefulness." He took the tin from her and opened it, fishing out a biscuit for her and one for himself. They ate in silence, occasionally feeling the raindrops that managed to infiltrate their leafy canopy. She handed him the water, and he took a sip, wiped the rim, and returned it to her.

A smile twitched, and she fought the urge to laugh.

"I would love to hear what you find so amusing." He took another biscuit from the tin.

She couldn't very well admit she found it silly that he would go to the trouble of wiping the rim of the water canteen so shortly after kissing her senseless on the beach. On a practical level it made sense, she supposed, and she took a sip of water. She should appreciate his thoughtful attempt at civility.

"When we were young, Isla, Hazel, and I used to enjoy impromptu picnics. When Isla's younger—and often irritating—sister, Melody, tagged along, we always insisted she clean the rim after taking a drink of communal punch."

"Did you consider packing more than one drink container?"

"Space was at a premium. Isla usually carried everything in a pack on her back. Does military protocol dictate you wipe the canteen before sharing with a fellow soldier?" She nibbled on her biscuit, hungry but slightly nauseated.

"More often than not, if we were in a position to be sharing water, nobody worried about such details."

She'd never heard his tales from the time spent at war in India. What she knew of Daniel, Sam, and Miles was that they didn't share much about those experiences either. Having arrived at a place where she cared about offending Oliver, she wasn't certain she should ask about it.

"Why did you decide to leave military service?" she asked, hoping the question was innocent enough. "I've heard you were a rising star."

"Were you asking about me?" He winked.

"I may have made some inquiries while looking for information to exploit."

He laughed. "Were you hoping to blackmail me into staying out of your way? I hear such tactics run in your family."

She smiled. Isla had blackmailed her way onto Daniel's airship when they first met. "Perhaps I was actually looking to understand you better but didn't realize it."

He looked at her thoughtfully while eating. "No, I believe your first admission was true. You were looking for information to exploit with no altruistic motives whatsoever."

She laughed. "Much more likely." The moment stretched into comfortable silence, and as she looked at him, she wondered when she'd begun to see him as devastatingly handsome. For nearly two years she'd thought him a gargoyle.

He offered her the open tin, but she waved it aside with a "No, thank you." He replaced the lid and turned it idly in his hands, studying it.

"I had thought to make a career in the military. My early years before were spent as a constable, and when I thought of the benefits of travel and adventure, military service seemed an excellent option. And it was. I just hadn't learned that my temperament isn't suited to that work for a lifetime."

She tilted her head. "I should think your temperament excels at leadership in any organization."

He nodded, still looking at the tin he turned slowly in his hands. "Leadership is one matter. Politics, purchased commissions, and non-merit-based advancement is another altogether."

She bit her lip and tried to keep from digging. It was a useless endeavor, but she congratulated herself for thinking she might manage it. "You face politics and troublesome colleagues working for the Yard, I am certain."

He glanced at her, one corner of his mouth turned upward. "Perceptive, of course." He paused and looked again at the tin. "I lost men in battle. I saw the futility in certain maneuvers but was obligated to follow orders from above. I saw—gruesome things." He traced his thumb along the edge of the lid. "Images that still haunt my sleeping hours." He abruptly spun the tin in his hands and returned it to her. "The horrors of my work now are mostly intermittent. The scope of it manageable. I do not ordinarily encounter large-scale slaughter."

She nodded and took the tin. She returned it to the bag, and, on impulse, closed her eyes and breathed in deeply, opening her senses to him. She felt a wave of grief and even anger before he abruptly shut it away. She looked at him, trying to mask her surprise.

"You have a door you close."

He blinked. "I'm sorry?"

"You shut your reactions away quite efficiently."

He tipped his head in thought before rubbing his eyes. He looked incredibly weary. "A door. Very apt description. One I keep closed and locked."

"I imagine your door resembles a bank vault. I fashioned my door when I was young—yellow with black hardware. Isla says it is dangerous to keep such doors closed. I say it is wise. But should you ever need a place to open your door safely, she is a good one."

He smiled. "Isla is a shifter empath, and I do not count shifting among my traits."

"She is an empath for animals of all sorts. Including the human kind." She closed the portmanteau and turned back to him with a small smile. "I am rarely a willing participant, but there are instances when she has been a great solace."

He lifted his arm, and she settled against his side. She yawned and moved her leg, wincing and groaning when it jostled her ankle. He rubbed her shoulder and dipped his head to look at her face. "We'll find medical help in a few hours."

She nodded and rested her head against his shoulder, blinking back the sting of unwelcome tears. She'd cried enough for a lifetime in one day, her emotions having exploded in a torrent she couldn't remember experiencing since childhood.

"Emme," he murmured, "I feel I should apologize for my actions earlier. I unwittingly took advantage of you in a vulnerable state."

The thought that he would apologize for kissing her caused her heart to drop. "It was lovely, and I do not wish to discuss it."

"I . . . very well." He rested his head against the tree trunk.

She lifted her head, and anger crept forward as she looked at his face, his closed eyes. "Why on earth would you apologize?" She tried to keep the hurt from her voice but heard it herself.

His eyes snapped open, and he lifted his head. "I thought you didn't wish to discuss it."

"Well, I do wish to. I'll thank you *not* to take ownership of a situation in which I was a willing participant. Perhaps it was I who took inappropriate advantage!"

He opened his mouth but said nothing. He studied her with those intuitive eyes that seemed to read everything at a glance. "If I encouraged something untoward, placed you in a position you may later regret, I apologize because it was unprofessional in the extreme. I would not cause you pain."

"You placed me in a position I very much appreciated." She felt herself blush, glad it was still dark.

His lips twitched, but he waited for her to continue. It was a tactic she knew he used as a detective—stop speaking, allow the suspect to fill the awkward silence.

"Insult me with something other than an apology for a kiss."

"You look like a hideous troll."

"That is ridiculous. No, I do not."

"No, you do not," he agreed. "Why on earth do you want to be insulted at all?"

"Anger at you, frustration with you, is much more comfortable." She swallowed. "You swept me out of the path of a careening carriage. You jumped from an airship despite your aversion to heights. You *could* have insisted that someone else take this job. Nobody else would have done it as well, I know that as surely as I breathe. You held me when I was terrified, and I fully participated in that kiss. Do not *ever* apologize to me again about that kiss."

He cleared his throat. "Fair enough." He paused, and this time *she* let the silence linger. "I like to know how to plan for the future, and am . . . unsettled that we have arrived at such an unexpected crossroad."

"Is it *really* so unexpected, Detective? Our reactions to one another have always been strong. Two sides of the same coin and all that."

He chuckled and tipped his head back against the tree. He closed his eyes again and added, "We've flipped the coin."

She nodded and settled against his shoulder. "This side is so much more pleasant," she whispered and closed her eyes, certain she'd not gain even a moment of sleep.

Chapter 12

Light finally crept over the horizon and into the trees. Oliver watched it approach, having slept little. His eyes were gritty, and he wished Emme had a pot of tea in her portmanteau. She still slept, the longest stretch throughout the night as far as he could tell. He knew her leg must throb and protest in pain while sitting still, let alone involuntarily moving in her sleep. He'd stretched out his legs so she could angle sideways toward him and rest her foot atop his shins.

If someone had told him even a week ago that he'd find himself sprawled with Emmeline O'Shea beneath the trees in an unknown countryside, he'd have laughed. Or sworn like a sailor. They'd been resting for a handful of hours, and the enforced stillness when he was desperate to be proactive was a test of his patience. He was exhausted and couldn't have carried her anymore, so when it had begun raining and she'd insisted they stop, he'd been able to retain his pride.

She'd been sleeping with her head on his shoulder, though it had now slid to his chest. He held her close to try to keep her from moving, because every time she did, she awoke with a pained gasp. He took the opportunity now to study her in better light. When compared so literally against his own height, she made him look like a giant.

Her hair was completely free of pins and ribbons. The strands were long, with a gradual curl at the end, and a good portion of the silky black mass was trapped beneath his arm. He wanted to lift it free, but she woke at the smallest of movements, and he desperately wanted her to rest. Her eyelids were swollen, her skin pale, and he knew her shoulders and chest would be aching at least as much as his were from maneuvering the Jump Wings.

He sighed softly and inched his far leg out from under her, bending it at the knee and feeling much like someone trying to keep a child napping. It was better to convince himself that was how he viewed the situation than to admit he had taken the proverbial plunge into abject insanity.

He loved her.

He didn't know why it surprised him. She had been paramount in his thoughts for months on end, and she was definitely correct—their intense emotional clash represented two sides of the same coin. Since taking on the role of her bodyguard, his drive to keep her safe had been as desperate and focused as before, when he was tasked with keeping her in check.

He suspected her feelings mirrored his. She was a constant surprise, however, so he could be completely wrong. Perhaps her affection wouldn't extend beyond gratitude for his friendship and the enjoyment of a kiss. She'd been hurt, though, when she thought he'd regretted kissing her on the beach. That may be nothing more than pride; many a modern woman found opportunities that allowed freedom from dependence on a man. Heaven knew Emme had established her place in the world all on her own, and he was fortunate to have fallen into her sphere. But if he knew anything about her, it was that whatever she did, she did with her whole heart. He didn't imagine she would be content with an occasional dalliance.

He wrapped his hand around his other wrist, encircling her in an embrace, and leaned his cheek against her head. They needed to reach civilization, and soon. Someone had paid Barclay to take them far away, and who that person was must know by now the plan had failed. Oliver had stashed their Jump Wings behind a large outcropping of rock before leaving the water's edge, but even so, he imagined it wouldn't be long before her enemies found their trail.

They ought to have been in Edinburgh by now, settling into the Grand Hotel near the heart of the Summit's festivities. He mentally reviewed Emme's schedule for the day. She was to have visited the International Village, where multiple temporary buildings had been constructed in the Princes Street Gardens to showcase varying countries' cultures with games, food, events, and items for purchase. She was also to have met with Giancarlo and the rest of the International SRO delegates to review the week's events.

As if she heard his thoughts, she stirred. He lifted his head, giving her some space. She planted her hand on his chest and shoved, pushing herself upright with a loud groan and then a wince.

"Oh, mercy. Everything hurts." She put a hand to her

head and rubbed her eyes before glancing at him. "I must look a fright," she mumbled. She gathered her hair in one hand and pulled the mass over her shoulder, grimacing as her fingers caught in the tangled strands.

"I need to . . ." She flushed and looked away. "I'll just go over there for a moment."

He understood her embarrassment and pushed himself to his feet, barely restraining his own groan. "Here, I'll help you stand. I'm going to take better stock of our surroundings now that it's daylight. I will just be out on the road. Call for me if you need me."

She nodded but wouldn't meet his eyes. He bent down behind her and put his arms beneath hers, lifting her carefully and wincing at her gasp of pain. He handed her the walking stick, feeling helpless and wishing there was a maid magically nearby who could help her.

When she was steady on her feet, he looked at her carefully. He could truthfully say he'd never seen her looking worse for the wear, and he'd seen her muddied from a demonstration involving water projectiles and dirt clods. She lifted her eyes to his, and his heart turned over. They were puffy from crying, her face was smudged with dirt, her clothing filthy, and her shoulders slumped.

His jaw tightened, and he cupped her cheek. "I will get you to Edinburgh. Do you trust me?"

She nodded and chewed on her lip. Feeling ridiculously tender, he cupped her other cheek and tilted her head, kissing first one closed eyelid and then the other. She was dejected, defeated, and it did not sit well with him. She was allowed a period of melancholy as much as anybody else, but in his mind, she was Emmeline O'Shea, firebrand and fierce defender of the wronged. To see her looking so crushed was disconcerting, and, he admitted, frightening. He realized then how much he'd come to expect her solidity, even as his adversary.

She must have sensed his thoughts, because when she opened her eyes, she managed a light scowl. "I am not broken."

He smiled. "Of course you're not."

"Then you should not look at me as though I'm already laid out in a coffin."

"Ah, good. There she is." He still held her face in his hands. "I confess, seeing you wounded is an unpleasant occurrence."

"You've seen me wounded plenty." She managed half an eye roll before wincing.

"No, I've seen you filthy from demonstrations gone awry, hair pulled from pins as I've tossed you over my shoulder or into carriages, and angrier than a nest full of wasps. Never wounded."

She cleared her throat, scowl deepening, and subtly straightened her shoulders. "*Wounded* is a subjective term. I've merely been inconvenienced by the actions of others."

He smiled and was surprised by his sense of relief. She was still in there despite her bruises and aches and pains. He kissed her forehead and released her. "I'll be out on the road," he repeated. He paused and turned back. "Emmeline, what would you have done if I hadn't followed you out of that airship?"

She sighed. "I suppose I'd still be sitting on the rocks, stuck in that infernal Jump Wing death trap."

He laughed and made his way to the road. She'd have managed, of that he had no doubt. Perhaps she'd still be near the beach, or taken a different direction, but she wouldn't have remained stationary.

The road was clear in both directions, but the stretch of coast where they'd landed was desolate for miles in either direction. He remembered seeing lights on the western horizon during the night, though.

"West, then," he said aloud and strolled a short distance down the road and then back again to the trees.

He'd begun to wonder if Emme had disappeared by the time he heard snapping twigs. She hobbled out of the trees, making good use of her walking stick. He took the portmanteau from her and eyed her up and down.

"How fares the ankle? Better or worse than last night?"

"Same." She'd cleaned her face and braided her hair, and while her eyes were still swollen and her face pale, she was looking more like herself.

He offered his arm, and she grasped it, and with a deep breath, she nodded at the road. They made their way slowly at first, until she found a rhythm in her limping gait. At one point she paused and withdrew her scriber from her pocket and handed it to him. "The radio signal still isn't strong enough, but perhaps as we get closer to town . . ."

He nodded and watched it periodically as they walked, hoping to see signs of life on the thing. He was looking at it for what seemed the millionth time when she looked behind them and stopped.

"Someone is coming!"

He followed her gaze and saw a horse-drawn cart with a solitary driver approaching.

"Here's hoping he's a friendly fellow," he said as the conveyance grew closer. The large horse's clop was muffled by the rain-softened path but grew in volume until the wagon drew up alongside them and stopped.

It was filled with pumpkins, and the driver was a trim, tidy-looking man with round spectacles, nondescript features, and a friendly, curious smile. He might have been twenty years old or fifty. He was the sort of person who would have been an excellent undercover detective. He would melt into a crowd and be utterly unremarkable.

"This is a long stretch of road to walk!" He bore the speech of an educated Englishman.

Oliver nodded. "I wonder if you are traveling in the direction of Edinburgh? If so, might we prevail upon you for a ride? We would certainly compensate you for it."

"No need for all that. I'm going there anyway." The smile seemed genuine, and Oliver glanced at Emme, who regarded their would-be rescuer with an assessing eye. He couldn't read her face.

She looked at Oliver and nodded. "We are grateful for the help," she finally said.

As the driver slid over on the seat, Oliver helped Emme up and then handed her the bag. She sat gingerly next to the man, her lip caught between her teeth as she carefully maneuvered her sore foot.

"Oooch," the driver said, watching her. "An injury?"

"A sprain," she said with a tilt of her head and a strained smile. "I was running along the rocky shore, foolish me."

"I shall deliver you directly to the hospital doorstep, if you wish, and would also be willing to remain and take you and your husband to your hotel of choice."

Emme looked at Oliver, her smile frozen in place.

"Excellent," Oliver told the man and extended his hand. "We are John and Mary Smith, and are very grateful for your assistance. Our Traveler malfunctioned a mile or so behind us, and we've had a rather long night of it."

"My name is Guster Gustavsen. Associates with a sense of humor call me Gus-Gus. Most simply call me Gus." He shook Oliver's hand and then tipped his hat to Emme. "Let's be about getting you to the doctor, then, dear lady."

Oliver nodded at the affable man, who carried the conversation with innocuous observations about the weather, upcoming holidays and fall festivals, and the multitudes already gathering for the Summit meeting.

The wagon rolled along, catching the occasional bump, and Emme's fist tightened on the bench between them. Oliver picked up her hand and threaded her arm through his. He placed his fingers around her fist and held it, maintaining the other end of the conversation with Gus.

Emme swayed against Oliver, trying to keep herself upright, but after a time, she leaned on his arm and shoulder.

Eventually, Edinburgh appeared on the horizon and grew larger as they approached, the humble wagon making its way into the heart of the city. A combination of ancient and newer architecture adorned the streets, and congestion in both traffic and pedestrian walkways slowed all movement.

The mood was festive, laughter abounded, and music poured from pubs, restaurants, and gathering spots.

They slowly made their way along the row of tents and temporary structures set up on the green lawns of Princes Street Gardens. Signs outside each building announced its function and activities to be found within. Emme, who betrayed her true depth of physical pain by the punishing grip she held on Oliver's hand, took in the city with eyes bright and a smile on her pale face. A large building came into view with the words "International Shifter Rights Organization" emblazoned on a sign above the door.

"Look!" She pointed with her free hand, the other still tightly clenching his. "Stop—we should tell Carlo we've arrived."

Finding treatment for her ankle was paramount, and Oliver told her so, motioning for Gus to keep going.

"I'm fine," she protested.

Oliver used the only thing he could think of to sway her. "You're the spokeswoman for the organization. We must treat your ankle and freshen your appearance before you arrive and are introduced to those you've yet to meet."

She side-eyed him but reluctantly nodded. "You are correct. I'll acquiesce this once." She looked at their joined hands as if only just realizing she was squeezing his fingers. She gasped a little and released his hand, which slowly regained its color.

"And we shall request something for the pain," he told her, his smile wry.

She shook her head. "I cannot have anything that will leave me feeling sluggish. I shall be well enough. Oh dear."

She pointed down the street. "Protesters?" As they drew closer, she frowned, looked pained. Some of the protesters held signs reading "Predatory shifters are dangerous!" and "Protect our children from shifters!"

The crowd was not large, but the effect on Emme was palpable. She bounced her knee, and her eyes widened as she sucked in her breath.

He picked up her hand again and held it between his. "Squeeze," he told her. "And do not fidget; it will only hurt more."

They passed another protester holding a sign reading "Vampires are monsters, not coworkers!"

Emme tightened her grip. "They protest vampire assimilation, too." She looked at Oliver and then at Gus. "Have these protests been continual?"

Gus side-eyed them both for a moment. "No, and they are quickly dispersed. Summit organizers have been quite diligent in securing peacekeepers." He paused before stating, "You are not John and Mary Smith, methinks." Gus's expression was grave as he studied Oliver. "As a matter of fact . . . Have you a brother named Lawrence Reed?"

Chapter 13

Oliver was impressed with the effectiveness Emme's title afforded her at the hospital. Staff were abuzz with the news that the missing spokeswoman for the ISRO had arrived in town and needed medical attention. Apparently word of her delay had spread, though no one knew what had caused it. She was whisked away from him, yelling over her shoulder that he should protect her portmanteau with life and limb.

He remained as close as he could, pacing up and down the long hallway outside the door to her examining room. It was not long before he spied Gus, who, true to his word, had returned to meet them after delivering his load of pumpkins. Gus's question about Lawrence had rattled Oliver more than he cared to admit. He'd put off conversation about him for the moment, but a full discussion about Lawrence was inevitable.

Gus approached him in the hallway. "How fares the lady?"

A scream followed by a torrent of angry almost-curses

sounded from behind Emme's closed door, and Oliver winced. He was torn between wishing he could be with her for support and feeling grateful that the stern-faced nurse had barred his entrance.

"Well enough, I suppose," Oliver said. "Alive, at any rate."

"Oh dear. She must be in horrible pain. Is she still insisting she not be dosed with laudanum?"

"Very insistent."

"Sir," Gus said, falling into step with Oliver as he began pacing again, "I was unable to fully explain my curiosity about your brother, and while I know the time is still inopportune, I feel I must pursue it."

Oliver glanced at the shorter man, whose spectacles perched in front of intense eyes. Sincere eyes, as far as Oliver could surmise. "I've told you he was turned into a vampire a few years ago and has not been in contact with me since."

"Yes." Gus nodded. "I must tell you, however, that—" He glanced over his shoulder and motioned for Oliver to join him in a small seating area adjacent to the corridor. "Lawrence Reed has risen through the powerful vampire Cadre ranks by deposing those above him with frightening speed. He plans to disrupt the Summit meetings, though how or when, I do not know. I have taken this information to the authorities, and they've assured me their security forces are prepared for any attack, but I remain uneasy."

"How are you privy to this information? Are you a private investigator?"

Gus's eyes slid away from Oliver's face for a moment, and he shrugged. "Of a sort. I am a jack-of-all-trades, and because I am unassuming in stature and personality, people do not guard their tongues in my presence." He paused. "I am hoping that, given this knowledge of your brother's plans, you will be vigilant both in protecting Miss O'Shea and listening for any additional information about your brother or his plans. I assume your role is indeed to protect the ISRO's spokeswoman?"

Oliver nodded. Since Gus had surmised they were not "John and Mary Smith," it seemed silly to continue using the pseudonyms with him.

"And will you pass along my concerns to your superiors at the Yard? I fear a Cadre attack would have far-reaching consequences. The innocent of the vampire population are especially at risk. They must live in the shadows now because the reputation of the Cadre terrifies the public. There is little human understanding for those vampires who simply wish to continue their lives in peace."

Oliver squinted. "I am afraid I do not follow. Who are these innocent vampires?"

Gus removed his spectacles and rubbed his eye. The little man suddenly seemed weary. "You are aware of the Soul Consistency factor among the shifter population? That a peace-loving person in human form is also nonviolent in animal form, even if that form is predatory?"

Oliver nodded. Soul Consistency was a theory that had recently been proven in multiple studies; it was the very heart of Emme's arguments. Although the scientific community had known of its verity for years, politicians continued to cast doubt on it to maintain control and take advantage of shifters and their sympathizers.

"The same factor applies to many who have been turned."

Oliver raised a skeptical brow. "Soul Consistency applies to vampires?"

Gus nodded, solemn.

Silence stretched between them.

Oliver finally asked, "How do you come by this information?"

"I know many personally. They have nobody to speak on their behalf. I quietly assess and observe, but I need help. I thought, given your situation and experience, that perhaps you and Miss O'Shea . . ."

Oliver sat back in his chair with a sigh. "Miss O'Shea will take this information and run with it," he muttered, adding, "once her ankle heals, I suppose."

Gus smiled. "Please, allow me to assist you this week. I know the city well, and I have many contacts. I will act as your personal valet and man of affairs. In years gone by, I was a solicitor. All I ask is that you grant me permission to quietly spread the word that you are willing to speak with your brother."

Oliver assessed him carefully. Gus might genuinely wish to help, or he could be a Trojan horse. Perhaps Emme might be willing to read his aura, check for any hint of deceit. "I am not certain meeting with Lawrence will yield any results. We were never close."

Gus opened his mouth, then closed it again.

"Speak, man."

"Sir, would you have described Lawrence as a good sort? Was he kind?"

Oliver's jaw tensed. "Lawrence was a dissatisfied sort.

Unhappy with his lot in life and resentful of any whose circumstances were better than his own."

"Vampirism heightens emotions that already exist, enhances traits one possessed in life. What you say of your brother makes sense." Gus rubbed his neck. "Lawrence Reed is not a good man, sir. He is among the most dangerous I've ever met."

"You've spent time with him? Often?"

"Not often, but enough. As I said, the innocent have no voice, and I quietly search for allies. They are, regrettably, few and far between."

Oliver finally nodded. "My priority is Miss O'Shea and ensuring her safety for the duration of the Summit. I hesitate for you to hint that I wish to see my brother because I will not have Emme put in harm's way. Should you come across further intelligence, however, pass it to me, and I'll see it is fed into the right channels."

Gus nodded, relief showing in his face. "It is more than I hoped for, sir. Thank you."

They were interrupted by the same severe nurse who had prevented him from entering Emme's examination room. "Miss O'Shea has been treated for a severe ankle sprain and multiple bruises but insists she must leave, despite the doctor's recommendation that she stay overnight." She sniffed and looked at Oliver in clear disapproval. "Miss O'Shea says she is to be remanded to your care."

He debated telling the woman that Emme's body was bruised because of an insane dive from an airship, but doubted even that would wipe the look of condemnation from her face. Oliver picked up Emme's carpetbag and nodded to the nurse. "Have you instructions for her care?"

"I gave them to the lady herself, who can read."

Oliver eyed her evenly. "I am well aware of her literary acumen. As her temporary caregiver, I would like to be apprised of any medical instructions you may have."

The nurse sniffed. "She has instructions and will share them if she wishes. We are securing a rolling chair for convenience in transporting her where stairs are a complication, and crutches she may utilize when she feels ready."

"Has she been medicated?"

"Did you not hear the screaming? The doctor prescribed laudanum, but she refused. She is insisting she does not need it and never will. Claims she has no time to waste in a lethargic state."

Oliver's lips twitched. "Time will tell."

"Indeed." She paused, examining him. "Perhaps I'll give you the bottle. Come along. Has she a maid or a female relative nearby?"

"I'll secure the services of a maid at the hotel." He followed the nurse, and Gus followed him. Her stride was surprisingly brisk, and he doubled his stride to keep up.

"Inform the maid that the cast on Miss O'Shea's foot is not to become wet. It's been bound with bandages soaked in plaster of Paris. They've hardened but must remain dry. The cast is small, but not enough to fit inside a boot."

"Madam, supposing the swelling recedes?" Gus asked, trotting alongside Oliver.

She stopped, and they nearly bumped into her. "Who is this?" she demanded.

Oliver swallowed. "My valet."

"Tell your valet that the physician attending Miss O'Shea is a sixty-year veteran of the profession. I should think he knows how to treat a patient." She spun on her heel and resumed her pace.

"Sir," Gus said quietly to Oliver, "it is only that I observed my nephew's condition after a nasty break, and—"

"Not now," Oliver muttered with a shake of his head. "The foot is already set. If it is loose in a day or two, I'll cut off the cast and rebandage it myself."

They reached the examination room just as another nurse wheeled Emme out in a rolling chair. She was pale and bedraggled, with tear smudges on her face.

He turned to Gus. "Will you arrange for a cab to the Grand Hotel?"

"Absolutely." Gus leaned forward to take Emme's hand. "Dear lady, you'll feel much better after a good cup of tea and some soup."

Emme's eyes glistened, and she cleared her throat. "Thank you, Gus." He moved on, and she looked up at Oliver, mouthing, "Get me out of here."

He needed no further urging. He took the bag holding the bottle of laudanum, placed the portmanteau on Emme's lap, grasped the chair's handles, and wheeled her through the halls. His pace was likely too quick for decorum, but she looked up at him with a grin. A weak grin, but he would take it.

Gus showed them to the cab and then informed Oliver he had some business to attend to and would find them at the hotel.

The ride through the streets to the hotel was bumpy, and Emme bore traces of strain around her mouth and eyes. He was casting about for something to distract her when she said, "John and Mary Smith? You are not a creative sort at all. Why not the pseudonyms Xavier and Guinevere? Alexander and Sophronia?"

"The beauty of John and Mary," Oliver said, "is that they are unremarkable. They would allow us to continue our journey without fuss or unwanted attention."

"You are far from unremarkable, John. One would know you as law enforcement at fifty paces."

"I do not care for your tone, Mary."

She smirked and turned her attention to the window. "There are so many people here," she breathed. "I hope . . . I hope . . ."

"The very size and scope of this gathering is proof of growing public awareness. You've been an instrumental part of that and should be proud." He touched her hand, and she turned it over, clasping his fingers but keeping her attention focused on the world outside.

They rode in silence for the remainder of the ride, and the driver pulled around to the back of the hotel, as Oliver had instructed. After much maneuvering and grunts of frustration and pain from Emme, he managed to get her and the rolling chair into the hotel. The halls were crowded with maids and bellboys, kitchen help and various administrative staff. Each walked quickly and with purpose, and Oliver quickly realized the chair was an obstacle.

The freight elevators used for luggage and larger items were crammed full, and two smaller elevators were too narrow for the chair. He flagged a passing employee, flashed his police identification, and requested attention from either the manager or someone at the registration desk.

Emme leaned forward and rested her head on the portmanteau in her lap. She had assured Oliver that she preferred to get cleaned up before being seen by other hotel guests, many of whom were colleagues.

Oliver reflected that they'd not slept decently for forty-eight hours, which explained why he was beginning to see enemies in every shadow. Finally, a front desk attendant, flustered that they'd entered through the servants' area, took their information and provided room keys.

Emme dismissed the harried young man with a smile of reassurance that dropped the moment he was out of sight.

Reasoning they could wait an eternity before a freight elevator was available, Oliver caught the attention of a young maid. "This chair," he told her, "must be delivered to room 407, along with these crutches." He must have looked stern, because she nodded with wide eyes and promised to see to it personally.

He scooped Emme out of the chair, portmanteau and all, and carried her into a personnel elevator. The bewildered maid closed the outer grate, and Oliver instructed Emme to push the button for their floor.

The compartment began climbing, and he shifted Emme in his arms with a grunt. "Ought to have requested a ground-floor room."

"Safer from miscreants when not on the ground floor. Every woman in the world knows that." Emme looked at him, humor touching her mouth. "Is your strength waning, Farmer John?"

"No," he panted, "but my arms are wickedly sore, and my wife's weight is doubled with her wretched carpetbag."

She tipped her head and raised her brows, affecting a picture of innocence. "Your wife can at least stand on her own now."

He took a deep breath. "It would take me an hour to pick you and the luggage up again."

She narrowed her eyes at him as they reached their floor. "I see good manners dissipate once vows are said." She managed to open the elevator gate for them.

"Good manners?" He carried her down the hall to the end, locating their room. "Woman, there is no better image of chivalry than this very moment."

She took the key and fit it into the lock, turning the handle and pushing the door open.

"Only fitting I carry you and your infernal luggage across the threshold, I suppose, since John and Mary have only recently wed."

Her mouth lifted at one corner as she looked at him, their heads very close together.

He entered and nudged the door shut with his foot. The main room was large and elegant, with an adjacent room sharing a connecting door. A sofa and chairs graced the hearth at one end, a large bed occupied the other, and an open door near the bed showed a small wash-and-dressing room.

Emme carefully dropped the luggage to the floor, and he slowly lowered her to sit on the edge of the bed.

They both exhaled, and he shook his sore arms.

"You needn't make such a show of it," she told him, scowling. "The detective I met two years ago could have carried me up a flight of stairs at a run."

He grinned despite his fatigue, despite his worry over her injury, and despite the unknown plans of her enemies. "The detective you met two years ago had no compunction about *how* he would have carried you up those stairs. You're fortunate John Smith is a gentleman."

"Well, Mary Smith is grossly insulted by your utter lack of circumspection. A lady needn't know a man's arms are sore from carrying her across her bridal threshold." She paused and looked at the room as if for the first time. She blew out a puff of air and rubbed her eyes. "Oliver," she said quietly, "thank you."

He managed a smile. "You're welcome." He ran a hand through his hair and scratched the back of his neck. A quick glance in the washroom showed a small bathing tub with plumbed water, which was a welcome sight.

He returned to Emme, who still sat, unmoving, on the bed. Her feet dangled a few inches from the floor, the casted foot marginally larger. "Gus suggested the swelling may reduce. If the cast becomes loose, tell me immediately."

She grimaced. "I do not wish to return to that hospital. Sam and Hazel will be here soon. They can tend to me, if needed."

He nodded and checked windows, the wardrobe, the security of the outer door, and the door connecting their rooms.

"When you wish it, I'll secure the services of a hotel maid. Human or 'ton, whichever you prefer."

"I'll need a human maid right away, actually. Without

my trunks, I'll need her to go to a local shop for a dinner dress. I have the ISRO meet-and-greet this evening. Dining and dancing." She looked dubiously at her foot.

"You'll be there, never fear. You may not dance much, but you'll be in attendance."

She smiled at him. "Thanks to you, Detective-Inspector. I owe you everything."

He waved a hand at her with a wink. "Promise me no shenanigans between now and the final Summit event, and your debt is paid." He picked up a telephone earpiece from the desk and dialed the office. He requested help for Emme's shopping errand, a tea tray, and a maid to help Emme freshen up. "We must keep up appearances," he told her as he hung up the phone, "and preserve your good standing."

"Or *your* continued good standing."

"Yes, also my continued good standing. There's little worse than a man's ruined reputation."

She rolled her eyes and looked at him. "A man's reputation is ruined due to unpaid debts or dishonest business practices. A woman's reputation is ruined if a man compromises her morally."

"I do see the inequity." He crossed the room and looked out the windows, taking stock of the yard behind the inn, the stables and autocar garage, and the neighboring businesses. "Regrettably, all I have to offer unjust society as a whole"—he twitched the curtain back in place and returned to her—"is a healthy, equitable respect for one Emmeline Castle O'Shea." He sat down next to her on the bed's edge. "The rights of women. I see another cause in your future."

She sighed. "It is a cause already underway. I have the energy for but one at a time."

"Fortuitous, then, that you'll be able to take on something already organized and in place. You would be welcomed with open arms."

She turned her head and offered a wry smile. "Mr. Reed, are you sympathetic to the suffragette cause?"

"I am sympathetic to any cause that rights an egregious wrong. My only request is that a semblance of civility is observed."

She looked at her foot for some time before murmuring, "I cannot believe this is happening. I do not have time for it!" Her eyes were huge when she turned them to him. "Oliver, what am I going to do?"

The fact that she was asking him such a thing spoke volumes about not only her anxiety level but her extreme fatigue. The Emme he knew formulated her own plans. The Emme he knew jumped out of airships. A glance at her foot was explanation enough, though. This injury heaped on the mountain of existing stress was enough to make anyone feel helpless.

"The first thing you are going to do is take a bath with the help of a maid. Then you will don the fluffy robe I spied in the dressing room and take a good, long nap."

She blinked, and he wondered if she'd understood a word he'd said.

"Yes. Very well." He carefully put her arm around his neck and lifted her to her feet. With his arm around her waist, he half carried her to the washroom, and, hooking his foot around a small stool near the sink, set her down. He turned on the water, hearing the hiss of the gas heating mechanism. He tested the water temperature, talking to Emme over his shoulder.

"My mother had a theory—everything in life was manageable after a nice, long warm bath. I'm inclined to agree with her." He stood up as the tub began to fill and looked at Emme, who stared back at him with unfocused eyes.

He sighed and knelt in front of Emme, carefully removing her other boot. She stared at her legs, one bare from the knee down and grotesquely discolored with bruises before disappearing into the plaster cast that looked like a hard white stocking.

He took her hands in his. "Emme."

She looked at him, unblinking.

"This could be much worse. Your family could be planning your funeral today."

Finally, she blinked slowly and took a breath. She exhaled and nodded. "Thank you," she whispered, touching her forehead to his.

"You're welcome. The maid should be here momentarily. I'll send her in."

She nodded. "I can manage in the meantime. My schedule for the day . . . there are people I must contact."

"Yes. I'll do that while you rest."

A knock sounded at the door. "That will be either the maid or our new friend, Gus." He nodded toward the filling tub. "Watch the water level." He turned to go.

"Oliver?"

"Yes?" He looked back over his shoulder, thinking she

would thank him yet again and preparing to dazzle her with a humble yet charming bow.

"There's something you should know about Gus."

He frowned. "What is it?"

"He's a vampire."

Chapter 14

She almost summoned enough energy to laugh at his reaction.

"A vamp—" Another knock sounded on the outer door, but he ignored it. "He's a what?"

"Get the door." She scooted the stool over to the bathtub and turned off the faucets. The water was delightfully warm, and for the moment, her only desire in life was to crawl inside the tub for an extended soak.

A knock sounded again, firmly, and she pointed.

"How do you know he's a vampire? Emme, he's far from handsome, he's . . . he's nondescript!"

"Vampires do not have an aura. I attempted to read Gus when he pulled alongside in his wagon. Besides, vampirism merely enhances the individual's best physical potential. That still leaves considerable room for variety."

He blinked. "How do you know he is safe?"

"I can still discern his feelings, his emotions. That man is as sincere as anyone I've ever met."

He opened his mouth, closed it, and repeated the process. By now the knocking had become insistent.

Emme shoved herself upright and hopped over to him. She nudged him out of the bathing room and shut the door behind him. She hopped back to the copper tub and began pulling off her torn, dirt-smudged clothing, deciding she couldn't wait for the maid's help.

She clumsily maneuvered her way into the hot bath while keeping the cast out of the water. Her sigh echoed around the small room, and she nearly cried from the relief of dunking herself completely. Steam rose from the water, and she exhaled wearily, resting her head against the back of the tub and closing her eyes.

She heard Oliver's voice in the other room, thanking someone for the delivery of her rolling chair and crutches, and then the outer door closed. She heard him continue to speak, making calls to Giancarlo, her mother, and possibly their friends. The floor creaked as he paced the room, undoubtedly wanting to solve every problem facing them.

She made use of the soaps lined on a small shelf next to the tub, scrubbing her hair and deciding Oliver's mother had been a wise woman, indeed. Freshly washed and rinsed, she felt armed to at least make a showing to the world, if not take it entirely by storm. She wrapped her hair in a towel and donned the robe Oliver had spied earlier.

She secured the robe as a knock sounded at the outer door, and she hobbled out of the bathing room. Oliver glanced at her as he opened the door, then back again, taking in the casual state of her attire. The robe covered her from neck to floor, but it was intimate wear. What had he expected her to do? Her options were limited, and if she didn't speak to an employee soon who could shop for her, she'd be obliged to wear the robe all over town.

"One moment," Oliver said and quickly closed the door. He frowned and approached her, but seemed unsure about gathering her up to carry her somewhere. He scratched his head as though considering the best way to move a bale of hay.

"For pity's sake," she muttered and hobbled across the room to the sofa.

He helped her sit on the couch and put her feet up, and then looked around, found a blanket, and covered her lap. To her amazement, he flushed. After the indelicate situation they'd been in for hours, he'd suddenly developed a bashful side?

"Oliver, open the door." She sounded cross, even to her own ears.

He obeyed, issuing apologies to Gus and the maid, who stood on the other side.

Emme made quick work of giving the young woman instructions for the clothing she required for the rest of the day and evening. The maid, Josephine, made notes on a piece of paper as Emme dictated. When she began giving her quantity and quality instructions for unmentionables, Oliver and Gus suddenly struck up a conversation about the weather.

"I'll choose carefully, miss, and I'll return straightaway. I know just the shops that carry everything you need." Josephine smiled brightly. "I'll give them this card and tell the sales clerks to send the bill here to you, yes? Oh, and if you've nobody else to help, I can style your hair."

Emme nodded, finally feeling back in control, and Oliver saw the young woman to the door. Gus remained with her near the hearth, and she turned to him. "Now, I hope you are willing to share your story with me. And you," she added as Oliver sat with them, "what do you know of your brother's activities?"

Oliver sighed. "Not much, other than being certain he's up to no good. Gus has a much better grasp of the situation. It's time I took my head out of the sand."

Gus looked at Oliver with sympathy, which reinforced Emme's prior assessment of their new acquaintance. "It is easy to don blinders where family is concerned. The most crucial information for you to know at this point is Lawrence Reed and the vampire Cadre, which he leads, are determined to prevent wide-scale acceptance of shifter reform."

"I can guess the reason," Emme said. "Lucy Blake is a botanist who has studied Assimilation Aid at length. She mentioned new theories of Soul Consistency concerning the vampire community."

Gus nodded. "Not merely theories—scientific studies published in recent journals. Proof of long-term, nonthreatening vampire populations has come to light. Accordingly, the Cadre's stranglehold on non-predatory vampires will soon lose its effectiveness."

Oliver whistled softly and sat back in his chair. "Of course."

Gus smiled wryly. "As law enforcement, you see the problem."

Emme frowned. "I do not follow."

"The Cadre oversees and benefits from extortion money, black-market Vampiric Assimilation Aids, and a host of other things you've likely never heard of. When the world accepts the reality that good, law-abiding vampires exist, Lawrence's tower will crumble."

The room fell silent. Oliver rubbed his eyes with one hand, and Emme's heart went out to him. With vampire discontent and protesters in the streets, Oliver would likely find himself confronting his brother at some point.

Seeking a momentary diversion, Emme nodded toward a small tiepin Gus wore. "Tell me about your pin," she said.

"It is a glass-blown heart that provides identification amongst vampires of goodwill. When I see a person wearing the heart, I know he or she is a non-predatory vampire or someone sympathetic to our cause. We have hidden in the shadows for so long we have learned how to survive by finding one another." He touched the pin with his fingertip. "The glass symbolizes transparency and pure intent, and the heart shape is for the heart inside us that ceased beating at the moment of Turning. Most people are unaware that the majority of the vampire population are Turned against their will. But truthfully, we want to remain in the earthly realm with friends and loved ones." He paused and then smiled. "I suppose the notion of a symbolic heart is at odds with your prior assumptions about vampires."

Emme nodded, her throat aching with the symbolism. "It is," she answered honestly, "but given what I know of the shifter community and the hatred they face, I am not surprised." She returned his smile. "The glass heart is beautiful—a lovely symbol."

"Thank you, dear lady. I confess, the Summit has given many of us a sense of hope. Heaven willing, we shall see clear skies between now and the week's end."

The Grand Hotel gathering hall that evening was a lavish affair, beautifully appointed and sparkling with light. The mood was festive, champagne flowed, and people laughed as they tried to overcome language barriers and mostly succeeded. Summit attendees and visitors from all around had descended upon Edinburgh, and the air was charged with excitement and possibility. The predinner social event was by invitation only, and as the face of the ISRO, Emme was well on display. Josephine, the maid, had outdone herself in selecting a ball gown for Emme to wear as well as choosing a hairstyle for her. Much to Emme's surprise and delight, Gus was also an adept hand at managing curling tongs and accessories.

Emme and Oliver had both managed a long nap, Oliver in his hotel room and she in hers, but with the adjoining door left ajar should something happen. As much as her ankle throbbed and her bruised body protested each movement, she felt rested enough to enjoy the gala and all it signified.

Their friends had arrived in time to check into their rooms and attend the dinner social, and her colleagues showered her with careful embraces and well-wishes. Signore Giancarlo helped her make the rounds of the room, speaking with ambassadors she'd previously met and a few whose faces were new to her. Her ankle throbbed, but her giddy relief at knowing they'd actually made it in relatively one piece to the Summit after all the months of preparation outweighed the pain.

As she moved through the room, one hand on Carlo's arm and the other maneuvering a crutch, Oliver was never far behind. She felt his presence constantly, and it gave her a sense of peace she wouldn't have imagined possible. He had met Carlo in London the day of the carriage "accident," and the two had developed a quiet communication as they navigated the crowd. Now and again, she would hear Oliver's low murmur and catch Carlo's subtle nod as she spoke with dignitaries, sharing the ISRO's mission and the benefits it brought to countries, cities, and towns.

She noted the military men and constabulary mingling subtly among the crowd; Carlo told her the entire city was guarded carefully after law enforcement had foiled two minor plots to disturb gatherings at the Princes Street Gardens pavilions.

The only dimming factor of the evening was her worry for Oliver. He did not verbalize concern for anything other than his mission to keep her safe, but since the discussion with Gus about Lawrence Reed's narcissistic and ruthless control over the vampire world, there was a heaviness to Oliver she'd not felt before. She wanted to take it from him, or at least help him shoulder it, but she was learning that sharing intimacies and personal concerns was not usually part of his repertoire. Perhaps in the future . . .

That she was considering a future involving Detective-Inspector Reed and his personal burdens was an irony not lost on her. It played in the back of her mind as she mingled and smiled, chatted and made lighthearted comments about her injured foot and her clumsy use of the crutch. She wanted to see Oliver smile, and knowing he felt responsible for all in his purview—whether the men under his command in India or the entirety of England itself—suddenly seemed grossly unfair. Little wonder he had been so fierce in disrupting *her* efforts at disruption; his determination to keep the peace and ensuring order was part of who he was.

Had it been only twenty-four hours since they boarded the airship in London? She thought of her mad leap from the airship, the soul-crushing fear as the ground had grown closer, and the relief mingled with guilt when she saw him touch down behind her.

The kiss—oh, the kiss. It had been one of the most majestic moments imaginable. She would remember it as long as she lived. She allowed herself the luxury of glancing at his mouth, his face, and the way his shoulders and frame perfectly filled the formal tuxedo.

He touched her shoulder and asked quietly if she felt well, and she nodded at him with a smile, missing Carlo's introduction to an ambassador from Port Lucy. Oliver inclined his head toward the guest, his lips twitching in a quick smile at her, and she whipped her attention back to the moment at hand. She flushed but figured she would be allowed an occasional moment of distraction—everybody knew she'd been in an accident of some sort. They needn't be privy to the fact that her distraction was wrapped around the memory of a desperate, frantic kiss in the dark on a lonely beach.

The dinner bell rang, and Carlo relinquished her to Oliver, telling her, "I took the liberty of seating you with friends. We will mingle more with others afterward."

Emme leaned toward him as he kissed both of her cheeks.

"Detective," Carlo murmured over her head, "when dinner finishes, we move into the ballroom. I'll join you there, and we shall decide how best to help our wounded spokeswoman circulate, as dancing seems out of reach for now." He winked at Emme, and his expression turned serious—a rarity. "I am happy you are here."

"Thank you, Carlo. This work means the world to me, and the thought I might miss it had me in knots."

He held up a finger. "You remain close to your bodyguard. No acts of bravery, at least until your foot heals."

"Noted." She smiled and took Oliver's arm, balancing on one crutch. He led her to wide double doors and into a dining room where round tables were set with glittering crystal stemware and silver polished to a bright shine.

Oliver walked Emme to the table where their names were scripted on place cards. To her delight, Sam and Hazel were already there, as were Daniel and Isla. Lucy and Miles had been snagged in conversation but were making their way to the table. Isla settled next to Emme, and when the ladies were seated, Oliver sat on Emme's other side.

Hazel, seated next to Oliver, leaned past him to regard Emme with huge eyes. "What were you *thinking*?"

"We had a devil of a time keeping the details from your mother," Isla said as she spread her napkin onto her lap. "Dearest, your escapade leaves me in horrified awe." She looked at Emme much as she had when they were younger and Isla was the eldest in charge.

Emme fought not to squirm. "I had no choice," she whispered back, glaring first at Isla and then Hazel.

"The captain was taking the ship to Portugal," Oliver murmured low, his eyes sweeping the room.

"Exactly." Emme motioned with her hand. "He was taking us to Portugal, where we would have likely been drugged and imprisoned. Possibly killed." She sighed. "Clearly our hasty departure from the ship was not one I would have chosen had there been any other option."

Miles and Lucy arrived at the table, and the gentlemen rose as Lucy was seated. She looked at Emme, eyes sparkling. "We have much to discuss! The *Journal of Paranormal Medicine* published only today their latest findings on Soul Consistency within the vampire community!"

Emme's smile spread across her face. "How wonderful! Fortuitous timing. The more credibility we can show, the better for everyone."

Lucy nodded and then paled as the introductory course was placed before her. Miles deftly moved it away and handed her a glass of water.

Emme frowned. "Are you ill, Lucy?"

Lucy shook her head and glanced at Miles, who winked at her.

"Oh, I do not believe traditional illness is at work," Hazel said.

Isla gasped quietly and turned to her husband. "Daniel, I believe congratulations are in order. You're about to become an uncle."

Daniel Pickett, Lucy's brother, turned to her, mouth slack. "Is it true?"

Lucy sipped her water and then placed the glass carefully on the table. "It is." She smiled, although her face remained a shade lighter than her normal, healthy hue.

Miles frowned. "She's not kept a decent meal down for weeks."

"Martha Watts insists I am perfectly fine."

Daniel raised eyebrows high with implied doubt. "Martha Watts, the stable mistress?"

"She has been a midwife for years," Lucy said, exasperation clear. "I have also consulted two obstetric physicians in London at this one's insistence." She motioned to her husband. "They validate Martha completely."

Hazel's attention was on Miles, and she chuckled softly. "I am certain Lucy really is fine." She elbowed Sam, who grinned at his friend's distress.

"I've reassured him repeatedly." Sam winked at Lucy. "Be strong, my lady. He may stop fussing before you deliver."

Isla and Hazel both looked at Sam. "How long have you known?" Isla demanded.

He lifted a shoulder. "Few weeks. This food is delightful. Will you be eating yours, Lucy?"

Emme laughed and glanced at Oliver, who smiled and seemed more relaxed than he'd been in days. He inclined his head at Lucy. "Congratulations to the both of you." He raised a glass and said, "To your continued good health."

They each raised a glass, and Emme had taken a sip when a hotel employee appeared at her elbow.

"For you, miss," the young man said, extending an envelope to her.

"Thank you." She took it from him, and Oliver tensed in his chair.

"A moment," he called to the messenger, who returned. "Who is the sender?"

He shook his head. "I received it from the front desk and was told to deliver it immediately."

"What is your name?"

"Edward, sir. Edward Smoot." The young man swallowed.

Oliver nodded and dismissed the boy.

"Is there a problem?" Miles asked quietly.

Emme swallowed. "I've received several cards and letters since arriving, but they've been delivered in bulk to the room."

Oliver held out his hand, and Emme gratefully gave him the envelope. The script appeared a match for the Bad Letter, and she hoped she was imagining it.

Oliver slit open the envelope with his knife while taking a quick look at the large dining room. He removed the card inside, touching only one edge.

"'Return to London, Miss O'Shea, or you shall bring wrath upon the world,'" Oliver read in a low voice.

Emme's lips pinched together, and she tried not to react.

"Do you believe the sender is in the room?" Daniel asked Oliver.

"Possibly." Oliver motioned to the nearest constable. He murmured something to the man, but Emme's ears were buzzing. The food on her plate suddenly seemed inedible as her stomach turned.

Isla gripped her hand. "Emme. Look at me."

"If I do not leave, everybody is in danger." Emme bit her lip and fought the burning sensation behind her eyes that signaled tears. She looked around the room at the sea of people who were having a lovely time.

Oliver's voice sounded low in her ear. "Your family is here. Far corner, left side."

Emme's eyes followed his directions, and she spied

Lysette, Sir Ronald, and Madeline. Seated next to Madeline was Nigel Crowe, and with him were Mr. Jenkins and another young man she didn't recognize. She swallowed. "How did they receive invitations?"

The event was an exclusive one for foreign dignitaries, members of Parliament or other influence, and presenters of note. Miles was an earl, and Lucy a well-respected botanist who was scheduled to present her work with Anti-Vampiric Assimilation Aid. Daniel Pickett owned the world's largest fleet of airships, and Dr. Isla Cooper-Pickett was well known in the shifter community as a therapist. Sam was a respected surgeon whose star was on the rise, and Hazel was presenting an address on the spiritual components of healing and potential applications in shifter medicine. To Emme's knowledge, in addition to her own circle, everyone in the room had a reason for being included on the guest list.

"Sir Ronald is a baron," Hazel said, mirroring Emme's thinking. "Perhaps that, along with your mother's status with Castles and your role here, provided incentive for their invitations?"

Emme lifted her shoulder. She couldn't allow her family's presence to tarnish her enjoyment of the evening; the fact that she'd just received a threatening note did seem suspicious, however. "Who is the younger man next to Jenkins?"

The others strained to see around the people in their various lines of sight. "Stuart Rawley," Miles said grimly. "Youngest member of the PSRC. I'm surprised they dare show their faces here this week, given the damage they've caused through the years."

Emme nudged Isla. "I thought you said your friend Nigel had turned over a new leaf. He's back on the Committee."

Isla squinted at the table across the room, and her mouth dropped open. "Why is he there?" she murmured.

Daniel's brow creased in concern. "He must have an explanation."

"Yes," Emme said hotly. "His explanation is that he is rotten."

Isla turned back to Emme. "Sweetheart, I am certain he has his reasons. He is not rotten."

"Where is your mother?" Hazel asked.

"In London with Isla's mother for a few more days. They were needed at the store." Emme was glad. The thought of seeing her mother sitting with people who bore her such ill will would have been especially cutting tonight.

They returned to their meal as the next course was served. Emme noted with some surprise that Gus had been standing watch in the shadows.

Oliver motioned to him and quietly instructed him to make inquiries with the front office about the message Emme had received, which was now nestled in Oliver's coat pocket.

She was unable to eat much but made a good show of regaining her spirits. Conversation continued, but a stressed undercurrent ran through it. One course followed another, Oliver discreetly telescribed Chief-Inspector Conley, and Gus returned to quietly report that the message had been left at the reception desk with written instructions to be delivered to Miss O'Shea during the meal.

As dessert drew to a close, Emme again looked across the room at the table where her family sat. Madeline turned then, and locked eyes with Emme. Her face was tense, her aqua-blue gaze haunted, even at a distance.

"Something is wrong with Madeline," Emme whispered.

"What is it?" Isla asked.

"I don't know. She's been . . . Her behavior has been . . . I don't know." As Emme watched, Nigel Crowe leaned closer to Madeline and said something. Madeline, clearly startled, turned to him with a response. Emme's lips thinned. "What does he want with her?"

Isla clasped Emme's cold fingers again. "I will find out."

An announcement was made for all to gather in the ballroom in fifteen minutes, and the guests rose and began to exit the room. People groaned and laughed about dancing on a full stomach, and Emme smiled at several guests she'd met earlier, laughing and exchanging noncommittal niceties even as her mind tumbled and worried.

She and her friends walked back through the main hall, the density of packed people easing as some made for powder rooms and others to the patio for some air or a quick cigar. Emme was dizzy with pain and fatigue, and she noted the crowd's movements as though they were all slow and underwater.

Carlo was making his way to where they stood near a bank of windows just outside the ballroom entrance. Gus quietly approached Oliver with a question, and her friends stood close by. A flash of light in her periphery was followed by shattering glass as an object with a lit fuse crashed through one of the windows and rolled to a stop near their feet.

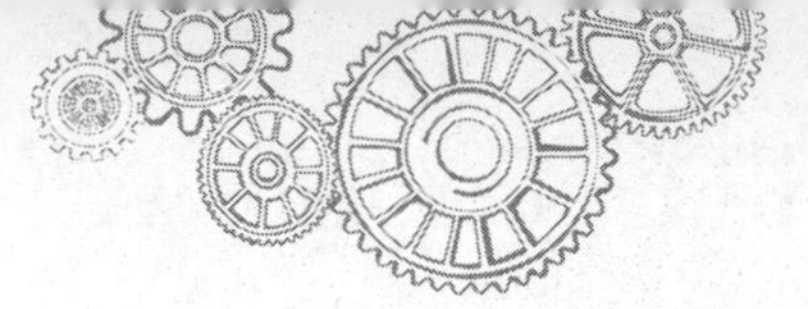

Chapter 15

Oliver's heart tripped as an incendiary device smashed through the hotel's massive windows and rolled to a stop on the thick rug. He wrapped both arms around Emme's head and shoulders and pulled her down to the floor as Miles picked up the device and jumped through the shattered glass.

The chaos was deafening, screaming from outside spreading inward like a wave. Isla pulled a knife from a sheath on her leg and leaped through the broken window, quick on Miles's heels. Oliver squinted and was just able to make out Miles, who drew his arm back and hurled the thing upward where an explosion rocked through the sky.

Daniel, cursing, yelled at Sam to remain behind as he jumped through the broken glass behind his wife.

Emme trembled but was shoving at Oliver's chest and arms. "What happened?"

He rose, pulling her upright and supporting her weight. He squeezed her so tightly she grunted and coughed. Moving quickly and staying close to the wall, he headed around a corner. The main hotel staircase was down a long hallway, but to his relief, three passenger elevators were situated to the right, and one was empty and open. He hauled Emme into the elevator, and she was barely able to drag her crutch into the compartment before he slammed the door and punched the button for their floor.

"What was that?" Her breath came in gasps, matching his.

"An explosive device packed into a bottle with a fuse. We called them 'cocktails.'" He leaned against the wall of the moving elevator, chest lifting and falling, and kept her close against his side. "Are you hurt?"

She shook her head.

"Are you lying?"

"Perhaps, just a bit." She looked up at him, eyes troubled. "People are in danger because of me. This is all my fault."

"This is not your fault. If you begin that line of reasoning, you'll have played nicely into his game. He is not going to win. They are not going to win." He tightened his hold on her shoulder. "Are you hearing me?"

She nodded. She swallowed, closed her eyes, and rested her head against his shoulder.

He released a deep, shuddering sigh and tipped his head back to the wall, closing his own eyes for a moment.

"I hope nobody was hurt," she said without lifting her head.

"I believe Miles solved the problem before it came to that."

"Did I see Isla run outside after him?"

He lifted his head, lips curling in a rueful smile. "She did. Daniel was not pleased."

She looked at him, her own grin threatening. "I am certain he wasn't. She makes him crazy. He should not worry so much. She is very, very competent, with years of experience running after dangerous predators and the like."

He shook his head, both pitying his friend and completely understanding. "Easier said than done. Mistakes happen no matter how competent someone might be. There are often variables out of one's control—and sometimes a person will rush in where fools fear to tread with no thought for self-preservation at all."

"Come now, Detective. That sounds rather like a pointed barb."

"Does it?" He tipped his head back against the wall again. "I wonder why that should be. Perhaps because it sounds oddly familiar."

The elevator bounced to a stop and settled in place. Oliver opened the door, scanned the hallway, and helped Emme walk to her room. Once he settled her near the hearth, he kindled a warm fire and rang for Josephine. Emme was quiet as they waited for the maid, and he wondered if she still blamed herself for the incident.

He opened the door between their rooms and, sighing, removed his jacket, cravat, and cuff links. The day had been long, it was late, and the threats against Emme were far from over. For all he knew, his own brother might have had a hand in it.

Emme's family's attendance was suspicious, if nothing else but for the timing. He would have to speak with Nigel Crowe about it. Oliver knew Nigel had resumed his position on the Committee, but this time as a spy. He wasn't at liberty to share the information but wondered if he should tell Emme so that she wouldn't push the issue. Illegal and unethical goings-on had been part of the Committee since its inception, and Conley was quietly hopeful Nigel would be able to collect useful information. Oliver was becoming more convinced that someone on the Committee was responsible for the threats against Emme.

A quiet knock sounded on Emme's door, and he hurried to answer it. A quick look through the peephole revealed Emme's stepsister, Madeline, and he frowned. He opened the door. "Yes, Miss O'Shea?"

"Detective, I must speak with Emmeline. Please, it is important." She darted a glance down the hallway.

He opened the door wider, suspicious, but allowed her entrance.

"Madeline?" Emme looked bewildered at her stepsister's appearance. "What is it? What's happened?" She paused. "Other than the explosive, I mean—is anyone hurt?"

Oliver motioned for Madeline to take a seat, and she perched on the sofa with Emme.

The young woman was pale, and she rubbed her forehead with her fingertips. Oliver noted the pink dress, which washed out her complexion, and the severity of the chignon fastened tightly at the back of her head and hiding the beautiful strands of brown, red, and gold hair. Her large aqua eyes seemed desperate and anxious.

Emme's voice was soft. "What is it, Maddie?"

Madeline's eyes were liquid, and she chewed on her lower lip for a moment. She shook her head. "I believe you are in danger, but I do not know why. I hear whispers behind closed doors but never see who is talking. I've heard your name more than once since our arrival, and . . . and Lysette has made 'secret plans' for the hunt." She winced. "She is not a good person, Emme. I know it as well as do you. I do not trust her, though I have been unable to discover her plans."

Emme's eyes widened, and a smile spread across her face. "Madeline O'Shea, have you been sneaking about?"

Maddie blushed even as she shook her head in denial and studied her hands. "Only enough to learn that her last secretive conversation was just before we left the lodge to come here. She specifically singled out Mr. Jenkins and Mr. Rawley. And now Mr. Crowe wishes to speak to me about bird-watching."

"What would they possibly be planning together? And what on earth is Nigel Crowe about? When did you take up bird-watching?"

Maddie shook her head. "I have not. One of the guests at the social was regaling me with her tales. I was only nodding in agreement."

Oliver leaned forward, bracing his arms on his knees, and rubbed the back of his neck. "I've no idea what they may be planning. I am aware of Mr. Crowe's activities, however."

Emme waited. "And they are?" she prompted.

"Confidential."

"Con . . . *confidential*?" Emme scowled at him. "We agreed not to keep secrets from each other."

He looked at her flatly. "We did not agree to any such thing. I cannot share police business. And to my knowledge, you still have 'confidential informants' inside the government whose identities *you* refuse to divulge."

"Of course," Madeline whispered.

They both turned to her. "I'm sorry?" Emme said.

She nodded slowly. "Mr. Crowe must be working undercover, spying on the other members of the Committee. It stands to reason; he doesn't seem to like any of them. Barely tolerates them. We've been at the lodge for two days now, and I've wondered why he bothers."

"Not a very effective way to foster trust," Emme muttered.

"I do not know if he was any different before, when he was one of them," Madeline said.

Emme looked at her stepsister. "You're very observant," she said quietly. "I'd no idea you were so perceptive. I am sorry, Maddie, for . . . many things. For always leaving you in that house."

Madeline lifted a shoulder. "I never gave you another option. You did try, long ago. You do not understand Lysette. Or rather," she admitted, "I suppose you do."

Oliver remained quiet, as was his habit; he listened, faded into the background so others would perhaps forget he was there.

"Why does she have such hold over you?" Emme asked. "I understand her tyrannical personality, of course, but Maddie, you are so much . . ." She spread her hands wide, searching for the words. "So much more everything."

Madeline was quiet, studying her hands. Her shoulders slumped as though she would sink in upon herself. "When we were young, she was merely cruel. Manipulative. She knew what bothered me and exploited it. A few years ago, however, she learned . . ." She lightly cleared her throat, and even with her face tilted down, the blush was clear. "She learned something dreadful about me."

Emme frowned and leaned forward. "What could it possibly be? And how are you certain it is truly dreadful?"

She laughed softly and finally looked at Emme. "It is."

"Maddie, it cannot be so awful. What on earth could she know that requires you to endure her continual abuse?"

Madeline shook her head. "It is ruinous."

Emme studied her for a moment. "If that is true, then your actions here tonight may cause problems for you with her."

"I do not believe she will divulge my secret—not yet. Once she does, she will have no more leverage."

Emme's hands tightened into fists on her lap. "Then let us find a way to take that power from her."

Madeline smiled. "As it happens, I do have a plan. When the time comes, I promise I will take you into my confidence. Until then, I must ask for your patience."

Emme released a breath and sat back. "Very well. I will honor your wishes. In the meantime"—she looked at Oliver—"is she correct? Is Nigel Crowe spying on the Committee?"

Oliver rolled his eyes the slightest bit before massaging his forehead with his thumb and forefinger. "I would not know, of course, Emmeline."

Emme smiled at Madeline in triumph. "Excellent observational skills, Maddie."

"You'll not repeat such a rumor to anyone, of course," Oliver said.

"Who on earth would I tell? Mr. Rawley? Other Committee members?"

Oliver sighed. "You know what I mean, Emme."

"Maddie, let me help you. You're a grown young woman. Lysette is like a poison. She has made my life miserable; I can only imagine how it has been for you."

Madeline's eyes were glossy with unshed tears.

Emme shook her head. "I have been so busy telling myself I am helping the downtrodden, yet I failed a sister in my own home."

Madeline bit her lip, wiping at the tear that spilled down her cheek with a hand that trembled. "You were surviving, Emme. Just as I was." She pulled in a deep breath. "Yes, perhaps we can stop her. Ruin whatever she has planned. If I can, I'll search her room. We've rooms for the night on the sixth floor."

"Have you noticed anything unusual in Lysette's attention to the Committee?" Oliver asked.

"I am not entirely certain, but I have noticed Lysette's affections turning quite heavily toward Mr. Rawley."

"An illicit assignation?" Emme asked. "Lysette is most particular about her potential suitors. I suppose that is irrelevant if her intentions are less than circumspect. She may not see him as a suitor at all."

"Mr. Rawley may not be titled, but he is in a position of some power. He has attended the last two hunting parties. He also seems taken with Lysette, but as I said, I do not know what her true intentions are." She blushed, then glanced at Oliver. "I know she does harbor a tendre for others who are also not titled but are men of some influence."

Emme gasped, looking at Oliver. "I knew it! She is in love with you!"

Oliver raised a brow. "That is preposterous. She does not even know me."

"Detective," Madeline said, "she has instructed the staff to inform her immediately of your arrival at the London home. She feigned tears, once, in a conversation with you, and keeps with her always the handkerchief you gave her. Additionally, I heard her once ranting about your attention to Emmeline."

His mouth dropped slightly. "My attention to Emmeline has never been social in nature. In fact, it has even been negatively confrontational at times."

"That is true," Emme muttered.

Madeline shrugged. "I see that. I believe everybody sees that." She paused. "Until now, I suppose—now that your role with Emme has shifted." She paused again, longer. "Since you were assigned as Emme's bodyguard, Lysette has been intolerably angry."

"Oh dear," Emme breathed. "Worse than usual?"

Madeline nodded. "Much. And she has railed at Father, of all things. Has him quite baffled."

"Yet you say she is showing attention to the young Committee member, Mr. Rawley." Emme frowned. "If she is seeking access to his power, she should know he is in danger of losing it if all goes well at the Summit and the government agrees to abolish the Regulations Committee."

Madeline looked at her in speculation. "All the more reason to hope it fails. You do have a tremendous gift with public address."

Emme's mouth slackened. "That is what I do not understand about these threats to me. It is ridiculous!"

Madeline shook her head. "You've never been in the audience of one of your own speeches."

Emme stared. "Have *you*?"

She nodded. "One afternoon, Lysette was shopping, so I snuck away to the Activity Hall. You were . . . It was enthralling. Everything seemed so clear when you spoke, it all made sense, and the feeling of goodwill toward one and all was just . . . overwhelming. Inspiring." Madeline smiled. "I was quite proud of you."

"Oh, Maddie. When this is all done, we have some things to change at home."

Madeline's smile faltered, but she nodded.

Oliver noted the slip. She was holding something back. He excused himself and stepped aside, telescribing the name Chief-Inspector Conley had given him if he needed to contact Nigel Crowe. He quickly asked if Crowe knew of secret conversations between Lysette O'Shea and any other Committee members. While he waited for a response, he listened to Madeline.

"Your mother sent a package with me, rather secretively," Madeline said. "I've only glanced at it, but it seems to contain two ensembles, colors I've never worn in my life. Lysette has always bullied her way into decisions about my wardrobe, so I wear pastels."

"Do you prefer pastels?"

"Not particularly. In fact, one of the dresses Mother sent is aqua in color, and shimmery." Madeline smiled. "I quite like the look of it."

"Excellent! It will match your eyes, and you will feel like a princess." Emme grinned at her.

Madeline sobered. "And Lysette will find a way to make me feel as though I've committed a criminal act for making a decision without first consulting her."

"Lysette can chew on an angry stick. You and I are finished allowing her to rule over us."

Oliver's telescriber dinged with Crowe's response.

Yes, secret conversations. Cannot ascertain the content.

Oliver frowned. He felt as though they were headed for disaster, and he was frustrated at his inability to see around the bend. He sent another message to Crowe.

When did Rawley become a close associate of Lysette O'Shea?

Crowe replied immediately.

Six months ago. Sir Ronald invited him on a big-game excursion to Africa. Most of the Committee are regular guests at the family hunting lodge here.

It was a pity Crowe hadn't returned to Town earlier; his presence embedded with the Committee was helpful now, but he was a step behind.

A knock sounded at his door, and he crossed into his room to find the Blakes, the Picketts, and the MacInneses in the corridor. He ushered the couples inside and led them to Emme's room.

Sam and Hazel joined Emme and Madeline on the sofa, while Lucy took an adjacent chair, her expression grim and eyes angry. Oliver had spent time with Lucy and Miles before they were married and Lucy had been a houseguest at Blackwell. Lucy had suffered a vampire attack, and Oliver and Miles had been her only company for a week as she convalesced. He recognized the frustration in her face at her inability to fix the situation, to solve everything immediately.

She looked at Emme. "Bryce Randolph hired someone to toss that explosive into the hall."

"We don't know it for certain, Luce," Daniel said to his sister and joined Isla at the hearth.

"Who else would it be?" Lucy snapped back. "That smarmy little miscreant described him to the last detail."

Oliver looked to Daniel. "You caught him?"

Daniel side-eyed his wife. "Isla ran him down. Surprised him with a throwing star to the back of the shoulder and then tackled him to the ground."

Emme clapped her hands. "Of course she did. Well done, cousin!"

Isla inclined her head, and Oliver noted Daniel's smile, his frustration and pride evident in equal measure.

Oliver looked at Emme's pale face, the dark smudges under her eyes that bore evidence of her continued fatigue, and the cast on her foot. The similarity in a penchant for action was evident in the cousins, and he knew a moment of rueful despair. He was in for it every bit as Daniel was.

Emme would never slow down, and he realized with some surprise that he felt it would be a pity if she did. She would always take life by the throat, and he would always chase after her in a heightened state of anxiety.

It was a truth he could no longer deny. He'd been chasing after Emmeline O'Shea for two years, and the thought that there might come a day when that pursuit was no longer his role did not sit well in his gut. The thought of her eventually as a friend, a lover, a wife to someone else made him irrationally angry. Perhaps his reaction wasn't so irrational, he mused as he looked at her. Any man would recoil at the idea of a woman he loved with another.

He looked back at Daniel, seeing a future version of himself in his friend. Daniel rested his hand beneath Isla's hair and massaged the back of her neck. In all likelihood, the contact was probably more a comfort to Daniel than Isla, who seemed perfectly composed. She leaned into her husband, comfortable and content.

The men in the room, his best friends, had reached a place in life that Oliver now envied for the first time. He wanted what they had. He'd spent time with them socially for months and had never felt a wisp of desire to walk the path they had each pursued. Now, however, everything had changed. His world had completely spun and shifted. He didn't want what they had with just anyone. He wanted it with the woman on the sofa who had turned her attention to him as the conversation continued.

She wrinkled her brow and tilted her head at him, and his heart thumped that even amidst the chaos of their circumstances, she was attuned enough to him to know his thoughts were elsewhere. Provided he could keep her alive, perhaps she might entertain the notion of receiving him in her drawing room for purposes other than arrest or interrogation.

". . . you heard what I said, Emme?" Isla was looking expectantly at her cousin.

Emme blinked and turned her attention away from him, and he bit back a smile. "I'm sorry?"

"You seem a mite distracted." Isla's lips twitched.

"I was conferring nonverbally with my paid companion," Emme said hotly.

Laughter met her remark, and Daniel, grinning, looked over Isla's head at Oliver. "Didn't realize you'd changed professions, Reed."

Lucy shot a look at her brother but also laughed. "Paid companions come in many forms, you know. Sometimes a young woman will travel with an elder aunt, or a family friend."

"Equally as amusing," Miles said, his mouth turned up in a grin. "And what did your 'nonverbal communication' tell you?"

Emme glared at the lot of them, even Madeline, who sat next to her and tried to cover her own mirth. Emme's lips twitched, and she huffed out a breath. "*I* am prepared to tell *him* very verbally to cast you all out into the corridor."

In truth, once he had the information the others had come to deliver, Oliver planned to do that very thing. Emme was tired, he was tired, and the hour grew late.

"Isla," he said as the laughter died down, "what did you learn from the man you took to the ground?"

She took a breath and sobered. "I questioned him before the police arrived, and he described the man who had hired him to lob the device through the window—'the one with the curtain drawn back'—as soon as he caught sight of a woman walking with the aid of a crutch."

All levity in the room settled. Oliver couldn't bring himself to look at the hurt he knew he'd see on Emme's face. "With the intent to kill her."

Isla shook her head. "I don't think so. He said he was to scare the woman, throw it when he saw her, not when he could hit her with it."

"So to frighten me," Emme said, "and everybody else in attendance. What if Miles hadn't been there? What if someone had been hurt because of me? I know you'll all say it's not my fault, but if I weren't here, it wouldn't have happened."

"Perhaps not," Miles said, "but likely, yes. The cocktail would have been thrown at someone else who represents the ISRO. The organization has risen to tremendous influence in the last year alone, and is ultimately the biggest threat to the Committee's existence." He paused, then added, "This is not your fault."

She bit her lip, and her knee bounced twice before she winced and stilled. "Nevertheless, I believe it in everyone's best interest if I remain in this room until the final night of festivities."

"Oh, Emme," Madeline breathed. "You have worked so long for this."

Emme reached over to clasp Madeline's hand. "And it will all be for naught if the whole thing is blown to kingdom come." She sighed and looked at Oliver. "I shall have Carlo present the address tomorrow on the history of the ISRO and its current mission. Perhaps if I remain scarce, the next couple of days will pass uneventfully and I shall still be able to address the final assembly before they vote to pass an international accord. *Hopefully*, they vote to pass it."

"They will pass it, Emme," Hazel said. "In the meantime, once I've finished my presentation tomorrow, I shall keep you company here."

"Likewise," Lucy added, and Isla nodded.

"No, no. You must all go out and enjoy it for me. Please. I caught only a glimpse of it today, and perhaps I can sneak out in a day or two, but I need you all to see everything and tell me about it." Emme smiled, but it was strained.

"Tomorrow evening, then." Lucy's tone was firm. "We will bring the celebrations to you. Leave everything to me."

"Excellent." Emme nodded. "And you'll join us, Maddie." She looked at her stepsister.

"Yes," Isla added. "It is lovely to see you here, Maddie."

Madeline blushed. "I'll make every effort." She glanced at the clock on the mantel. "Oh, mercy. The hour is late." The blush faded from her face, and she looked ill.

"Miles!" Lucy jumped up from her seat. "Thank you, Madeline, for noting the time. We must go but shall see the rest of you tomorrow." She planted a quick kiss on Emme's cheek, and Miles nodded to them all before making a quick exit with Lucy.

Madeline looked in confusion after them as she stood. Oliver realized that while Emme knew of Miles's condition as a predatory shifter, she would not have told her family. He thought to make an excuse for their hasty departure, but Madeline said quietly to Emme, "I must be back in my room. Lysette will have noted my absence by now."

"Yes, very well. The sixth floor."

Madeline nodded. "We return to the lodge tomorrow evening following dinner with Father's associates at a restaurant down the street."

Emme reached up and grabbed her hand. "Visit with us tomorrow night before you leave, if possible. I shall be in touch."

Madeline nodded, squeezed Emme's hand, and left. The Picketts and MacInneses also made their farewells as Gus entered Oliver's room with Josephine. Leaving Emme in the young maid's capable hands, Oliver brought Gus up-to-date with news of the perpetrator. Gus had little to report other than having heard continued rumblings about a planned attack sometime during the week.

Oliver called Conley to compare notes and learned that Bryce Randolph, the head of the Predatory Shifter Regulations Committee, had indeed hired the man to throw the cocktail through the hotel window when he saw Emme. Randolph had taken to the shadows; a team had been tasked with his arrest.

Oliver felt fortunate so much law enforcement and military presence had descended upon the city; this latest disturbance was now heaped upon the usual round of increased activity visited upon a host city. In addition to several thefts and two minor assaults, six missing persons reports had been filed in the prior twelve hours.

At length, Josephine left via the connecting door between rooms, as he had instructed everybody to contact Emme through him. The door between their rooms was still ajar, and he poked his head inside to see Emme seated on the couch in a robe, legs drawn up and arms wrapped around them. She stared into the fire, barely blinking.

He knocked on the doorframe. "May I?"

She lifted her head, gesturing to the space next to her on the sofa.

"Bryce Randolph was responsible for this evening, and the search for him is on. Perhaps now that he knows he has been identified, the threats will cease."

She nodded but didn't seem convinced. In truth, he wasn't settled either.

"We'll remain vigilant. Have you contacted Giancarlo regarding tomorrow's address?"

She nodded again, and this time, a sheen covered her eyes. She cleared her throat as if she might speak but then swallowed and looked again at the fire. A tear trickled down her cheek. It was sadder than any she'd shed over the past many hours since her frightening jump from the sky, and his heart turned over. How did one comfort a woman? He would have to ask Sam about such things. In the meantime, he scooted closer to her and put an arm around her shoulders.

She sniffled and blinked, then leaned back, resting against his side. "He hasn't won," she murmured, and he was relieved at the statement.

"No, he definitely has not. We are outmaneuvering him. Keeping you hidden is strategically sound, should he have other weapons in his quiver." He settled comfortably and stretched his legs on the coffee table before them. "I'm curious," he said after they'd sat in silence for a moment, "why you'd never referred to Randolph as your nemesis. I know I have the honor of that title and that Nigel Crowe is 'nemesis number two,' but surely you have a pet name for the worst of us all."

She turned her face toward his and arched a brow. "I do, indeed. His name is 'Devil.'"

"Ah. Very good." The firelight flickered warm against their faces, and he cupped her cheek, rubbing his thumb softly across her skin. His heart thumped hard in his chest. Her head lay against his shoulder, and he thought of the times he'd been close to her and not nearly so content.

"Are you in much pain?" He traced her brow with a fingertip.

She blinked slowly. "Yes, but I'm growing accustomed to it. Hardly notice it anymore."

"I have some laudanum to help you sleep, if you wish."

The corner of her mouth lifted. "Detective-Inspector, is it your goal to render me defenseless?"

He smiled. "I would never waste energy on the impossible."

"How is it that a handful of days ago I quite detested the sight of you?"

He chuckled softly and brushed strands of her long, dark hair from her face. "We had a good, long run on the enemy front, did we not?"

"We did, indeed. Where are we now?"

He pursed his lips as if giving the matter thought. "Unfamiliar territory. Are you concerned?"

Her brow wrinkled. "Stunned, more like. Are you concerned?"

He smiled. "Extremely. I am afraid if I do not kiss you again, we'll not know whether our feelings on the beach were simply a reaction to stress or something more."

"Mmm, yes. I see the need to investigate." Her eyelids fluttered closed as he shifted, intending to place his lips on hers.

They were separated by a fraction of an inch when a quick knock sounded at the door, and Emme jumped, bumping their noses together.

"Miss Emmeline, I wonder if you—oh my! Oh, do forgive me." Gus stood in the doorway between rooms, mouth agape.

Oliver closed his eyes and tipped his head forward, resting it against Emme, who stared at Gus, wide-eyed.

She shook Oliver's shoulder. "Gus has a question."

"I know." Still, his eyes remained closed.

She cleared her throat, and when he made no attempt to move, she said, "What is it, Gus?"

"Forgive me, miss. Josephine has sent word that she is not scheduled to work tomorrow morning but would be glad to come in anyway and offer her assistance."

Emme sighed, her breath falling softly against Oliver's neck. "That would be lovely, Gus. In fact, I mean to speak with her about the possibility of a more permanent position."

"Very good, miss. And . . . well . . . as you were."

The room was again quiet, and he felt her laughing softly before he finally lifted his head and settled for a kiss on her forehead.

"It is late," he said with a sigh and a smile.

"And the moment has passed." She shook her head, but the corners of her mouth tilted upward.

The phone rang in the other room, and Gus answered it, pausing as he tripped over himself explaining that the detective was out . . . er . . . not out, but occupied . . .

"I'll be right there," Oliver yelled to Gus, who relayed the information to the caller.

"Go." She nudged him. "I am falling asleep anyway. I'll sit here another moment and then climb into bed."

"Very well." He paused, wishing he could say something poignant, or at least witty. Instead, he stood, making his way to the door. "Call out if you need anything—Gus and I will sleep lightly. Keep the corridor door locked, and do not open it for any reason."

She saluted him, and he smiled. Perhaps a quiet day spent together would be a good thing.

Chapter 16

Emme felt crazed by noon the next day. She knew everybody was out enjoying the festival, and she was stuck indoors. She paced awkwardly, sometimes with both crutches, sometimes with one, and other times limped around without either. She made a circuit around her room and into Oliver's more times than she could count.

Josephine had arrived at breakfast time and was delighted at the possibility of future, full-time employment with Emme. In addition to duties as a maid, she was also an excellent seamstress and proficient on a typewriting machine. Emme was in the process of checking references, but she already knew Josephine had the temperament to deal with Emme's restless energy. She was efficient and possessed good taste in clothing and manners. Emme had sent her out shopping again for more clothing and necessaries, and she envied the young woman her ability to leave the hotel, even if it was for only an hour.

Emme had tried to convince Oliver that the threat to her well-being no longer existed since Bryce Randolph knew he'd been found out. Oliver had reasoned that Randolph was still on the run, and he was surely not the only one involved in trying to silence both her and the ISRO. As much as she wished otherwise, she couldn't argue with his logic.

She received a message from Madeline on her telescriber that read, *I know what's happening. I will stop by* . . . and then it ended. She didn't say when she would stop by—presumably before the family left for the hunting lodge, but Emme wasn't sure. She'd returned a message that went unanswered, and instead called the front desk. She was informed that her family had taken three rooms on the sixth floor, but Sir Ronald had checked them out earlier in the morning. Madeline's cryptic message played in her thoughts, and she felt uneasy for her stepsister. She did not trust Lysette.

Gus came and went, gathering what little crumbs of information he could without raising suspicion. His network of acquaintances was impressive, in both the underground vampire world and the unsuspecting society of humans with which he mingled.

He took daily medication that was an improvement on Vampiric Assimilation Aid, which allowed vampires to walk in the daylight and eat regular food. It was also incredibly expensive, and the vampire Cadre controlled both the medicine and its distribution. Yet another reason the Cadre did not want to see vampires as a whole accepted within human society. If vamps did not feel the need to hide any longer, the Assimilation Aid would become obsolete.

Carlo made one of the presentations she had been scheduled to give, and visiting her later, gave her details of all who were present and an accounting of the conversations occurring before and after the address. He expressed regret that she had been unable to speak herself and patted her hand, promising that she would be safe and the "scoundrels rounded up" before the night of the midnight vote.

After Carlo left, Emme wandered into Oliver's room to find him sitting at a small table, writing a letter. He looked up at her entrance and smiled, oozing charm. The more irritated she grew with their enforced confinement, the more affable he became. It was insufferable.

"Why have you never married?" she asked Oliver bluntly.

He gave a startled laugh, and she looked at him, determined not to flush or feel awkward.

"Who says I've not?"

She froze in place, aghast. "You're married?"

His mouth quirked in that smile that was now more infuriating than charming. "No. I am not married. Have never been."

She looked at him in silence, wondering why it mattered.

"You would be unhappy if I were?" His brows rose innocently, and yet a smug undercurrent rolled from him in waves.

"I would feel an enormous amount of pity for your wife, knowing her husband was tasked with the personal protection of another woman who does *not* look like a hideous troll."

He nodded sagely. "Fortunate, then, that I've managed to beat back the pressing horde of women who want nothing more than to be the wife of a detective. Especially if my career continues on its current trajectory. Perhaps I shall move into the knight-in-shining-armor business, make a living protecting damsels in distress."

She frowned, not caring for the sound of that option, either. Then an equally irritating thought struck. "I am not a damsel in distress."

"No. You are not." His expression sobered. "You're in need of protection from enemies unseen, but you are not in distress. That is an important distinction to you."

She nodded. "It is, but I hate to think you are placating me."

"Never. I do not find you helpless, never have." He sighed. "My work would have been infinitely less complicated if you were. The helpless refrain from tearing into the fray, heedless of worry for life and limb."

"Ah, but then you might find yourself facing a nasty case of ennui, no?"

He laughed, and it warmed her heart. "Rich man's boredom? I hardly think I shall ever be bothered by such a thing. If I were ever at risk of it, however, I've you to thank for keeping it away."

"You are most welcome." Her mouth curved into a smile. The world had righted itself, mostly. He was not married, had never been, and did not consider her helpless or distressed.

Why did it matter so much to her?

Probably because he was handsome, of course, and she was of marriageable age. He was a fine specimen of manhood, and both nature and science practically *dictated* she should find herself drawn to him. She'd had an almost-kiss with him the night before, and even as tired as she'd been, the thought of it, the memory of his tender closeness, had kept her awake for some time. She paused at the mantel, trying to untangle the knot of her emotions.

"Would you care to share your thoughts, Miss O'Shea?"

She *could* tell him what she'd been thinking. She could admit that she felt herself falling through a cloud of her own emotions and desires and hoping he would be on the other side to catch her. She could admit that she was depending on him more than she'd ever depended on anyone before, and as much as it was frightening, there was also a heady delight in it.

He would defend her with everything he had; she knew it in her soul. What she did not know, however, was what a passionate kiss meant, one which might not otherwise have transpired had they not just cheated death. If she gave him her heart, even if he didn't know she'd done it, he might not be interested in keeping it. She knew he was developing a reluctant affection for her, but she very deliberately did not open herself to his emotions because she was afraid of what she might *not* find. And if she did find something significant, what on earth was she to do with it?

"I was thinking of all the times we met as antagonists," she finally said. "We'd never have believed in a future that saw us working together." It wasn't entirely a lie, more of an evasion. An omission of some details.

He rose from the table and joined her at the hearth. He took her hands, one at a time, and held them between his own. "You're cold," he said as though she'd done it on purpose.

"I suppose the turning weather has seeped under my skin." As if to punctuate her statement, a flash outside the window signaled lightning, followed by a clap of thunder.

He rubbed her hands briskly. "The storm is blowing in

quickly. You ought to have said something. I'll build up the fires."

She shook her head. "It is plenty warm in here. Likely it is a case of nerves. I am unsettled, and now that the rain is beginning to fall on the festivalgoers, I am feeling quite bad for them."

His lips quirked, and he held one of her hands up to his mouth, cupping it in his and softly blowing warm air onto it. "You feel bad for the festivalgoers whose parade is literally getting rained upon. Festivalgoers who have been the target of your envy all day."

"Certainly! I hate to see their fun come to an end."

He chuckled and repeated the warming process with her other hand. The small gesture was proving so effective she found herself quite warm all over.

"You are amazingly good at playing nursemaid. Did you know that? Have you had occasion before to be so . . . motherly?"

One eyebrow shot up. "Does my attention to you truly feel maternal?"

She swallowed. His nearness was deliciously warm, and she wanted to snuggle against him and hold him tightly. Maternal? She sighed. Not in the least.

She looked up at him, and those intense golden-brown eyes held a hint of laughter, mixed with an exasperated smirk she was certain should spark her temper.

"Not *maternal*, I suppose, but you seem very . . . natural . . . at all of this." She waved her hand in a small circle. "This caring-for-an-invalid sort of thing."

"I'll be honest."

"Please."

"I could care for you as an invalid with much less familiarity and significantly more professional efficiency."

Her cheeks warmed. "I suppose you could." She cleared her throat and tried for an expression that would read Mature Conversation Between Two Adults, Neither of Whom Feel Self-Conscious. "And you've another situation with which to compare?"

His lips twitched. "Another situation where I've cared for an invalid with more professionalism? Less familiarity?"

"Yes. Just so."

"I believe I can gather a memory or two. Between military service and police work, I've been occasionally called upon to lend aid." He paused. "Heaven knows I ought to be reprimanded at the very least for my presumption. Would you rather I establish clearer boundaries? More distance?" His voice was low and wrapped around everything in her that still felt chilled.

She felt fairly breathless. "I believe that would be counterintuitive, wouldn't you say? How can you keep me safe from a distance?"

He tucked her hair behind her ear. "An emotional distance, perhaps, would be more appropriate. Less of this sort of thing." He trailed his finger softly along the curve of her neck.

She licked her lips. "But Josephine is off on an errand, so it naturally falls to you to fix my hair . . . warm my hands. And after falling from the sky, it would have been positively criminal for you to neglect me."

"I do admire your logic." He put his hands in his pockets,

and she swayed slightly forward, regretting the loss of contact. "One might suggest those hours directly following the 'sky falling' were a natural response to fear of death or paralysis."

That didn't account for the night before, when the prospect of another lovely kiss had been unintentionally curtailed by one well-meaning vampire-valet.

Oliver sobered, and she knew he laced his flirtation with honesty. "If I were any sort of gentleman, I would treat you now with less familiarity, not more."

"You are more of a gentleman than the majority of men I know." Her throat felt thick, and she swallowed. Honesty was painfully emotional, and she didn't want tears threatening when she had entirely too much time to wallow in it. She gave him a half smile. "I am still quite traumatized, you know. Any sudden change in your treatment of me could be awfully dangerous and extremely irresponsible on your part."

He lifted that one brow, but for the first time, it didn't feel condescending. In fact, when combined with the smile that played at the edges of his mouth, the warmth she felt turned to heat.

"I should hate to be accused of neglecting my duty to you, Miss O'Shea."

She nodded. "I should hate to feel obliged to report your dereliction to your superior."

"Speaking of my duties." He nodded toward the sofa. "You ought to sit. Rest your ankle."

She sighed. "Perhaps in a moment." She smoothed the lines of his vest. "I am too restless to sit." She fiddled with a button on his chest and lifted her eyes to his, stepping a few inches closer.

He pulled his hands from his pockets and cupped her elbows, slowly inching his way up her arms to her face. "You're playing with fire," he murmured.

"Perhaps."

"Do you ever do anything by halves?"

She smiled. "What would be the point?"

He chuckled softly and shook his head, finally lowering his mouth to hers in a kiss that robbed her of breath and coherent thought. He braced her against him with an arm around her waist and one at the back of her neck. She clutched his vest in tight fists.

The shrill ring of the telephone intruded, and Emme was content to ignore it, but then Oliver broke contact with a sigh. She swallowed, overwhelmed, and when he straightened, she relaxed her fingers and tried to smooth the mess she'd made of his vest.

Oliver clasped her hands in his, kissing her knuckles. "Probably a timely interruption," he whispered and left her to answer the call.

She placed her fingertips against her lips and watched him walk away, running a hand through his hair. He picked up the receiver, his back still to her, and she sank slowly onto the sofa, enjoying the simple pleasure of watching him move.

The tone of his voice was professional, as always, and he leaned down to jot notes on a paper. He listened, then responded, turning to lean against the table, one hand on his hip. His shirtsleeves were turned up at the cuffs, revealing arms she'd felt around her more times than she could count, and she couldn't help but smile.

He looked at her as he concluded the conversation,

finally hanging up. He leaned against the desk and folded his arms over his chest. A flash of lightning showed outside the windows, where a relentless rain hit the glass.

Emme sat back against the sofa cushions, and she grinned even as her heart thumped with a mixture of daring and fear prompted by self-preservation. "You're not going to come back over here, are you."

"No, I am not."

"Was that the Chief-Inspector?"

"Yes."

"With an update?"

"Yes."

She nodded. "Any news of consequence?"

"Nothing useful to us."

She felt a thrill at his use of the word *us*. It tied them together as a unit and almost gave her the courage to ask him what his feelings for her entailed. Almost. As much as she was reckless and an odd sort of brave, she couldn't make the words leave her mouth.

"I suspect Gus or the others may return soon, and we would be well advised to turn our attention to more . . . constructive things," he said.

She'd had things on her mind before they'd begun flirting like a couple at a society ball—well, she amended, perhaps a couple outside in the moonlit gardens at a society ball. She was hard-pressed to remember what had been occupying her thoughts, and for a moment her mind was blank.

She took a deep breath and released it in a sigh, then pulled her telescriber from her pocket. Constructive. She could be constructive and professional and not at all affected by something as simple as a harmless attraction to a man whose job it was to protect her at all costs. That was the problem, really. The relationship had been unusual from the beginning, and now had twisted into something equally strange. She was a modern, adult woman, and she would act like one.

She straightened in her seat and cleared her throat. "Something is bothering me, as a matter of fact."

He raised a brow, the picture of a calm professional. Pleasant but back down to the business at hand. "What is bothering you?"

She frowned. "Something about Madeline. Nothing negative, but there is definitely something odd happening. I cannot put my finger on it. Perhaps if Maddie visits later, Isla might discover it. She's dangerously good at coaxing conversation from the most reluctant of people."

"Madeline has not yet responded to your telescribed message?"

Emme shook her head. "Nothing. The family is supposed to hunt tonight. I know she dislikes it as much as I do, and I wish she would come here instead."

"I do not suppose much hunting will take place if this weather continues."

She rolled her eyes. "They may wait until it clears. Of course, they do like to make a show of their masculine prowess in times of difficulty. Hunting in a rainstorm at night might be just the thing."

"Do they customarily hunt at night?"

Emme sighed. "Yes. Again, anything to prove their prowess."

Oliver frowned. "They're fortunate nobody has been accidentally shot."

"So they say," she muttered. "I would put nothing past them. For all I know, there could be graves all over the property." She glanced at Oliver. "You should check your missing-persons lists."

"I'd like to believe you jest."

"Of course." She smiled and shifted on the sofa to warm her back at the fire.

"What do they hunt? Small game, I should think?"

"Yes, small game here. They travel to Africa for the larger, more dangerous kills. Lysette pouts at being excluded from the big-game expeditions abroad, and the household is obliged to weather her foul mood until Sir Ronald returns with his grand stories and even grander trophies." She smiled grimly. "My mother put her foot down when he threatened to station a lion and hyena in the London townhome."

"Does she spend much time at the lodge?"

"No, but now and again, she likes to assert her position."

Oliver looked surprised. "He does not control the money?"

Emme smiled. "Women and property law was an issue barely in its infancy when my mother married Sir Ronald. She refused to step one foot near an altar unless he signed away his rights to her portion of Castles' Boutique and any income it may ever generate."

Oliver whistled low. "Very intuitive of her. How was she certain to avoid loopholes?"

"Our solicitor is an old family friend. By the time he finished drafting the documents, my mother's interests were carved in stone, as were my aunt Bella's, Isla's mother." Emme felt immense satisfaction in that fact. She remembered the ruckus it had caused, having been old enough to understand her mother's fierce determination and her insistence that she would cancel the wedding. "Sir Ronald was not pleased but eventually capitulated. What else could he have done? He got his money for estate repairs, and Mama bought a title. She thought it would be good for the business."

Oliver nodded slowly and quirked a half smile. "The apple has not fallen far, I see."

Emme sniffed. "I'm sure I do not understand your insinuation."

"That you inherited your persistence from your mother?"

"Persistence. I shall take it as a compliment."

"It was intended as such."

She glanced at him with sudden suspicion. "Have you endeavored these last several minutes to distract me? Keep me from crippling boredom?"

"Has it been effective?"

She frowned. "Spectacularly."

He laughed softly. "Excellent. My work here is done."

"If only that were true," she muttered. "I'd rest easier."

"Come now." He made his way to the sofa and sat down. "I thought we had moved beyond our mutual distrust."

"No," she said, glancing at him. "I mean I'd rest easier knowing you were away from harm." Her cheeks warmed.

Her thoughts returned to their Wing Jump landing on the rocky shoreline. She knew she'd babbled unintelligibly when he'd landed on the beach after they'd jumped, though she couldn't exactly remember what she'd said. She was certain it ran in the vein of "I couldn't bear it if anything happened to you." That was entirely true. And then there had been "The Kiss," which she now amended to "The First Kiss." But the words she'd used in that frantic moment of fear—she didn't *think* she'd admitted she loved him . . .

The thought stopped her cold. She swallowed, her eyes fixed on the fire grate and definitely not on him. She had fallen in love with her nemesis, her greatest enemy. She frowned deeply and chewed the inside of her lip. She tried repeating to herself all the excuses she'd manufactured over the last week regarding her growing attraction to him but could not make any of them stick.

She sighed. "This is a disaster."

"Which part?"

"I ought to have insisted you replace yourself with someone else."

He was quiet, and she finally braved looking at his face. He was guarded. She'd not seen that expression for some time, and that she'd put it there filled her with regret.

"I do not mean to offend, I only . . ." She twisted her fingers together. "Do you understand? I—please understand—Oliver, I could not bear it if you are harmed in defense of me." She shook her head. "I do not want to see you harmed at all, under any circumstances, but were it to happen while protecting me would be the cruelest of all things. Especially since I really did detest you only a short time ago, and—"

He laughed, then, and leaned close to her. Just when she thought he might kiss her again, he took her hand in his and patted it, which made her scowl. Perhaps he *was* only feeling maternal now. He'd kissed her twice and had every opportunity to make it a nice, round three. They were quite alone, she was *not* a young debutante in danger of ruination, and she doubted Gus would return within the next few minutes, or however long it would take for Oliver to indulge her with one more kiss.

Men were amorous, or so she'd been told; what man wouldn't take advantage of the moment and claim one more kiss? Maybe he found her lacking or had simply indulged her because she'd had a traumatic forty-eight hours and he knew she desired the closeness. He *had* tried to step back. She had pressed the advantage.

"You, Miss O'Shea, are enchanting." He smiled and squeezed her hand, giving it one last friendly pat.

She looked at him flatly. "I am going to read now. Excuse me."

Still smiling and trying to stifle a laugh but clearly failing, he helped her rise, and she hopped with as much dignity as she could manage back to her own room.

Emme did manage to read for a time, reviewing some passages in Miles Blake's old family journals, about people who, to their horror, had begun shifting into predatory animals three nights per month. The pain, the fear, the humanity of the stories never failed to move her, and she planned to share some of them at the end of the week. She wanted to hold up one of the journals, show the physical proof of living, breathing people who were unjustly terrorized because the majority didn't understand them.

The day dragged on interminably, until finally Josephine presented her with a lovely dark-green dress and helped her get ready for dinner with her friends. The young woman had also procured a black stocking that she stretched over

Emme's casted foot, and while they laughed at the silliness of it, Emme decided it was much better than staring at the ugly white plaster.

She had sent a note inviting Madeline to join them for dinner and a visit but hadn't heard anything in return. She worried, remembering Madeline had said she was going to try to do some snooping around Lysette's room.

She had discussed the next day's activities with Oliver, Gus, and Carlo, and they had agreed to wait to see what news came from local law enforcement before deciding whether she would remain sequestered for another day. Gus had thought of a few other associates who might have knowledge of Bryce Randolph's whereabouts, and had promised to speak with them later that evening. The thought of remaining alone with Oliver after she'd all but thrown herself at him that afternoon was not something she wanted to contemplate. She would insist Josephine remain with her and save herself the embarrassment of dwelling on the fact that Oliver Reed had probably just been placating her. It was just as well. Distance from him was safe. He was doing her a kindness, really.

Finally, a knock on the door signaled it was time for what Oliver had described as "a secret gathering." She grabbed one of the crutches and made her way into the corridor with Oliver.

"Where are we going?" she asked.

"Not far." He grinned and led her to the room adjacent his. "This room was unexpectedly vacated this morning, and Lucy snapped it up. It is now fit for a queen's celebration."

Emme laughed as they entered the hotel room, which had been rearranged to hold a large dining table. Lucy directed the guests to their seats and made use of two hotel staff, who served the meal according to her instructions.

"Lucy, this is lovely!" Emme smiled as Oliver took her crutch and held out the chair for her. "And you've brought souvenirs!" Flags, scarves, and bits and pieces of the countries represented at the festival were placed all around the room. "You've gone to so much trouble."

Miles shook his head. "My wife could do this in her sleep. You've made her most happy by providing a reason for a gathering." Lucy eyed her husband askance but nodded in agreement as she gave a final instruction to one of the servers. Miles waited for her to finish and then held out her seat. She made a remark to him over her shoulder as he seated her, and he chuckled and murmured something back. The words might have been whispered, but the affection was clear.

The gentlemen sat, the meal began, and Emme's friends regaled her with tales of the day. She laughed with them, soaked up each detail, and felt extraordinarily fortunate to have loved ones who cared for her. It helped ease the sting of the last few days—weeks, even. The sadness and frustration she'd felt while at home, her current worry about the shifter cause, and the self-doubt in the back of her thoughts that often crept forward and taunted her belief in herself were banished in the warm glow of friendship.

They finished the meal, and Lucy directed the removal of the table and dishes. The furniture in the room had been pushed back, leaving a large empty space that Lucy proclaimed was now a dance floor. She produced a Victrola that Emme was fairly certain hadn't been there moments before and cranked the handle, producing the sounds of a recorded waltz.

Amidst laughter and cheers, the couples matched up. Emme looked awkwardly at Oliver, who extended his hand. "May I have this dance?"

She looked down at her foot, unwilling to spoil Lucy's fun but doubtful about her ability to participate.

"We shall move in very small circles," Oliver promised. "I'll support you."

His words echoed through her head, and she nearly grew emotional. He was her support, always. Even in times of stress and antagonism, he hauled her away from danger. She thought of all the times he'd disrupted rallies, jumped into the thick of the melee, and while his primary aim had been to stop the chaos, he always managed to snatch her from harm's way just as it was about to descend upon her. Looking at him now, appreciating the broad shoulders, the sun-kissed face and hands that evidenced time spent outdoors in the warm summer months, she thought of all the times he'd bodily tossed her about in the name of law and order and regretted she hadn't known at the time to appreciate it.

She smiled and took his hand. "I must apologize in advance for your sore feet."

"Nonsense. I've seen you dance before. You'll manage an injured ankle without fuss. Would you be more comfortable with the crutch?"

She laughed. "No. Remember to be patient, though."

"Always." He stepped close and splayed his hand wide across her back, holding her right hand securely. She placed her other hand on his shoulder and leaned on him for support. True to his word, he moved slowly and in small steps to accommodate her limp.

They swayed in silence for a moment, and she looked at the others, who were so clearly happy together. She loved them all, had grown up with Isla and Hazel, and her heart was full as she watched them dance with their husbands. She laughed self-consciously and shook her head. "I am sorry you are saddled with a wounded partner."

"I am not. As a matter of fact," he said, his mouth close to her ear, "I believe the benefits far outweigh any negative."

She smiled. "And how is that?"

"I am holding you much closer than propriety allows. But I must, you see, or you will fall."

She tipped her head up and laughed, torn between affection and frustration. "I do believe you are a shameless flirt at heart."

The surprise in his eyes was genuine. "Now *there* is one thing I have never stood accused of."

She was dubious. "Truly? You've never used your considerable charm to comfort or placate a desperately pathetic woman laboring under a mountain of stress?"

"My considerable charm?" His eyebrows rose high, and he stopped moving altogether before something dawned in his eyes and he shook his head. He began moving again, turning her away from the others before ducking his head to catch her eye.

"You are somehow under the impression that my . . . attention to you this afternoon was prompted by an errant sense of duty to a woman who is most certainly *not* pathetic?"

He laughed softly, continuing, "And with my *considerable charm*? Emmeline. Have you forgotten who I am?"

She wrinkled her brow, disgruntled. "My nemesis."

"That is correct. Your number-one nemesis, who has managed a small smattering of charm because of the one woman alive capable of bringing it to the surface." He paused, and when she remained silent, he added, "Emme, I am not toying with you. If you believe nothing else, you must know that."

"You patted my hand," she muttered and tried to look anywhere but at him. His broad shoulders blocked her view of the room, however, so her efforts were for naught.

"I patted your—"

She looked up at him. "You patted my hand and called me 'enchanting.'"

The corner of his mouth curled up even as his eyes held clear astonishment. "You are enchanting—I apologize if you find it offensive. And as for patting your hand . . ." He paused and glanced over his shoulder. "Would you rather I had kissed you again?"

"Yes, as a matter of fact. Anything other than a brotherly pat on the hand and a laugh."

"Emme."

She looked up at his eyes, which was a mistake. They were warm and astute and saw into her soul.

"I would love nothing more than to lock the world away and spend the day alone with you. We cannot do that, so I settled for a compliment—a sincere one, mind you—and an innocent pat on your hand."

"At least it wasn't on my head," she muttered but was inwardly mollified, even happy.

He chuckled, and she braved another look at his eyes, at the mouth so close to her own that had kissed her so desperately back on the beach when he'd been terrified for her.

"Ah, Emmeline," he murmured, "you mustn't look at me like that."

"Why not?"

"Because I shall have to stop right here and kiss you. Perhaps that would prove my sincerity and disabuse your notions about my flirtatious proclivities."

Her lips curved. "In a room full of people? Detective, how absolutely shocking. You would never dare."

His eyes glinted. "I never could resist a dare. You might consider watching what you wish for."

They were barely moving; Emme realized their embrace could be called a "dance" only in the loosest of terms. He pulled her fractionally closer, and she choked back a horrified laugh, turning her face into his shoulder with a quiet squeal.

"Aha," he said, and she heard the smile in his voice. "Finally."

She looked up at him. "What does that mean—'finally'?"

"It means you flinched first, and I have finally called your bluff. I have outshocked the unshockable Emmeline."

"So you do *not* wish to kiss me," she murmured.

"Oh, no, I most definitely do. I am not one for exhibition, however."

She had a difficult time catching her breath, and it had nothing to do with an aching foot. Her feelings for him had always been extreme, and she remembered the conversation they'd had the night they'd spent under the tree. It should be little wonder that she would love him now so much it filled her entire heart, when before, her frustration with him had existed in equal measure.

He was reading her thoughts, he must be, because he said quietly, "You and I have some things to discuss."

She swallowed. "Oh?"

He nodded.

"What sort of things?"

The music drew to a close, and the others clapped and chatted. Oliver still held her, and she had no desire to move away. Ever.

Eventually, he shifted, and she blinked. He helped her to a settee pushed against the wall, and she sank down, quietly releasing a slow breath. Hazel caught her eye from across the room and raised a single brow before curving her lips in a smile. Sam drew her attention, and she turned her gaze from Emme, who realized she wasn't fooling anyone. They must all see that something was simmering between Emme and the detective, and she wasn't certain what she would say if any of them asked.

Oliver sat with her while the others danced three more waltzes. Eventually coffee and cake were delivered, which Lucy had, of course, arranged, and while the group enjoyed the treats, they played several hands of cards. Emme was pleased to note that she and Oliver made quite a competitive team.

The friends traded stories and memories, and Emme was delighted to hear the gentlemen tease each other and share amusing anecdotes. Each man had his own talents and strengths, and they complemented one another well. Emme had never seen Oliver with them in prolonged, casual interaction, and she realized that, in some ways, he was still their captain. He was older than the rest by a handful of years, but aside from that, he carried an air of authority about him the other three respected.

As the hour grew late, the little party naturally disbanded. Emme thanked Lucy profusely and embraced them all. Each couple left and headed toward their own rooms, and Emme entered through Oliver's door.

Oliver quietly closed the door and looked at her for a moment before removing his jacket and then his cuff links, setting them on the small writing table. He smiled. "A lovely evening."

"Yes." She was finally feeling the strain of having put weight on her foot most of the day, but she didn't want to leave him just yet. She told herself she would wait for Gus's return with whatever news he might have discovered and then turn in for the evening. She sank into a soft chair by the fireplace and sighed.

"I mentioned the need for a discussion, of sorts."

She leaned back in the chair. "Yes, you did."

"No time like the present."

Chapter 17

Emme's heart stuttered. "Perhaps we ought not speak of anything theoretical until the Summit is finished. It is possible your intentions may change or diminish when there is no longer any danger to me."

"Perhaps it is your intentions that may change or diminish?" He sat in a chair by her, leaning forward, closer to her, and bracing elbows on knees.

"I know my own feelings," she whispered, "and they will not change."

His lips curved in a smile. "I know my feelings as well. Nor will they change."

She swallowed and looked away. "You might change your mind. One never knows which way the bonds of affection will turn."

Her family circle had been small and secure until her mother had met Ronald O'Shea. Everything had changed, and if a mother's love was not constant, what hope was there for anyone else?

"Emmeline." He waited until she turned her gaze to him.

"Do you remember our first true conversation in your library? What was my point of reasoning when we spoke that night?"

Her brow creased. "I confess, it is rather a blur. You said many things that night."

"The most pivotal of which is that I am constant. I use all information at my disposal, but I also trust my instincts. Implicitly. In this, we are not so very different. Yours is a world of feelings, of emotions. And I also know mine."

Her eyes burned with tears, and she drew in a shallow breath.

"Emme, you have been riddled with doubt about the Summit meetings and your abilities. I've seen it under the surface. Combine that with a spectacular dive from a commercial airship with its subsequent consequences, and I believe you are strung tighter than a bow, taut with uncertainty."

She looked away, and he rubbed her knee. "I believe wholeheartedly in you, Emmeline O'Shea. I have seen you at your fiercest, and you are magnificent."

She rolled her eyes. "To you, I am a menace."

"To me, you are a force of nature. You are stunning and brilliant and possess a heart big enough to care for the entire world. I am not one to express my thoughts much, and in the last few days, I believe I've spoken to you more than I've done to all others in my life combined."

She smiled and stretched her hand out. He took it and rested it on her knee.

"I love you, Emme."

Her mouth dropped open.

"I apologize for burdening you with it now, but perhaps

it will serve as a support in the days to come." He swallowed, waiting for her to respond.

She tugged on his hand, pulling him to her. He knelt next to her chair, and she placed her hands on his face. She kissed him. It was soft and tender, and she pulled back slightly before he'd even had a chance to respond.

"You could return the gesture," she said against his lips.

"You could be patient and give me a moment." He straightened up on his knees and wrapped both arms around her, pulling her close.

She smiled, her hands still on either side of his face, and kissed him again. She moved her hands and wrapped her arms around his neck, burying her fingers in his hair and sighing as he deepened the kiss. She wished the world would melt away, that they could go someplace safe and alone, no threats, no enemies, no danger. She reveled in the fact that he kissed her because he loved her, because he wanted her—*her*, not her beautiful sister or someone less complicated who respected convention and always followed the rules.

The door to the corridor rattled. Oliver tensed, and they both looked at it. Before they could move, a key turned in the lock, and the door swung open. It was Gus, wide-eyed and breathless, one hand braced on the doorframe, the other against his chest.

Oliver's hands still rested on Emme's waist, her arms still around his shoulders. "I didn't realize a vampire could become winded," Emme said.

"I suppose the level of prowess is commensurate with prior abilities." Oliver sighed quietly and rose, and Emme grasped his hand to pull herself up. He retained hold of her fingers, intertwining them with his.

"Apologies," Gus said, "but I bear distressing news."

"What is it?" she asked.

"Your brother," Gus said to Oliver.

"Lawrence?" Oliver's features froze. "What of him?"

"He is here."

Emme stared at Gus, uncertain how to process what he'd said.

Oliver tensed, and his fingers tightened on hers. "Where? When?" he barked at Gus.

"Outside the hotel. I saw him through the window. I crept out for a look but didn't see him. I did catch his scent." He swallowed. "I did not search long or far, however."

Oliver ran his hand through his hair. "I would not expect you to, Gus. Thank you for even this much. We do not know what he's capable of."

"I do know what he's capable of," Gus murmured. "Sir, I have not spread the word that you wish to speak with him. It is possible he is here to spy on the Summit meeting attendees; perhaps this has nothing to do with you or Miss O'Shea."

"Regardless of his aims, it is time I met with him. I must learn his game, once and for all."

Gus moved forward. "I am a very good tracker, sir. When I was an ordinary human, I was known for my exceptional culinary skills, especially as it concerned herbs and spices. Now that I am, er, enhanced, my sense of smell is exceptional. That is what I meant earlier when I said I smelled Mr. Reed—Lawrence, that is. I can help you track him, if you wish."

Oliver shook his head. He released Emme's hand and paced the length of the room. Emme's anxiety rose, and she felt as though the walls were closing in. She had only two days until she was to speak to the council that would meet before the midnight vote, and she couldn't believe another block had been tossed in their path.

Oliver stopped pacing. "Gus, I will do a quick search of the grounds around the hotel. If Lawrence is here to see me, he will know I'm there. You must remain with Emmeline."

She shook her head. "Oliver, that seems rash. Why not wait to see if he contacts you?"

"I would rather draw him as far away from you as possible. That is why Gus must remain with you." He turned to Gus and pinned him with a stern look. "At all times. You understand?"

Gus swallowed and straightened his spine. "Indeed, sir."

Emme rubbed her forehead. Everything was moving too quickly, and she wasn't settled with any of it.

Oliver grasped her shoulders and turned her toward him. "I will find Lawrence, ascertain his intentions, and return quickly. I'll not even interact, if possible."

"He will know your scent! Oliver, I do not feel right about any of this."

He sighed, still holding her shoulders. He was quiet for a moment, thinking, and then shook his head. "We've no choice. I'd rather end it now."

He released her and retrieved his cuff links and jacket, his expression a thundercloud. "I ought to have known," he muttered, shaking his head. "I should have become familiar with his life and dealings long before now. It is so very typical of him. A showman. Manipulative. Plays games and fancies himself cleverer than the rest of the world."

Gus nodded. "An amazingly accurate assessment."

Oliver adjusted his collar. "Emmeline, do not leave your room. Do not leave Gus." He looked at her, eyes fierce. "I promise—"

"Go, find your brother, and for heaven's sake, take someone with you—not Miles, of course, but Daniel or Sam. You have a silver knife?"

He pointed at his boot. "If Madeline ever returns your message, ask her if Crowe mentioned anything to her, anything at all. I've not heard from him since last evening."

She nodded, her worry about Madeline growing afresh. Her concern that Lysette was dangerous to her twin was real. With the family keeping company with Committee members, Madeline was sitting in a viper pit.

Oliver turned around from the bed where he was pocketing his police-issue ray gun in his holster. "Gus, do not leave her. And bite anyone who threatens."

Emme blinked. "I do not know that I want such extremes on my conscience."

"Bite," Oliver repeated, looking at Gus.

Gus nodded. "Sir."

Oliver grasped Emme's shoulders again, pulled her forward, and placed a firm kiss on her lips. "I'll not be long."

"I do not like it."

"Remain. Here."

She scowled. "Go, Oliver, and if something happens to you, I shall never, ever forgive you."

With a final stern look at Gus, he left the room and locked the door behind him.

Emme looked at the closed door for a few moments before picking up the telephone. She called the hotel's front desk and asked if any rooms remained rented under Sir Ronald's name. The attendant informed her that the O'Sheas had retained one room on the sixth floor should they decide later to stay in town. As Sir Ronald's stepdaughter, she requested a key to the room be delivered immediately.

She hung up the phone and relayed the news to Gus. "We must go to that room. Perhaps Madeline left something behind that will give me a clue about what happened this morning."

"Forgive me for asking, but have you considered that Miss Madeline may be acting on behalf of her sister?" Gus looked as though he would rather broach any other subject.

"You think Maddie is manipulating me?" Emme couldn't believe that. She wouldn't believe it.

"I am not suggesting it as a fact, Miss Emmeline. I only wonder—I do not know your family at all, but from an outside perspective . . . She is hiding something significant. I do not know the nature of it, only that I sense it."

Emme frowned. "She mentioned something Lysette knows, something ruinous . . ." She paused. "I would be very surprised to learn Maddie works in subterfuge." She grasped her crutch and did her best to pace about the room.

Gus paced opposite Emme, occasionally peering through the closed, heavy drapes.

She glanced at the clock on the mantel for what seemed

the millionth time. The minutes ticked by, and Oliver hadn't returned.

At a knock on the door, Gus answered it and accepted the key from the employee. Emme joined him at the door, and when Gus hesitated, she said, "I am going to that room, Gus. You may join me or wait here."

He capitulated quickly and followed her down the corridor to the elevator. They rode up in silence, and Emme was anxious. When they reached the sixth floor, they found the room in question. Their knocking was met with silence, so Emme took the key from Gus and opened the door.

The room was dark, and after switching on a lamp, Emme saw that it looked completely uninhabited.

"Hello?" She spoke to the empty room as if expecting a response.

She heard a thump coming from the bathing room, and with a quick look at Gus, crossed the room. The door was locked, and at Emme's urging, Gus shouldered it open. He entered the room first and caught his breath.

"Oh, Miss O'Shea!"

Emme shoved into the room and saw Madeline, her hands tied behind her back and secured to a thick water pipe, her ankles bound, her mouth gagged. Her hair was down and in tangles, and she wore only a white shirt and a simple skirt.

"Maddie!" Emme dropped to her side and pulled at the gag. "Untie her feet, Gus," she said as she fumbled with the knot at the back of the cloth until it finally loosened. She pushed away strands of Madeline's beautiful hair and murmured an apology.

Maddie sobbed with relief, and as Gus moved behind her

to untie her hands, Emme cupped her cheeks. "What *happened*?"

Maddie tried to speak but coughed roughly.

Gus gently released Maddie's arms, and she pulled them around her middle, rubbing briskly.

Emme grabbed a glass from a counter in the bathing room and filled it with water. "Did Lysette do this to you?" She handed her the water and sat next to her on the floor.

She nodded and swallowed a gulp of water too quickly, choking and sputtering, before she was able to say, "Yes. I discovered their plans." Her aqua eyes widened. "What hour is it? It cannot be midnight yet but must be close."

Emme nodded. "We've an hour until midnight. Why?"

Gus helped Madeline and then Emme to stand. Madeline threaded her arm through Emme's and guided her from the bathroom with a quiet grunt of pain. "We can make it to the lodge and into the woods before then. We must. Emme, they have abducted shifters."

Emme's heart pounded in her throat. A horrible notion formed in her head, too horrible to believe. "What do you mean?"

"They have abducted at least six people, perhaps more, and locked them in a cage Sir Ronald has built on the property. I only know of its location because Lysette lured me out there weeks ago. Called it a 'dungeon.'"

Emme's head spun with questions. "The abducted people—they are shifters?"

Madeline nodded and looked quickly around the room, her lips tightening. "They've taken my things, of course. She meant for me to die." She urged Emme and Gus toward the door. "We must hurry. The dungeon door will automatically open five minutes before midnight. Hopefully, the abductees do not begin shifting early."

Emme's mouth dropped at the implication. "Some people do! And I'm assuming, of course, they have kidnapped predatory shifters?"

Madeline nodded and ushered her into the corridor and toward the elevator. "The most satisfying big game of all, apparently."

"Miss O'Shea, are we to understand that your father, sister, and members of a government committee make sport of hunting people after midnight when they shift?" Gus sounded horrified.

She nodded, and they stepped into the elevator. Gus closed the door, and Madeline pushed the button for the main level. "I must go now, straightaway. I'll have the stables bring a fast auto-curricle. You remain here, Emme." Madeline rubbed her forehead with a shaking hand. "I only hope—" she whispered. "Time, not enough time . . ." She stretched her arms and legs, wincing.

"Maddie, you cannot go alone!"

"Where is the detective?" Madeline looked at the two of them as though only then realizing Oliver was missing.

Emme closed her eyes. "Looking for his vampire brother. And he has been gone much too long." She paused. Madeline shivered violently, though she was clearly trying to hold herself still. "Are you cold, Maddie? Here, take my jacket."

"No, no. I . . ." She coughed and trembled again. "It's happened only twice. I am still adjusting—" She coughed again and gagged. She drew in a breath through her nose and out through her mouth.

Emme narrowed her eyes. "*What* has only happened twice? Maddie, has someone hurt you?" She glanced at Gus, who looked away, and whispered, "Are you with child?"

"What? No!" Madeline's brow creased even as her eyes widened in shock. "No, I . . ."

Emme glanced at Gus and, remembering his earlier concern about Madeline's loyalties, quickly opened herself to the young woman's aura.

She was nearly blinded by the anxiety and fear swirling in blues and dark greens emanating from her stepsister. There was no malice or deception to be had, but so much terror Emme was swamped by it. There was an additional glow on the fringes, something she only saw when working with the Shifting community, and she stared at Madeline, stunned.

"Oh, Maddie. Is this what Lysette knows? That you're a shifter?"

Maddie's eyes widened, and she shook her head quickly. "How do you . . . No! No, no, she doesn't—please, Emmeline, you mustn't tell her. She will kill me."

Emme took her stepsister's hand; it was cold. "Of course I would never breathe a word."

Madeline's aqua eyes filled with tears she furtively wiped away. "I—it makes sense now, so many things."

"Does your father know?"

Maddie sniffed in derision. "He's not my father."

The elevator came to a bumpy halt at the main level, and they exited into the corridor.

Emme turned to Gus. "This is what we must do. Oliver

wouldn't have stayed away so long without sending a message. Something isn't right." Her heart pounded as the words flew from her mouth. "You must find him. Alert Sam and Daniel. I will accompany Madeline to the hunting lodge, so I need you to inform the authorities immediately about what is happening there. Insist they send someone right away—several someones."

Madeline shook her head. "You should stay here. I can manage now. There is one other at the lodge who knows what I . . . what I am—what I do."

Emme ignored her. "Gus, as soon as you find Oliver, bring him to the lodge. Also notify Chief-Inspector Conley." She fired off the last bit as she guided Maddie to the doors, leaving Gus in the lobby.

Fumbling with the crutch slowed her down, so she tossed it aside when they exited the hotel. A quick look over her shoulder showed Gus running to get help, and Madeline quickly requested an auto-curricle from a doorman.

The earlier storm continued still. Rain fell steadily, and lightning flashed in the distance.

Emme told the employee they were Sir Ronald's family, at which point he jumped into action and whistled to a 'ton standing near a line of empty vehicles. While they waited for the curricle to circle around, Emme clutched Madeline's arm and rubbed her back.

"I'll drive," Emme said, and Madeline nodded. They clambered inside the vehicle, and Emme released the brake. The small two-seater lurched forward and swung hard to the left before Emme righted it, swerving out of the way of startled attendants.

"You've driven before?" Maddie asked.

"Yes. Every curricle is different, though." She glanced at her stepsister as they pulled away from the hotel entrance and headed down the street. Traffic was light due to the late hour, but many Summit revelers apparently celebrated until the early hours. The rain made the whole business trickier, and she fumbled until she found a switch to power the glass-wiper blades.

"Maddie, what do you mean Sir Ronald isn't your father?"

Maddie took a shuddering breath. "Seven months ago, Lysette was searching for something in his room and found a letter he'd hidden. It was from Sir Ronald's sister, who begged him to take her infant daughter, who shared the same birthday as his own newborn. His wife had just died in childbirth, and since a nanny would raise his daughter, why not two?" Maddie winced. "The letter stated that her baby had been born out of wedlock, and since the parents of the baby's father refused to acknowledge the relationship, she didn't know what else to do. The baby was illegitimate, of course, and if Sir Ronald would take her, she wouldn't be a bastard in society's eyes."

Emme maneuvered the vehicle carefully down the street, avoiding singing pub-goers and vehicles that couldn't seem to find the correct side of the road. She glanced at Madeline and then back at the road. "What happened to Sir Ronald's sister?"

"I do not know. She said he owed her this favor because of all the times she had covered for his misdeeds through the years. And that she had named her baby 'Madeline,' after their great-grandmother." Madeline bit her lip as tears gathered again.

"Oh, Maddie." Emme turned from the busy street onto a quieter one and followed Maddie's instructions to turn again to the right. "I am so sorry. Lysette has been holding this information to keep you under her thumb, yes?"

"She boosts herself up high by standing on me. But I am finished." Maddie shuddered, wrapping her arms tightly around her torso. "When this is over, I am going to leave. Find my real mother."

Emme looked at Maddie in shock until Maddie shrieked and pointed; Emme swerved to avoid colliding with a stone gate and quickly steered back onto the road. "How can I help? Do you need money?"

Maddie shook her head. "I've been saving. Please do not alert anyone of this until I'm gone."

"I'll not breathe a word of it. But you must promise to communicate with me." The road opened up as they moved farther away from the center of town, and before long, Emme was able to pick up speed. "Where is she—your mother? Do you know?"

"The letter said she'd been in Venice."

Emme nodded, and they rode in silence for a time. She wanted desperately to ask Maddie about her Shifting condition. Which form did she take when she Shifted? She settled for a less obtrusive question. "You mentioned someone at the lodge knowing of your Shifting."

Maddie nodded, but her eyes were troubled. "I did not believe I could trust him, but he reasoned it out on his own."

"Who?"

"Mr. Crowe."

Emme stared. "Nigel Crowe?"

Madeline pointed again at the street, and Emme jerked out of the path of a scuttling creature. "He said he recognized something in me, something that reminded him of someone else he once knew. A nontraditional shifter." She closed her mouth and winced. "If you don't mind, I'd rather not discuss it."

"Of course. Please know, though, I have a good listening ear. Isla, too. She would be a wonderful resource."

The small auto-curricle raced through the night, away from city lights, and Emme was obliged to drive by moonlight.

Maddie pulled a pocket watch from her skirt and released a slow breath. "Twenty minutes—if we are fortunate."

Emme pushed the car to its limit, and they rode in silence; the only sounds came from the car mechanisms and the steady patter of rain. They eventually wound down the heavily wooded road leading to the family hunting lodge. The huge structure came into view, lit dimly from the interior due to the late hour. She squinted into the darkness, spotting several of her stepfather's guests gathered at the back lawn, some with lanterns, most with umbrellas or coverings, and nearly all with weapons that glinted in the torchlight.

She pulled the vehicle to the roadside under the trees a distance from the wide front doors. They were ill-prepared for the weather, which grew colder by the minute. Madeline ran quickly around the car to Emme and grasped her arm. "I must retrieve the dungeon keys. I know where Sir Ronald keeps an extra set. We shall have to take a horse through the woods, as it isn't accessible by auto-curricle."

They dashed and limped through the rain, and Maddie nudged Emme toward the stables. "Wait here for me. I'll be five minutes."

Emme hid in the shadows, and true to her word, Madeline quickly returned. She handed Emme a jacket and thrust her arms into another. She patted her pockets, and a muffled clunk sounded from the keys within.

They skirted the main portion of the garage, and Madeline shoved her behind a barrel when a groom crossed their path. When they were alone again, Maddie quickly pulled out her telescriber and punched in a message.

"Who are you messaging?"

Madeline's eyes were wide with fear and determination. "Hopefully, an ally."

They slipped into the stalls where the natural horses were kept, hiding again when a groom called out an answer to someone on the other side of the building. He left the horse he'd been guiding, grumbling about constant interruptions when he had work to do, and slowly ambled away.

"You take that horse," Madeline whispered, pointing to the animal the groom had just left. "I can ride my own horse bareback."

As Madeline fetched her mount, Emme moved to the side of the saddled horse. After a few clumsy attempts with fingers that were cold and wet, she managed to pull herself into the saddle, gasping in pain. The stirrups were too long, and she hurriedly adjusted them, grimacing at the condition of her plaster cast, which was wet and muddy.

Maddie emerged from the stall on her mare. "Follow me," she said, and as Emme drew alongside her, added, "I'll lead you there, but I may have to get to the lake, if . . . if . . ."

Emme blinked. The lake? She reached over, squeezing Maddie's hand as they moved forward. "It will be fine. You'll have time." She hoped desperately she was right.

Emme fell into line behind her stepsister, following her breakneck pace and feeling a combination of shame and amazement that she'd been so unaware of Maddie's accomplishments. She spent so much time away from the family that the only time she actually saw her quiet stepsister was when they were all together and Maddie was literally in Lysette's shadow, likely not cowed but cleverly keeping herself safe.

They wound through the trees, and Emme held her breath as the pain in her ankle exploded. They moved at a pace that made adjusting her foot in the stirrup impossible, and she clenched her teeth to keep from crying out. She shifted and leaned low over the animal's neck, murmuring quietly, trying to let it have its head, and hoping it would freely follow Madeline's mare. The horse seemed to understand and put up with Emme's miserable grasping as it followed the other horse deeper into the woods.

The forest was dark and cold, and the rain continued to fall in steady sheets. The ground was saturated, and the horses' hooves threw mud behind them as they thundered through the trees and foliage. Madeline occasionally slowed and turned, and after a while, produced a small Tesla torch from her jacket pocket. She switched it on, took a quick look at their location, and then turned her mare again. She switched the light back off, and Emme knew she was avoiding the hunters who had spread out over the acreage. Logic dictated that the hunters would be a fair pace behind, as they were on foot, but Emme's sense of dread remained.

The horror of what her stepfamily was doing made her ill to the point of nausea. She couldn't think about it completely, could only hope Madeline would lead her to the place where they could free the imprisoned people before they began to shift. The cruelty of it and the utter humiliation inflicted upon the victims made Emme so angry that tears formed in her eyes.

Madeline veered sharply to the left, around a berm hidden in a thicket, and quickly dismounted. Emme followed, limping to her side at a metal gate that was covered with vines and leaves. Both women breathed heavily, and as Emme gulped and tried to calm her racing heart, she heard faint shouts coming from the other side of the gate.

Madeline again produced her torch, handing it to Emme. Emme shined the light on the gate, finding the locking mechanism. Madeline pulled a pair of large keys from her pocket and with shaking hands tried the lock. Neither one seemed to fit, and Madeline gasped in desperation. She looked up as though searching for the moon, and Emme knew they were nearly out of time.

Hoofbeats thundered in the distance but grew closer.

They stared at each other. Madeline's eyes were huge and liquid, and she clutched her stomach, crying out in pain.

Emme grasped the keys from her stepsister's cold hands and said, "Go! Go to the lake now!"

More shouts sounded from within the locked cavern, and Emme felt a terror born of helplessness.

The hoofbeats drew closer, and as Emme shoved one of the keys into the lock with enough force to hurt her hand, a horse and rider flew around the bend. Nigel Crowe sat atop a huge black steed that seemed an extension of him, and Emme gasped. Still trying to turn the key, she threw her other arm around Madeline, who was doubled over in pain.

"Stand aside," Nigel shouted.

Emme dropped the keys and nudged Madeline to the side, holding her close. Nigel lifted a sledgehammer and swung at the gate. The lock gave way with a deafening crash and screech of metal, and he dropped the hammer. Reaching for Madeline, he pulled her roughly from Emme's arms.

"She must get to the lake," Emme gasped as he hauled Madeline onto the saddle in front of him.

"I know." He pulled on the reins, the horse reared, and he was off with a whirlwind of leaves and branches.

Shaking and bewildered, Emme shoved open the gate, picking up the keys. Using Maddie's torch, she moved quickly into the deeper recesses of the dungeon, uncertain of what she'd find.

She came across another gate, and the torchlight shone on hands that shook the bars. Cries from within hastened her movements, and she again shoved one of the keys into a lock. Twisting it, she felt profound relief when the bolt slid back.

She tore the gate open. "Run, quickly," she said as a handful of people, mostly men, wide-eyed and terrified, some bent in pain, rushed out of the gate.

She hurried with them to the entrance, adding, "Do you

know where you are? The lake on the O'Shea property is in that direction, northward. Separate quickly, but head in that direction. It's the fastest way out of the forest."

One man grasped her hand and kissed her knuckles, and a few others shouted their thanks as they all disappeared into the night.

She moved forward, training the light on the ground, noting articles of clothing the fleeing prisoners were shedding. They had to, of course, but they were leaving a trail the hunters would easily find.

She heard a grinding of gears, and looking back at the exterior gate, realized it had been mechanized and timed to open just before midnight. The interior gate also clicked, but faltered and stopped since the gate was already open.

Her breath came in painful bursts, and she wrapped her arm around herself. She wasn't sure if any members of the hunting party would come straight to the dungeon or were hoping for more sport by giving the prey a chance to spread out through the forest.

She would need to find her way back to the lodge immediately. Knowing where the lake was gave her a sense of place, but as she looked at the horse, which had remained faithfully in place despite the chaos, she didn't know how she could possibly climb up on its back.

She had no idea where Oliver was, and knowing he might be in his awful brother's clutches added to her worry until she didn't think she could hold one more drop. The list was long and daunting. The shifters might not get far enough away to avoid the hunters, or they might come upon Madeline and Nigel. She had to hope the shifters were all well-intentioned people. Madeline may not have made it to the lake in time, which begged the question that had been nagging at Emme for some time—what sort of shifter was Maddie? A fish? She'd never heard of a nautical shifter.

She leaned against the horse's side and rested her head, which ached along with everything else. After a moment, she stepped away from it, shining the light on a discarded shirt on the ground, and bent over to pick it up. She could at least gather the clothing close by, hopefully eliminating some of the trail.

She stood, dizzy, and turned back to the horse when her breath caught in her throat. Lysette stood behind her, her venomous anger so thick in the air that Emme felt it without trying. Lysette looked at her as though searching for words she was too angry to even express.

"You released the beasts," she finally bit out, her voice low and even.

"I released the *people.*" Emme remained still.

"I have been planning this event for months. *Months.*"

"Is your father aware of the details?" For one small moment, Emme hoped Ronald O'Shea was only irritating, not murderous.

"Of course he is. When I told him about it, he said if the hunt was a success, I could accompany him on his next safari." She paused, regarding Emme dispassionately. "Now you have ruined it."

Emme was more concerned about Lysette's cooling emotion than an outburst. Her demeanor had turned calculating. "And the Committee members? Are they aware of the nature of this hunt?"

"Of course they are. All the members join Father on his safaris. The prey there is of the same kind I had corralled here. The Committee enjoy the irony of that variety especially."

Horror settled over Emme, and she felt faint. "Those trophies," she said, her lips numb, "the trophies inside were shape-shifting *humans*?"

"Such a ridiculous girl, you are." Lysette's eyes hardened, and she inched closer to Emme. "Where is Madeline?"

Emme remained silent.

"Where is she?"

"Gone. She has left. You cannot harm her anymore."

A muscle worked in Lysette's jaw. "Then your fate is sealed, Emmeline. The detective was showing interest in *me* until you intentionally sent him on a merry chase after *you*. Then you wrangled compliments out of Papa. And now you've sent Madeline away. You have taken everything that was mine." She smiled. "Now it is my turn."

"Lysette—"

"You ought to have stayed on the airship. You'd have been safer in Portugal."

Emme's heart leapt into her throat.

"I shall take you back to Edinburgh. I would hate for you to miss your Summit address."

Lysette struck so swiftly that Emme's world turned completely black before she hit the ground.

Chapter 18

Oliver's head pounded, and he swayed with the even movement of a well-sprung carriage. He rested against comfortable cushions and was warm and dry despite the obvious sound of rain on the roof.

He squinted at the low light of a small Tesla sconce mounted to the interior wall beside a window adorned with closed velvet drapes. The light pierced the back of his skull, and as he lifted his hand to rub his eyes, the other hand came with it. His wrists were tied securely with rope that bit into his skin when he tried to separate his hands.

He had no idea where he was, or why. He tried opening his eyes again and sat up. The pain in his head intensified to nausea. He took a shallow breath and lifted his hands again and felt along his head to a bump on the back that was raised—and bloody, if the stickiness was any indication.

He opened his eyes a crack to see a bright-red smear on his fingertips. A dry chuckle sounded from a blurred form opposite him, and his heart beat faster. He would know that voice anywhere.

"I would have tried to speak with you using less brutish means, but you've built a reputation, brother, as quite a brutish man yourself."

"Worried I would hurt you, Lawrence?" he mumbled and winced again as he sat up straight.

His brother laughed, but this time there was a sharper edge to it, a coldness. "Of course! Couldn't have you catching me by surprise, especially with a silver dagger in your boot." Lawrence leaned forward, and Oliver's vision finally focused.

He caught his breath. He'd not seen his brother since he was turned, and where he had been handsome before, now he was arresting. He had the undead quality that enhanced every good physical trait, and Oliver had no doubts about how his brother had risen through the underworld ranks. He had always been smart, and now he was more handsome than seemed real.

Each negative trait, those that had driven the brothers apart many years earlier, was also magnified. Oliver felt it as Lawrence smiled and narrowed his eyes. His ability to manipulate, his desire to play to a crowd—those would be enhanced, doubled. Regrettably, the desires that fed the traits would be also.

"Where are you taking me?" It seemed the simplest question to begin the conversation. He realized he'd not made it more than four steps outside the hotel before he'd been assaulted. Emme had been right—he had been in danger. To have remained in the hotel, though—that was unthinkable now. He'd have brought this horror directly to Emme's feet. She was safe with Gus, and he had to be grateful for that much.

"Only a ride around town so we can renew our bonds of fraternal affection."

Oliver closed his eyes and leaned his head back, carefully avoiding the lump. "What could you possibly want with me, Lawrence? You and I were getting along well by ignoring each other."

"Yes. We've been ignoring each other for some time. You did not even come to my aid when I was bitten."

"I contacted you, told you I would catch the first flight to your side. You told me you'd solicited the bite and that I no longer need tell the world I had a brother."

"Yes, I suppose I did. You irritated me, Oliver. Always did. Always the good one, always doing what you were told, forever currying favor with authority. Until you became the authority yourself." The sneer was subtle but there.

"And you never wanted a thing to do with pleasing anyone but yourself. Seems we both achieved our ends." Oliver's eyes were still closed—it hurt less.

"Are you not worried about exposing your neck to me?" Lawrence's voice was smooth and low.

Oliver cracked open one eye. "You'd have torn out my throat by now if it suited you. I can only imagine you want to play with me for a time. Like a lion with a mouse."

"Smug, arrogant. Nothing changes." Lawrence was across the carriage before Oliver could blink, and the thing baring its teeth and digging its fingernails into his throat was no longer his brother but something else entirely. "Ahh, *now* your heart beats faster."

Oliver met his brother's angry gaze and blinked, but remained silent.

Lawrence slowly released his throat and sank back into his seat, his teeth retracting, the smooth façade returning.

Oliver rubbed his neck. "Of course my heart beat faster." He coughed, clearing his throat. "I'm not dead." It seemed counterintuitive to taunt a vampire when he wanted very much to remain alive and spend that life with a feisty social activist, but he was testing Lawrence, searching for his limits, for the odds of finding any remaining humanity.

"I am curious," he continued, and Lawrence politely inclined his head and gestured for Oliver to continue. "I know a vampire who is a very amiable fellow, seeks for nothing more than to get along with his fellow man. He tells me there are many more like him."

"Guster Gustavsen?" Lawrence grinned. "Yes. Industrious, kind fellow, wears one of those ridiculous glass-heart tiepins. Stays out of my way, and I allow him to scurry along his own little path. Allowing him to see me tonight was part of my plan. He is nearly as predictable as are you."

"Are you working with Ronald O'Shea?"

Lawrence arched a perfect brow. "Ronald? Oh, no. His daughter is so much brighter. He jumps at her commands, and as our end goals meet in the same place, a liaison with Lysette O'Shea has been the natural course of things."

"What are those end goals?" Oliver swallowed, his head still pounding, the nausea still threatening.

"The Predatory Shifter Regulations Committee wants the Summit meetings to fail, but they are under such scrutiny that they have been forced to go about their objective differently. Removing Emmeline O'Shea from the proceedings will go a long way toward achieving that end. Removing

Emmeline O'Shea is also Miss Lysette's primary objective. Since Lysette holds the reins of her titled father and soon, the family money, you see why an alliance with her is beneficial to me."

Oliver bit his tongue. Lysette O'Shea would never see a penny of the "family money" but probably didn't realize it. He made a side note to have Conley assign a bodyguard to protect Emme's mother.

"So an alliance between you and the PSRC, along with the O'Shea influence, is worth all of this trouble? And I suppose you wrote the letter to Emmeline that caused such alarm?"

Lawrence chuckled. "No, that was the creative work of Lysette. Dictated to the young Mr. Stuart Rawley, who was only too happy to act as scribe. He is enamored of Lysette, Lysette hates Emmeline, and thus you have the makings of a perfect family tragedy."

Oliver clenched his jaw until it ached. "I am going to enjoy ending Mr. Rawley. And the carriage accident?"

"Mr. Randolph arranged it, but at the time, Lysette hadn't realized you would be keeping Miss Emmeline company. I understand she was most worried about your safety." He paused. "And my, but you are determined to protect your ladylove."

Oliver fought to remain impassive. "She is my charge, the object of my work task, not my ladylove."

"Ah, good. Then you'll not be alarmed when I tell you what Lysette has planned for her."

Oliver's anger grew, and for the first time since awakening, he knew he was in danger of reacting to Lawrence's taunts. "Lysette will be forced to get past a vampire, who although mild-mannered, has been instructed to protect Emmeline with deadly force."

"But, brother, mayhem erupted at the Grand Hotel after you and I departed." He held up a transcriber. "Lysette is not a happy young woman right now because Emmeline foiled some carefully constructed plans. It appears Emmeline arrived at the lodge just in time—and without our friend Gus."

Oliver looked at the curtained window, his fear and anger mounting.

"Regrettably, she is separated from her valiant little vampire, so you see, not only have you managed to get yourself captured, you failed her as well. Provided I can use my powers of persuasion on Lysette and prevent her from killing the little activist outright, I may just satisfy my own curiosity about the woman who has finally captured your heart. I'll turn her, and then"—he smiled with malicious facetiousness—"she'll have an eternity to convince the world that all creatures under the sun deserve the same rights."

Oliver lunged across the carriage, enjoying the satisfaction of catching Lawrence off guard before Lawrence responded and sent him back into the dark.

Chapter 19

Emme shivered and groaned as she shifted against the cold ground. Light and warmth flickered a short distance away, and she opened her eyes, struggling to reach the surface of her sluggish thoughts. She'd had laudanum once before, when she was young and had fallen out of a tree. Her mother had panicked, convinced that Emme's pain was worse than it was, and Emme had slept for two days.

The feeling now was exactly the same, and she gritted her teeth against the fog and dizziness. The fact that she was waking up was the one bright thought she could manage. The downside, of course, was that whatever benefit the drug provided against pain was also wearing off. Her ankle was on fire, everything ached from her head to her feet, and as she shoved herself upright, a wave of nausea nearly overwhelmed her.

What time was it? How long had she been asleep, and who had given her laudanum? She blinked at her surroundings, her eyes adjusting to the darkness. She was in some kind of cave, or maybe an underground dwelling. It was carved out, man-made, with low stone ceilings, walls, and floors.

It wasn't the dungeon that had held the shifters; the construction there had been largely earthen. The firelight flickering in the far corner finally became bearable enough to look at, despite the pain in her skull, and she saw Lysette seated on a low stool next to the flames.

"I was beginning to worry I'd given you too much. You've slept an entire day and another night." She smiled, and Emme's blood ran cold.

"Where are we?" she croaked, and coughed.

Lysette pointed with her chin. "There is water for you. Can't have you dying just yet."

Emme grabbed the water pitcher and drank straight from it, bypassing the cup that sat beside it.

"Manners, Emmeline. What would Mother say?"

Emme swallowed the cold water, hoping Lysette hadn't put anything nasty in it. "Where are we?" she repeated.

"You are in Edinburgh's underground, where only undesirables live, mostly the undead kind. You are in a far corner where nobody will ever find you, and your bones will waste away until there is nothing left."

Emme bit her tongue rather than snap that bones did not waste away for a very long time and that a scientist somewhere in the future would surely excavate before she disappeared permanently.

Think, Emme. Think. She had to get free. Lysette's weak spot was always her arrogant pride, and Emme hoped she could manipulate it enough to buy herself some time.

"I realize you clearly want me to suffer before you leave me forever, so I'm certain you've devised something delightful." She tried to shift and possibly stand but realized belatedly that a large manacle encircled her wounded ankle. She might inch forward, but she wouldn't reach Lysette, the fire, or the gated door.

"Very well. This is my plan, Emmeline." She pulled a bag to her side, and Emme realized it was her portmanteau, the one she'd managed to keep safe for days against all odds. Lysette pulled two small books from inside, and Emme's heart beat so hard she feared it would explode.

"No. Lysette, you do not need to do anything with those. Send them to Blackwell Manor."

Lysette smiled and set the first of the two ancient books on the fire.

Emme cried out and lunged forward only to be caught up in the chain which pulled so painfully against her ankle that spots formed in her vision. "No! Lysette, no! They are not mine!"

She lifted the second book. "Also not yours." She added it to the fire, and Emme stared through horrified tears as the pages burned.

Lysette checked a pocket watch pinned to her waist. "It is now late morning, although you wouldn't know it down here. As we speak, Lady Blackwell is presenting information about scientific research and all that rot. Pity she doesn't know her husband's family journals have been destroyed. I wonder if he will hold her responsible."

Emme stared at her stepsister, tears flowing. "Let me go, Lysette. You need never see me again."

Lysette reached again into the bag. "Hmm. Now this *is* yours. By my best guess, it is two years of research, notes, journals, documentation, firsthand anecdotes, and various ramblings about the shifter population and society's cruel and unjust treatment of them." The portfolio holding Emme's work was well-worn, and she knew every last crease and ink-smudged page. She closed her eyes and choked back another sob.

Lysette waited until Emme opened her eyes again before carefully setting the portfolio atop the other burning papers. She paused and watched as the flames curled around the parchment, lighting each piece before devouring it.

"I know you were to address the international body of distinguished guests tonight at the old castle. Your beautifully written notes—I've read them twice now—were crucial to your remarks. As you do not possess your dear friend Hazel's permanent recall, the loss of those pages is significant." Lysette paused. "Of course, you won't be there to give the address, so perhaps it doesn't matter."

Emme shook her head in mute denial of everything Lysette was saying.

"You know, the hunting party managed to take down four of the captured shifters you set free. Thank heavens for it! The hunters prevented what might have been an ugly rash of murderous crime. The city is afire with rumors about the increased shifter and vampire violence. People are afraid. Perhaps the present time may not be ideal to discuss loosening the proverbial reins of those monsters." She placed a hand on her heart. "If only there were someone to speak on their behalf, someone who could not only prove the recent murders were committed to resemble shifter attacks but who also had the emotional gifts to deliver the information compellingly."

Emme clenched her jaw, wishing she could rip the manacle off her ankle with her bare hands.

Lysette tapped her lip thoughtfully. "But considering the last several months have seen a concerted effort by influential parties to skew public perception of shifters"—she blinked and smiled slowly—"and good-hearted vampires as well, could just one person really change things?"

Emme swallowed hard. Everything she had worked for, everything she wanted to accomplish, was turning to ash right before her eyes.

Lysette dropped her hands back to her lap. "You could tell the truth, and with your reputation, *you* would be believed. Sadly, you and I have gone missing, presumed killed by the shifters that escaped my hunters. I will miraculously appear at the proper time to tell my tale of bravery and escape. I will cry quiet tears as I recount the violent nature of your death at the hands of a human wolf. I shall comfort Mama when I explain that there is naught left of you even to bury."

Emme kept her mouth closed, and the tears flowed unchecked. The quiet hatred in Lysette's eyes bore no mercy and never would.

"Oh, Emmeline, I do believe you are finally crushed." Lysette's bright-blue eyes shone, but not with compassion, and her beautiful face took on a sorrowful countenance that anyone who did not know her might have believed authentic.

"Why do you hate me so much? From the beginning, I wanted only to be your friend."

"And from the beginning, I knew you would always be in my way." She lifted a shoulder. "I couldn't very well have competition when I wanted a mother. And then as I grew older, when I wanted her money."

Emme's brow creased. "Her money?"

Lysette leaned forward and raised her voice. "Yes, Emmeline, her money."

Emme shook her head. "My mother's money is hers."

"Yes, until she passes, at which point it goes to you." Lysette paused. "Except that, sadly, you will already be gone."

Emme looked at her dully, wondering if she should correct her. Would it make a difference? "That is not how the inheritance on my mother's money works. I will tell you the details of it, but only once we are free from this place."

Lysette turned her head but kept her eyes on Emme. "I do not believe you."

"You were younger so you do not remember the stipulations my mother insisted upon before marrying your father."

Her mouth settled into a line. "Explain."

"No. Not until you set me free."

"That does not serve me one whit. No matter. I'll draw the truth from your mother." She put her hand to her chest. "Excuse me, *our* mother. Soon to be *my* mother. I'll be her support through her mourning period."

Hester Castle's money would go to Emmeline in the event of Hester's death, but unless Emme altered the will then, at *her* death, the money would remain in trust for Isla, and Emme's aunt, Bella, to either distribute to charities or hold indefinitely. The money would stay solely with the Castle women unless they stipulated otherwise.

Emme might die in the catacombs, but she could protect her mother. "You'll never get Castle money, Lysette," she said wearily. "Do what you will with me, but please do not kill my mother. The inheritance line remains with her family, so you'll get more from her if she's alive and well." She waved her hand and sat back, bringing her knees to her chest with a clanging of metal against the stone floor. "Be the perfect daughter, enjoy her as your own, but do not hurt her, if for no other reason than she will not be able to give you anything if she's dead."

"Mmm. Sound advice. Perhaps I will be such a good daughter to her that she will find it best for her heart and soul to place me where you once were, in her affections and in her will. I will be the new Castle daughter, and you will be a sad memory."

Emme wrapped her arms around her knees, numb. Short of tearing her hip from its socket, she had no way of rushing Lysette when she opened the door. Thoughts of what might have happened to Oliver were too painful to contemplate, and she wouldn't give Lysette the satisfaction of asking after him. He'd have found her by now if he'd managed to return from his brother unmolested. If Lysette had been telling the truth, it had been nearly thirty-six hours.

She didn't mention Madeline either, in hopes of keeping Lysette's attention completely away from her twin. She hoped her own suppositions about Maddie had been correct, that she had begun to imagine a way to live away from her toxic sister.

It was not to be. As though the very thought of Madeline slipping through Emme's mind printed her name in the air, Lysette said, "Where is my sister?"

Emme rested her forehead on her arms. "I do not know."

"Where *is* she?" For the first time, Lysette's voice trembled in anger.

"I do not know." Emme lifted her head and allowed her fury to show in her eyes. "If she is lucky, somewhere far, far away from you. I have not seen her since the night you took me from the forest."

"Lies!" Lysette's voice echoed through the cavern. "She is nowhere in the hotel, the hunting lodge, or the grounds. She has disappeared!"

Emme allowed a small, satisfied smile to lift her lips. "Excellent. Were you ever planning to release her from the hotel room? It was very clever of you to request the room not receive maid service for the rest of the week. Fortunate, really, that I took your father's last name. As an O'Shea, I had means of entry."

Lysette launched herself at Emme in a fury, catching her on the side of the head with her fist and knocking her to the floor.

Emme immediately wrapped both arms around Lysette's legs and pulled her over.

Lysette kicked, catching Emme in the jaw, and then the stomach, freeing herself and lunging across the room. Emme coughed, unable to catch her breath, and curled in on herself in pain. She watched through watering eyes as Lysette snatched up the keyring, ran out the door, and slammed it closed, locking it with a definitive grind of metal. She grasped the bars of the gate and snarled at Emme, shouting obscenities, her fury echoing down the dark halls.

Emme waited until Lysette had calmed herself and straightened her clothing before speaking. "You are not a shifter, but you are more of a monster than anyone I have ever met."

Lysette grasped the bars once again and tightened her fists, and Emme awaited another explosion. With any luck, it might bring someone to investigate. As long as that person wasn't worse than Lysette was, there might be hope.

Lysette smoothed her hair and repinned a few curls. "The fire will soon die out, Emmeline, and with it all light and warmth. The world's most important people will gather but will not hear you speak, and the changes to which you have dedicated your life will die just like that fire. A pity. With the recent violence, there are several ambassadors who are leery of signing the accord. You might have swayed them."

Lysette released one bar and smiled, her eyes cruel. "Do not hope for your fair detective to come to your rescue. His brother has taken care of him."

Emme stared as her stepsister finally turned to leave. "I will haunt you, Lysette O'Shea," she said, glad when the woman's step faltered.

"Chew on that, you wretch," she muttered once Lysette was gone. Emme had no idea how to haunt someone, or even if it was possible, but as long as it played in Lysette's thoughts, Emme would be satisfied she'd hit a parting shot.

The silence that settled, though, was oppressive. The fire still crackled, and as Emme watched the flames, she thought of the material Lysette had burned, and her eyes filled again with tears.

And Oliver.

Had Lawrence killed him? Turned him? Her grief broke free, and she sobbed. If he were alive, he would never know how to find her, and if he did, she might already be dead. She ached for just one more kiss, one more moment with him. It wouldn't be enough, though. A million moments, an eternity of moments, would never be enough. She loved him so much she hurt with it, and she would never see him again.

Something scuttled in a distant passageway, followed by a shriek. She was terrified to bring something worse down upon her head and tried to quiet her sobs. She lay down on her arms, prostrate on the floor, and her tears dripped into the dirt. She felt despair unlike any she'd known. Her heart opened up, and the emotions she usually kept behind the closed door flooded out, filling the air around her until she could barely breathe.

She'd dreamed of helping people, of being the voice they did not have. She had worked and clawed and scraped—literally—through masses of ignorant people bent on keeping themselves at the top of the human heap and all others squashed below. Her dreams were a farce, they would not come true, and she would die alone, abandoned in a tomb far beneath the earth. She and her idealism would disappear, and her family and friends would never know where she had gone.

"I do not understand," she whispered as the tears dripped down her nose. For the first time in her life, her optimism deserted her, and all hope was extinguished. She had nearly achieved all she had wished and had nearly claimed a life for herself with a man who was a prince among men. He had been keeping her safe since the very beginning. He was noble and good and cared about doing what was right. He was her prince, and she loved him, yet she had never said the words. Had he died not knowing she loved him?

"Oliver," she murmured. "I love you." Her eyes drifted closed, and she took a shuddering breath. She remembered him in every encounter, visualized each scrape, each verbal sparring match, each glare and resentful spat. Each uneasy glance, each careful maneuver, each quiet conversation, each kiss. Each wonderful, dream-worthy embrace. The terrifying moments after she landed hard on the beach only to see him close behind, running desperately to free her from the Jump Wings and chastise her and scold her and hold her as though he would never in a million years let her go.

She smiled, even laughed at his incredulity that she would risk her safety for the carpetbag that carried her treasures. Hot tears quickly filled her eyes again as she realized those treasures were now nothing more than ash.

Everything. Gone.

She paused, then lifted her head and sniffled. "Not everything," she mumbled. She looked over her shoulder at the fire that still burned, thanks to the heaps of paper on it, but also the stool and the carpetbag.

The portmanteau full of her things.

She scrambled up and lunged for it, but the bag was just out of reach. Her fingers brushed against the stool, and she swiped once, twice, three times and then finally grasped it. She pulled it close and stood up, every muscle and bone protesting the movement, and then lifted the stool high above her head.

She hurled it to the ground at her feet with all her strength and shut her eyes as it broke apart and bounced haphazardly into pieces. She grasped one of the legs, stretched her petite frame to its full length, and snagged the ragged wood around the bag's handle. With a soft laugh, she pulled it toward her. She sat up and held it tight to her chest.

That bag of treasures would lead to her freedom.

Chapter 20

Oliver staggered along Edinburgh's Princes Street Gardens, eyeing the structures that had been constructed for the Summit week activities and tried to remain upright until he found the building he sought. The ragged wound on his neck burned, and the pain grew more intense with every passing minute.

He pulled his collar higher and mumbled an apology when he bumped into a gentleman carrying an armful of purchases piled high. He sidestepped a gaggle of children who ran past, their faces and fingers sticky with spun candy and salt-taffy treats, and looked up to see the ISRO building.

He approached the woman at the front desk, knowing his appearance was probably alarming in the extreme, and said, "I must see Signore Giancarlo immediately."

"Apologies, sir," she said, wide-eyed and in heavily accented English, "but he is occupied."

Oliver planted both hands on the desktop. "Unless you want me to collapse right here in the next two minutes, either fetch Giancarlo or tell me which office is his."

Just then, the man himself poked his head outside the door directly behind the reception area. "*Dio mio!* Detective!" Carlo rushed to his side and helped him step around the bewildered receptionist and into his office. Oliver collapsed into a chair, and his head fell back.

A quick stream of Italian flew from Giancarlo's lips, and Oliver vaguely registered the man opening cabinet doors in quick succession until he returned to Oliver's side. His eyes drifted closed, and he fought another wave of nausea, breathing shallowly, before managing to say, "Emmeline has been abducted . . . believe she's somewhere here . . ."

"Shh, here now. Be still a moment." Giancarlo clucked his tongue in alarm. "This wound—it's already turned green . . ."

Oliver heard the rapid swirl of a spoon against a bowl and hoped Giancarlo was mixing anti-venom. The icy sting of the medicine against the jagged wound on his neck made him hiss through his teeth. Then he felt the lifesaving serum seeping into the wound, spreading instant relief through his neck, down his throat, and within a few precious moments, his heart regulated itself and he was able to take a full breath.

He was exhausted, limbs aching from prolonged systemic exposure to the vampire venom. Lawrence had left him for dead, but he hadn't killed him outright or completely exsanguinated him, which suggested he hadn't truly wanted him dead. Either that or he'd underestimated Oliver's resilience and partial immunity to the venom he'd developed over time as a police program safeguard.

Giancarlo rested one hip against the edge of his desk and wiped his hands with a cloth. He adjusted his spectacles and regarded Oliver with understandably serious concern. "Who did this to you, my friend?"

Oliver managed an ironic smile as he put a hand to the bandage Carlo had fasted on the wound. "My brother."

His eyes widened. "Your broth—" He clearly made the connection and nodded. "Ah. I have heard of him." He frowned. "Have you information about our Emmeline? Your Chief-Inspector has a small army searching for you both."

Oliver shook his head and swallowed, shoving himself upright.

Carlo grabbed a pitcher and glass and poured him some water. He handed it to Oliver with an admonition to sip slowly.

Oliver's hand shook, but he managed to keep the water inside the cup. He swallowed gratefully and took a deep breath, blowing it out slowly. "Thank you, *signore*. When I couldn't find a medical or police tent, I came looking for you. I knew you would have medicine at the ready." He winced at the pain that continued to pound in his head. "Emmeline was taken from the Grand Hotel the night before last."

Giancarlo nodded. "Inspector Conley traced her last whereabouts to the O'Shea hunting lodge. Quite a police presence there now, given the hunting scandal and abductions. Mr. O'Shea is being held in a jail cell while the investigation continues."

Oliver frowned and rubbed his temple. "I'm afraid I am unaware of the particulars. My brother took me shortly before Miss Lysette O'Shea absconded with Emmeline. Or so he claimed. I awoke less than an hour ago in a field outside town."

Carlo walked behind his desk to a small dry sink where he dampened a clean cloth and handed it to Oliver. Oliver gratefully held it to his face and wiped it from hairline to neck, relishing in the simple pleasure of a cool cloth against his skin. Carlo picked up a telephone on his desk and rang out, requesting something in rapid Italian, though Oliver caught Conley's name in the mix.

"I've sent word to your chief inspector." Carlo sat in a chair next to Oliver and leaned forward, his dark-brown eyes full of worry. "Where would this Lysette take our girl?" A muscle moved in his lean jaw, signaling his distress.

Oliver felt his eyes burn. He was exhausted, in pain, bruised from his brother's lethal attack, and so afraid for Emme he was sick with it. "I wish I knew," he said, clearing his throat and shoving his emotions into submission. He straightened in the chair, feeling stronger as the medicine continued to work its magic. "I fear time is of the essence, however. Lysette is unhinged, and her hatred of Emmeline is severe."

Carlo nodded. "Especially as Emmeline foiled the hunting plans."

Oliver was frustrated with how little he knew of what had happened after Lawrence took him from the hotel. "What did she do, exactly?"

Carlo smiled grimly. "The O'Sheas had abducted several local predatory shifters and held them captive, intending to hunt them once they had changed after midnight."

Oliver's mouth dropped open in spite of himself. He stared at the Italian, who slowly nodded.

"According to Mr. Gustavsen, the other O'Shea sister alerted Emmeline to the problem, and Emmeline sent

Gustavsen to find you while she went with the sister to free the captives."

Oliver's heart thumped. Of course she would do that, and he couldn't blame her. He'd foolishly walked into his brother's trap, even as she'd warned against it, and because of it, he'd not been there to help. "My fault," he mumbled, trying not to lose himself in self-pity. "Had I stayed with her—"

Carlo held up a hand. "No time for recrimination. These villains are devious and would have achieved their plans one way or another. Now, why do you believe Emmeline is somewhere in the city?"

"A comment my brother made. He said Lysette would see that Emmeline arrived here before the meetings conclude. He was speaking in veiled layers, of course, and I'm certain Lysette isn't planning for Emme to arrive in time to safely speak to the assembly."

Giancarlo sat back in his chair and tapped his fingers against the armrest. "Someone like Lysette would want Emmeline to suffer greatly. Stash her somewhere close enough to realize the festivities are commencing without her." He muttered a string of Italian words under his breath.

Oliver nodded his agreement, not needing to speak Italian to understand the sentiment. Voices sounded from the outer office, and then Conley appeared in the doorway, followed by three detectives from the Yard and two local constables. Oliver rose halfway from his chair and gasped when Conley grabbed him around the middle and clapped his back in a firm embrace.

"What the devil happened to you?" Conley pulled back,

grasping his shoulders and looking him up and down. "You look like you've been attacked by a mob."

"Later. But if you aren't already, we need to be on the lookout for my brother. Looks like me, only younger and significantly more handsome. Until he bares his teeth." Oliver sank back into the chair and quickly relayed the basic information he had for Conley.

Conley gave instructions to the other men and connected his scriber to relay the information to others out investigating.

Oliver turned to Giancarlo. "You mentioned Mr. Gustavsen. Do you know where he is now?"

Giancarlo nodded. "He is out 'sniffing the air' for our girl." The Italian shrugged. "The little man seemed most concerned and insisted he must do something. He feels horribly responsible. Said he would attempt to track her and the wretched sister and would alert us if he found anything."

Oliver's eyes burned, and he felt oddly sentimental toward the man who had so earnestly sought to protect both Emme and him. He couldn't be angry. Further commotion sounded in the outer office, and a desperate female cry sounded through the closed door.

Conley looked up from his discussions with his men. "Mrs. O'Shea," he said grimly.

Oliver stood and opened the door, and Emme's mother barreled into him. He steadied her and waited for the shock of his bruised appearance to recede from her stunned face. He quietly closed the door and ushered her into the chair he'd vacated. He knelt next to it and took her hand.

"What are you doing?" she asked, and her eyes filmed. "Do not *dare* tell me she's gone."

"No, no," he said. "We will find her. I will not rest until we do."

"What happened to you?" Her voice had dropped in volume, but the pitch remained high, as if the slightest nudge would send her into mania.

"I was accosted. Have you been apprised of the happenings at the lodge? Do you know where the twins are—where Lysette might go here in town?" He glanced up at Conley. He hadn't even asked about Madeline's welfare, and nobody had mentioned her.

Mrs. O'Shea sniffed, and then the tears escaped. "My . . . my husband and Lysette have been accused of some awful things, and they"—she glanced at Conley—"tell me Lysette has taken Emmeline. Why would she do that? Why would they do such awful things?"

Giancarlo offered Mrs. O'Shea a snow-white handkerchief and opened the door, quietly requesting a fresh pot of tea from the harried receptionist.

Oliver bit back an extremely judgmental comment regarding Mrs. O'Shea's inability to see the drama between the young women in her own home. Had she never truly realized how toxic Lysette was toward Emme and Madeline both?

He wouldn't insult her, but the time for blissful ignorance had come to an end. "Mrs. O'Shea, Lysette is a jealous and vindictive young woman. She has been extremely unkind to Emmeline for some time, and I fear her envy and cruelty have reached new heights. Have you no idea at all where she might take your daughter?"

Mrs. O'Shea stared at him for a long time before finally releasing a quiet breath. She dabbed at her nose with the handkerchief and then said, "I suppose I have seen such behavior. I haven't wanted to, and Emme is so fiercely independent. So competent. She was running our household long before I married, and she is so willful I never imagined she needed . . ." Her voice wobbled. "Protection." She swallowed and looked at Oliver. The room was silent. "I do not know where Lysette might take Emmeline, but I do know her tastes are extravagant. Hotels? Boardinghouses in New Town?"

Oliver looked at Conley, who nodded. "We've men searching everywhere right now. Most rooms and accommodations have been reserved for months in advance, however, and thus far, nobody meeting the young women's descriptions have been noticed."

Oliver stood and motioned to Conley as a soft knock on the door heralded fresh tea. Giancarlo busied himself tending to Mrs. O'Shea, and Oliver's anxiety climbed as he considered possible options.

"Sir," he said quietly to Conley, "if you were going to abduct someone and keep them from view, where in this city would you take them? I imagine there are poorer areas, workhouses, unsavory spots where people might turn a blind eye for a few coin."

Conley nodded. "I've spoken with local officials, and constabulary are searching Old Town and pockets outside the city." He scratched the back of his neck, and Oliver noted the signs of fatigue and stress on his superior's face. "What of this 'Gus' fellow? He seems to have contacts in nearly every nook and cranny I search. Ought I to send men with him? He may be the best resource here."

Oliver nodded. "Do you know where he is now?"

"No, and he is easily lost in a crowd." Conley frowned. "I've heard something about him I'm finding difficult to believe."

"That he is not . . . alive?"

The confusion on Conley's face was comical. "How can it be, though—"

"I'm learning there are many things about that part of the population we've yet to understand."

"He'd make a fine detective."

Oliver nodded. He thought of Gus's easy movements through the countryside, of his network of people who trusted him and with whom he traded favors and information. "I must find him. If anybody can track her, I believe he can."

Oliver left the ISRO building, promising to check in with Conley every hour. They met several times as the day wore on, comparing notes and marking spots on a large map of the city, places they had looked but failed to find any trace of either Lysette, Emme, or even Gus. He thought he spied his brother in the crowded streets more than once, but quick chases proved fruitless.

The skies were gray, and a light rain sprinkled intermittently. Throngs of people enjoying the festivities popped open umbrellas and continued visiting tents and buildings that hosted contingencies from various countries. Music sounded from multiple establishments up and down the Royal Mile and along Princes Street Gardens. The gardens were full to bursting with people from all walks of life, enjoying games, treats, and trying foods from foreign lands.

He was famished and weak and realized it only when he

received a message from Miles that he and their friends were meeting for a quick dinner.

He met up with them but didn't stay; Isla and Daniel went with him to purchase a meat pie from a vendor, and they searched together while the others ate at the hotel. They set up a command center of their own in Sam and Hazel's room, and between that support and his communication with Conley and law enforcement, he had a sense of which ground had been covered.

The hours marched forward relentlessly, and as outdoor lights twinkled to life and the daylight faded into darkness, the world seemed to celebrate in cozy oblivion while Oliver held on to his hope with only the most tenuous of threads. Isla was sick with worry; she was also a person who solved problems with action, and that they were met time after time with blank faces and negative responses was clearly wearing on her.

They separated to cover more ground, but he honestly couldn't imagine a corner of the city that hadn't been combed by now by the small army of people out searching. He trudged toward the old castle, which was lit with torches and played host to a double-stringed quartet that entertained those gathering for the final remarks.

Twelve state representatives and their staffs were gathering for the event, and according to all accounts, were prepared to vote on a multinational agreement adopting new standards and legislation for shape-shifter rights. Oliver swallowed past a lump in his throat when he considered all of the meetings, dinners, gatherings, and festivities Emme had missed. Local news reports splashed headlines that proclaimed the Summit an incredible success, a touchstone, and tremendous beginning to a new era.

News that Emme was missing was also spreading. Giancarlo told Oliver that in the last several days, her absence at multiple events had been remarked upon. Now that a small force of people was out looking for her prompted chatter that was spreading like wildfire. It told Oliver that the world did indeed know who Emmeline O'Shea was and that she was admired more than she knew. The only bright spot was that the entire city seemed to know something had happened to her, and having more eyes looking for her was a good turn of fortune.

He paused at the fountain at the base of the castle, looking up at the outer courtyard, where people were gathering, laughing, and enjoying the music while waiting for the Summit organizers to share remarks. Giancarlo would speak, and musical numbers would follow, but the final time segment before the midnight vote was reserved for Emme.

His eyes burned in earnest now, and he leaned against a tree for support. He put a hand to his chest, rubbing it in a vain attempt to soothe his heart. Never one for poetic drama, he couldn't dispute the fact that it felt as though his heart was made of glass and would shatter into a million shards if Emme was dead.

Suddenly, a hand clamped on his neck from behind, nails digging into his skin.

"Come quietly with me, brother, and nobody will be harmed." Lawrence pulled him from the courtyard with dizzying speed. Mayhem erupted as several figures dressed in formal attire began to storm the area and climb the sides of the castle.

Lawrence's vampires were attacking, and Oliver's blood boiled even as he was dragged along like a rag doll. He hadn't found Emme, but he wouldn't allow his brother to ruin his life. He would fight with everything he had.

Chaos abounded as people ran, screaming, but to Oliver's satisfaction, members of the military who were tasked with security, as well as dozens of constabulary armed with appropriate weaponry responded to the attack. Vampire after vampire fell, and Oliver marked the moment his brother realized they were losing numbers at an alarming rate.

"No matter. You'll be my consolation prize," Lawrence snarled in his ear as he dragged him farther from the castle. "Lysette has hers, and you will die knowing how closely you came to a lovely reunion."

"Not today." Oliver went limp, mimicking a deadweight ploy Emme had once used on him. It gave him a fraction of a second's advantage. As Lawrence paused in surprise, he shoved his elbow hard into his brother's abdomen. He pushed away just enough to reach the new silver knife in his boot and pull it free, but Lawrence knocked it from his hand, sending it flying.

Oliver scrambled toward the knife, but Lawrence lunged at him, fangs extended. Oliver punched and struggled like a man possessed, but Lawrence easily tore the bandage from his neck and reopened the wound. He lifted his head and smiled at Oliver in a grotesque mockery of joy, and Oliver struggled, shoving away with everything he had. Lawrence laughed, and Oliver knew he was going to end him.

Suddenly, a blur of movement pulled Lawrence away from him long enough that Oliver was able to wrench himself free.

Lawrence gasped and stumbled back. Embedded in his chest was Oliver's silver knife, and standing to the side was Gus.

Lawrence sank to the ground, mouth open in a silent scream, and as he fell backward, Gus pulled the knife from his chest. "You are finished," the calm man told Lawrence, who twitched once and then was still, destroyed.

Gus pulled a clean handkerchief from his pocket and wiped off Oliver's knife. "A man shouldn't have to kill his own brother," he said quietly, then returned Oliver's knife to him.

Oliver took the knife, dumbfounded and feeling a profound sense of shock at the diminutive, unassuming little vampire who looked more accountant than warrior.

Gus quickly helped Oliver to his feet. "Sir, I have credible information on Miss Emmeline's whereabouts." He stopped with a sharp intake of breath. "Your throat, sir! We must heal you immediately!"

"Gus." Oliver clutched at his burning neck, feeling the venom again beginning to spread. "Go, find her. Quickly. I'll get help."

By now, a crowd was gathering, and in his periphery, Oliver saw Conley running toward them.

"But, sir," Gus said, "you should be Miss Emmeline's hero!"

Oliver coughed and spat, too dizzy to remain upright. He staggered against the smaller man and then shoved at him.

"Finding her is the priority. We must reach her before Lysette realizes the Cadre's plan has been foiled! If Emme isn't dead already, I fear she will be soon. Go, and do not tell her I've been bitten!"

Gus turned, running through the crowd and out of sight.

Oliver clutched his neck and looked at the castle and surrounding area. Military and police had made quick work of containing the attack. Thanks in part to Gus's information, they'd already doubled security around the gathering of diplomats and dignitaries, and archers armed with silver-tipped arrows had been standing as sentries high on the castle walls.

Oliver dropped to one knee, pressing his hand against the wound at his throat, trying to stop the flow of blood.

Conley rushed up and caught him, yelling over his shoulder for a medic. "Do not even think about escaping your responsibilities now, Reed." Conley was pale, and a sheen of sweat dotted his forehead. "If you leave me alone to deal with Lady O'Shea . . ."

Oliver managed a weak laugh. "She respects you enormously. You'll be fine. How many others wounded?"

"Very few, from what I've seen. No, do not lie down! Stay awake!" Conley shook him, and Oliver wished he would just leave him be for a moment.

Oliver tried to swallow. "Gus . . . might have found Emme. Tell her, tell Emme—"

"Blast it, Oliver! You tell her yourself!" Conley yelled over his shoulder again for medical help.

The venom spread, moving faster than before because of Oliver's already weakened state. His head spun, and a fierce ache throbbed behind his eyes. His grip on Conley's jacket began to slacken, even as he tried to maintain hold. Numbness spread into his fingers, and they slipped from Conley's sleeve.

His thoughts turned to Emme. If Gus could reach her in time, she would still be able to address the assembly. Even if Lysette had hurt her, as long as Emme was conscious, she would fight to take her place before the midnight vote.

"Don't tell her about me until after . . . after she speaks . . ." Oliver mumbled to Conley.

"What did you say? Stay with me, man!"

". . . so proud. So proud of her . . . proud to have been her protector . . ."

Conley cursed, yelling again for help, but the sound faded away until Oliver felt nothing but blissful calm.

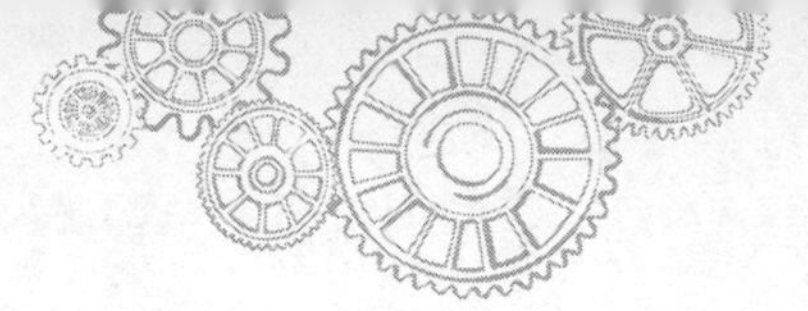

Chapter 21

Emme's fingers were bloody and raw as she tried one last, desperate time to unlock the gate with the long hatpin she'd found in the portmanteau. Lysette had removed the pair of shears Emme kept inside, and her tool options were limited. She'd been able to free herself from the manacle using the pin, but the entire plaster cast, already weakened from running in the rain on wet ground, finally cracked and broke. She'd wrenched the thing from her foot, nearly passing out from the pain. Her ankle was swelling again, and her skin showed a dark array of bruises and scrapes.

Her eyes were gritty, and she'd drunk the last of the water and eaten the rest of the crackers in the tin she'd shared with Oliver only days before. She'd been able to keep the small fire going by burning the stool, but it was nearly out now. She'd given up on the worry she might attract an enemy by screaming—she'd been yelling for hours, to no avail. Three mice paused outside the gate and twitched their whiskers at her, but otherwise she was alone.

The pin was bent and broken until it was almost too small for her to insert into the mechanism. She was forced to thread her hand through the bars, though they were so close together the angle was nearly impossible to manage. Finally, after what felt like hours, she managed to slip the pin directly into the center of the lock.

"Yes!" Her heart jumped, and she bit her lip as she twisted as gingerly as possible. She tasted freedom—was nearly there—when the pin snapped off in the lock and she was left holding an inch of useless metal adornment.

The air left her lungs in a rush, and she fell to her knees, her arm still threaded through the bars and twisting painfully. She barely registered the pain, could hardly think. She pulled her arm back to her side and sank completely to the floor, resting against the gate. The tears did not come. She was entirely numb. She would die in this small room beneath the city.

"Oliver," she whispered, and then the pain hit her with a vengeance that was nearly unbearable. Sobs erupted from her heart, but she was so exhausted the sound was sad and quiet. She closed her eyes, one hand wrapped loosely around a metal bar, and imagined his face. She would think of his face, she would live the few days she had remaining by reviewing every conversation, every interaction she'd ever had with him. She would close her eyes now and leave them closed, and she would imagine him until she breathed her last.

She lay for an eternity against the gate, tears slowing, as she absently hummed a song her mother had sung at her bedside every night when she'd been young. The soft sound echoed through the little room, and she repeated the tune again and again.

"Oh, Miss Emmeline!"

Eyes still closed, she smiled, deciding she was hallucinating. At least she wouldn't be alone anymore. "Gus," she whispered. "How wonderful." She drew in a shaky breath. "I've nothing to offer for tea . . ."

"Miss Emmeline!" Gus's voice drew closer, and she felt a gentle touch on her fingers still wrapped around one of the bars. "Oh, my dear sweet girl, can you move? It took me ever so long, but nobody was certain, and then a few of my sources lied out of fear."

Emme blinked and swallowed. The touch on her hand grew firmer. The light from the fire was nearly extinguished, and she had to squint to make out the features.

She slowly sat up. "Gus? Am I dreaming?"

"Dearest girl, of course not. Oh! We must be quick. You've nearly run out of time, but I've brought some things, and if we make haste, you'll arrive before it's over."

"What? What—"

Gus released her hand and stood up. He had a large satchel with him, and he pulled out a lockpick, which he used to make quick work of the lock. A few seconds later, the gate swung open, and she stood up and stumbled into his arms.

"Gus! How did you find me?"

"Now, now, we must hurry. Poor Mr. Reed is beside himself, of course, and—"

She clutched his arms. "He's alive?"

Gus nodded and pulled the large carpetbag closer. "There's no time, miss. I tasked Miss Josephine with procuring you a suitable dress earlier today in the hope I could finally discover your location." He withdrew a Tesla torch from the bag and switched it on. He set it down on the floor, and it illuminated the space, chasing shadows into the corners. "She included a few other necessities, and we shall do the best we can under the circumstances."

He spied the manacle in the corner. "You were restrained?" His lips thinned. "That woman has some explaining to do, does she not?"

Emme nodded and lifted her aching foot that bore traces of her struggle with the manacle.

Gus winced and tsked, and made a swirling motion with his finger. "Turn around. I'll unbutton and then avert my eyes. At the top of the clothing pile are the layers you'll need; don the first, and I'll help with the rest."

Emme's eyes burned even as a laugh escaped. She felt the darling little man tugging on the filthy dress. The clothing loosened, and he said, "Very well. Hurry, now!"

She looked over her shoulder to see him bent near the fire. As she quickly changed clothing, he poked at the ashes and looked inside her portmanteau. "She burned your precious books and papers?" His voice was as forlorn and dismayed as her thoughts when she considered the loss.

"Yes. I do not know how I shall explain it to Lady and Lord Blackwell." She blinked, rubbing her eyes and wondering if she would ever stop crying. "I'm ready." She sniffled, and he turned around.

He sighed. "She will pay for what she has done." He bent quickly to his bag and pulled out a dress of shimmering ice-blue. As he lifted it, yards of crushed silk and tulle fluffed out to reveal a gown to rival the original her mother had sent with her from Castles'.

"Oh, Gus. It is so lovely."

"Yes, yes. Turn quickly, now." He helped her step into it, tucking her petticoat and shift in place as he pulled it up and helped her thread her arms through the sleeves.

She winced as she looked at the bruises, cuts, and general scrapes from her fingertips to her shoulders. The dress settled into place, resting just at the edge of her shoulders, and fell below the smooth line of her collarbone. As he fastened the back buttons, the bodice tightened like a comfortable glove, and the skirts belled in perfect length to the floor.

He turned her shoulders gently to peruse his handiwork, and she glanced apologetically at her chest and arms. "I am all bruised and messy. Your beautiful dress is wasted on me." She tried to smile but felt very much like crying. "I am not usually vain—"

"Shh, now." Gus took her face gently in his hands. "Dearest girl, you put this dress to shame. Your wounds are evidence of your bravery and perseverance. I heard your song, I saw your efforts at the gate—you never quit. You are a warrior, and I am honored to be called your friend." He took the glass heart pin from his jacket and pinned it to her dress, just above her own heart.

"Oh, Gus." Tears flowed in earnest, and she hugged him gently. "You have saved me, sweet man. I thought I would die in this place."

He patted her back and released her. "Never. You've a life ahead of you, and if we hurry, one very important speech to make. At least three of the gathered dignitaries are still unsure about signing the accord. The truth of Lawrence's and the Committee's villainy in framing the shifter community for various murders over the last months is circulating, but I do not know how many yet believe it."

Her eyes widened. "I've missed some news, it seems."

"We are in the eleventh hour and must hurry. Miss Josephine included a few items in the bag to fix your hair." He tapped his fingertip against his lip. "Come, we shall finish your toilette in the carriage."

She clasped his hands. "Gus, I hardly know how to—"

"Yes, dearest, hold that for later. I've paid a man an inordinate amount of coinage to hold a carriage outside, but we are under quite a labyrinth, and finding our way out may take time."

"How did you find me?" She hopped over to her tattered and dirty portmanteau, determined to take it with her.

"An underground resident led me most of the way. For the remainder, I followed the sound of your voice." He pulled a pair of shoes from his satchel and held them for a moment, studying her. "You'll have to put these on when we get there."

She blinked as he put the shoes back in his bag and snapped it shut. "Underground resident? People live down here?"

He nodded sadly as he offered her his arm and led her quickly from the room. "Nonaggressive vampires have been forced into hiding by the Cadre. Though, we are already seeing a shift in the public's attitude regarding vampires like me versus the Cadre and their ilk."

He led her along the dark corridors, and she gritted her teeth to keep from crying out at the pain in her ankle. She leaned heavily on her escort, who took the brunt of her weight. He had them turning and twisting so many times she would have been hopelessly lost even had she managed to break out of her room. The feel of the place was oppressive, heavy, and she commented on it to Gus.

He nodded. "Haunted. Which is why I could find only one person brave enough to walk me through it."

Eventually they heard voices echoing through the corridors, and Gus walked her past people who seemed to actually live down there. She was horrified for them, and as they nodded to Gus, she said, "We must do something about this."

He smiled and nodded back to the underground residents. "I was hoping you would feel that way."

A cold blast of air swept through the tunnel, and he led her upward and out into the night. She turned her face to the sky. There was no rain, but she smelled it in the air. Spotty clouds shifted overhead to show a few sparkling stars blinking down at her.

"Oh, Gus, how lovely it is—"

"Yes, yes—" He clicked his pocket watch closed and nudged her ahead, mumbling an apology as she stumbled but shoving her forward at the same pace. They rounded a building to see a carriage in the street. It was made of bright, gleaming brass with jeweled handles, large windows, and a lush, red-velvet interior.

She gasped, and her heart jumped, as for a fraction of a moment she imagined it was one of the Yard's brass carriages, which would mean Oliver was nearby. But it was too fine for common criminals. This brass carriage was fit for royalty.

He opened the carriage door and helped her climb inside. "Take us up to the castle immediately," he told the driver. He climbed in behind Emme, and as the coach began to move forward, he once more reached inside Josephine's magic bag of tricks. He withdrew a bag of hair-styling supplies and ordered Emme to turn in the seat.

"Quite a mass of tangles, isn't it?" he asked.

"I'm afraid so."

"Hmm. Very well, we shall use it to our advantage."

He pieced and pinned, taking segments of knotted hair, twisting and braiding some, and before long, pronounced the result satisfactory. "The snarls actually provide volume," he commented as he reached into the valise for a small water canteen and cloth. "Not bad." He looked critically at her hair from one side and the other as he dampened the cloth with water.

"Oh, you'll want a drink, perhaps?"

She gratefully took the canteen and swallowed a large gulp of water, and he began dabbing and then scrubbing at her cheek until she felt much as she had as a young girl when her mother had cleaned her face vigorously every night after a day full of escapades outside.

"I wonder if my mother is here," she murmured.

He paused and looked at her. "Is she here? Dear girl, she has run the Chief-Inspector ragged turning this city upside down to find you. She is desperate to see you." He continued working on her face, then stopped and eyed her critically. "One more thing. For the princess that you are." He reached back inside the bag and pulled out a thin tiara, a double line of small diamond chips in a silver circlet that he nestled carefully in her hair. "Subtle, not ostentatious, but will twinkle just so in the light."

"Oh, Gus." Her throat burned with emotion.

"And the shoes." Gus handed her a pair of beautiful high-heeled shoes that sparkled with encrusted stones that looked like starlit diamonds.

"They're lovely," she said and smiled. She slipped the right shoe on her foot, and then, as the carriage moved forward, studied the other. Given how swollen her ankle was, there was no way the shoe would fit.

"Perhaps put it on just before you speak," he suggested, patting her knee.

She grasped his fingers and held his hand tightly, looking out the window at the sparkling city, profoundly grateful to be alive and not locked in a quiet, solitary tomb. She leaned closer to the window, watching the people who milled around the streets amidst the light and the music despite the late hour.

The carriage was beautiful, the cushion like a cloud, and she clasped her shoe in one hand and her gentle savior's hand in the other. She looked at Gus with wide eyes, hoping to keep the tears from falling and making tracks along her face. "Gus, thank you." She kissed his cheek, and he closed his eyes with a nod and a smile.

"Dear lady, it was my pleasure. I have learned more about you today—wonderful things—and am amazed at your humility. You are quite a celebrity, did you know? Your disappearance has been news for days."

She shook her head. "I didn't know. I'm glad to have been missed." Her brow creased in worry, though, when she thought of Lysette. "My mother, my family, may not be safe from Lysette. Have you heard from Madeline? Or Mr. Crowe?"

"The Chief-Inspector has placed additional security around your family, and the hunt is on for Miss Lysette." He paused as though carefully choosing his words. "Mr. Lawrence has been dispatched." He patted her hand. "You are not alone in this—it has become much bigger than we imagined."

"And Oliver?" She swallowed. "Where is he?"

Again, the small man paused, and a curl of dread snaked up her spine.

"When I last saw him, he was near the castle courtyard. I cannot speak to his current whereabouts, but I give you my word that I will find him the moment we deliver you to your destination." He was serious but sincere, and she had little choice but to trust him.

The carriage continued toward the ancient castle that sat alongside a cliff, the water down below. They neared the castle base and climbed upward, the crowd parting for the carriage as they traveled.

Finally, it rolled to a gentle stop, swaying as the driver descended from his perch. Emme looked at her forlorn carpetbag, her faithful portmanteau that had held priceless treasures inside. "Gus, she burned my notes, the pages I'd prepared for this speech." Apprehension shot through her. "I've never spoken to a gathering of such significance, and after all of this, what if—"

"Shh, none of that." He patted her hand and gave her fingers a gentle squeeze. "The words you need to share tonight are in your heart, not on a paper."

She looked at his kind, serious face and closed her eyes as he kissed her forehead. "Now, off you go, princess. Your time is here."

He passed her through the door to the driver. Clutching her shoe with one hand and the driver's arm with the other, she walked to the base of the stairs and began to climb. When they reached the top, she thanked him, and he offered a deep bow before disappearing back down to the carriage below.

She took a deep breath and turned her face into a soft breeze, feeling the chill but welcoming the fresh air. A few moments more brought stronger winds, and she realized she should make for the relative shelter of the common area where people had gathered to hear final remarks.

She leaned down to slip her foot into the shoe only to lose her grip and watch as it tumbled down the stairs. A small cry of dismay escaped her lips. The staircase was empty, with guards down below preventing anyone else from ascending.

She heard voices in the courtyard where the esteemed group was gathered. Her shoe lay too far away to retrieve, and time was running out. She turned to the courtyard and slipped off the other shoe. The stone was cold on her feet, but she hardly felt it as she made her way through the arched opening.

Heads turned toward her, faces showing shock and then delight. A murmur spread through the small crowd and grew in volume. She spied Giancarlo, who clapped his hands and leapt forward with a cheer. He grasped her to him and led her to the podium, where the Summit director smiled at her in surprise and said, "She is here, after all!"

She had hidden her remaining shoe in the folds of her

skirt and dropped it carefully behind the podium. She ran her hands along her midsection, trying to still her nerves as exclamations of delight flowed from the crowd through the courtyard and down the stairs. She licked her lips, feeling bruised, battered, and utterly overwhelmed.

It was so much to absorb. Less than an hour ago, she'd been locked in a cavern, and now she stood at the castle. Carlo was the only familiar face in the crowd, and she wished desperately that Oliver and her family were there. She knew as she spied a clock that had been placed on the podium to monitor time, however, that her moment was at hand and would pass whether or not she uttered a word.

She cleared her throat, took a breath, and smiled. "Esteemed ladies and gentlemen, it is my honor and privilege to speak with you on this momentous occasion. My name is Emmeline Castle O'Shea, and I represent the International Shifter Rights Organization . . ."

Chapter 22

" . . . going to check with the other inspector . . . young woman in custody matching Miss Lysette O'Shea's description . . ." Conley's voice sounded through a fog that Oliver tried to navigate. His limbs were heavy, his eyes burned, and his throat felt like sandpaper.

"Keep an eye on Detective-Inspector Reed, do you understand?"

"Yes, sir."

Oliver heard the soft whisper of a tent flap closing, and for a moment, he wondered why the Chief-Inspector was with him in India. His thoughts tumbled and churned until he finally broke the surface and cracked open his eyes and saw a pair of young constables standing guard over him.

He shoved himself up on one elbow and then to a sitting position with a groan, feeling much as he had when he'd awoken in Lawrence's carriage. With sudden clarity, his memories shuffled and then slammed into place, and he realized he was in the makeshift medical tent near the castle.

The constables looked at him uneasily.

"Sir, ye've had a horse's ration of anti-venom. Ye need rest," one of them said.

He nodded, but the movement hurt his head. "I will tell Chief-Inspector Conley that you both performed your duties admirably, but I must be on my way. Have either of you seen a small man named Gustavsen?"

They shook their heads, and his heart sank. He looked at his pocket watch and swallowed in grief and disappointment. The time was at hand, and unless Gus had managed a miracle, they had lost.

He pushed himself to his feet and noted his bloodied, filthy shirtsleeves and vest. He located his suit coat at the foot of the cot and shook it, failing to brush away most of the dirt, and shrugged into it anyway. He bent his head and exited the tent, standing still for a moment while the world spun.

The outer courtyard was still a hub of activity, wet but not under a deluge of rain, and he walked across it numbly, moving because he didn't know what else to do. He must find Gus, and if Emme wasn't with him, Oliver would turn the city inside out until he found her. He needed to think, but his brain was a tangled mess. He felt nauseated and quickly moved to the base of a tree where he lost whatever was in his stomach. He heard a woman squeal, and a man's chastising *tsk* about knowing when one more drink was too many.

Wiping his mouth with his handkerchief, he focused on doing nothing except slowly inhaling and exhaling. A young man who was manning a food stand approached with some water and held it to Oliver at arm's length. Oliver accepted it gratefully, rinsed his mouth, and then took a long drink.

He straightened and stretched muscles that screamed

with the aftereffects of vampire venom. He'd been injected twice in the last forty-eight hours, and he knew enough to be grateful he was still alive. He slowly made his way toward the castle, thinking to wait there for Gus. If he didn't show soon, Oliver hoped he would return to their hotel room.

A murmur swept through the crowd at the base of the castle, and Oliver looked up. He was unable to see much from where he stood, but then chatter and exclamations of surprise sounded from above, and he thought he heard Giancarlo's exuberant voice. He didn't know how the man could even manufacture joy when Emme was missing.

He massaged the back of his neck and stopped at a large fountain, dipping his hands in the cold water and then scrubbing his face and hair. He couldn't fault Carlo for maintaining his professionalism. The man had a job to do whether Emme was there or not. This thing was bigger than any one person. Even if that one person was the one who meant the world to Oliver.

He moved to the base of the stairs, irrationally angry at the happy people all around him. He leaned a shoulder against the cold stone, reflecting on the structure that had seen a thousand years of human drama and would likely see a thousand more. He rubbed his eyes and sighed, resting his head against the rock.

His gaze fell on an object halfway up the staircase. He narrowed his focus and realized it was a shoe. Someone had lost a shoe unaware? Who would do that in such cold temperatures, on wet ground, and not notice it missing? Another shout came from above, followed by laughter and scattered applause.

He began climbing the stairs, only to be stopped by a pair of security guards. He fumbled impatiently in his pocket for his identification before flashing it at the men, who nodded at him.

He continued climbing, reached the shoe, and picked it up. It was delicate, stylish, and small. Just the right size . . . and it was for a left foot . . .

Calling himself a million times a fool for raising his hopes, he climbed the rest of the stairs increasing in speed until he was running and dizzy by the time he reached the top. Security guards at the upper courtyard entrance attempted to bar his way, but he stared daggers at them, and fortunately, one guard recognized him.

"Sir," he said, nodding, and allowed him to pass.

He crept forward, moving toward the wall to avoid the crush of the crowd, and heard someone speaking.

". . . I represent the International Shifter Rights Organization . . ."

A buzzing sounded in Oliver's ear until he felt faint, and the closer he moved to the arched entrance, the farther away it seemed. He finally reached it and, hugging the wall, peered inside.

She was alive, and whole, and speaking. She was a vision of loveliness that stole the breath from his lungs, and his knees buckled. He clutched the shoe in his hand as he leaned against the wall for support. After a moment, he quietly skirted around the entrance and crept to the shadows in the back.

Emme.

Her image blurred through his tears, the ice-blue of her dress glowing, and he blinked, bringing into focus her black hair, beautifully accented with a tiny band of jewels that twinkled with movement.

His heart turned over when he realized the smudges along her collarbone, her jaw, and her forehead were bruises. She smoothly lifted her hands to emphasize a point, and he noted long scratches and bruising around one wrist. What on earth had she been through?

She wove a spell in the courtyard that seemed to isolate it from the world, filling it with words that carried with them her sense of love and justice for those she represented. An energy threaded from person to person, spreading a shared sense of grief and outrage at the personal examples she shared. She discounted the crimes erroneously attributed to the shifter community by the Committee, and by her and Oliver's individual families.

She held the assembly riveted, spellbound, and while he'd experienced pieces of that enthrallment over the past several days with her, to hear her present a cohesive, protracted yet concise argument for a cause that affected real lives was unimaginably powerful. He understood her power, the reason her enemies feared her. Her compassion and sense of justice were formidable, and because she possessed a gift that allowed her to share it with hundreds at one time, she was truly a force.

So much love in a tiny frame. He watched as she delivered a powerful appeal for an affirmative vote. Her eyes swept those gathered, and she made eye contact with each one. When her gaze finally fell upon him, he could see that her breath caught. He smiled and put his hand on his heart, his vision blurring behind tears. She smiled back, and he heard a few audible sighs as she finished her speech with respect and gratitude for those gathered. She inclined her head and stepped back from the podium.

Applause was instantaneous, with those assembled coming to their feet. She seemed stunned and put her hand to her midsection. Giancarlo joined her at the podium, as did the Summit president, who thanked her profusely and presented her with a huge bouquet of irises and lilies.

Oliver glanced to the side, gratified to see their friends gathered, all except Miles, and realized they must have entered just before he had. He hadn't seen them because he'd only had eyes for Emme.

He released a deep breath as the crowd settled, and a member of the international body announced that they would vote immediately, which was met with another round of applause. Once the excitement settled, the dignitaries seated at the front of the courtyard began a roll-call vote. There were twelve representatives, and each one voted in the affirmative, pledging that their countries would protect the rights of shifters within their borders and continue to work for the betterment of all beings worldwide.

The applause was deafening, and Oliver leaned against the wall for support, clutching one small, fancy shoe. Emme stood close to Carlo, who was propping her up, and her tears flowed unchecked, along with her laughter. She had done it. Against all odds, she had delivered her heart and bright mind to the world, and they would all be better for it. Suddenly all of the protests, rallies, unrest, and disruption that had marked his early association with the woman took on a beautifully sentimental hue.

He loved her more than life. He would endure every last battle with her for an eternity if it meant staying by her side.

Word spread like wildfire down the castle stairs and into the lower courtyard and then into streets beyond. Cheers could be heard for miles, and as the clock struck midnight and the dignitaries signed their names to a ceremonial document with large, plumed pens, fireworks exploded in the sky. The moment was magical, a miracle, and as people moved and embraced and laughed and cried, he caught glimpses of Emme. She looked so incredibly small, and her bruises attested to treatment at Lysette's hands he did not want to contemplate just yet, but she stood straight, hands occasionally clenching against pain, and he realized she was probably the strongest person he knew.

She moved into the crowd and was swarmed by her sobbing mother, friends, and several foreign visitors who awaited an introduction. He smiled. He was weary and sore from head to toe, but as he watched Emmeline, he'd never been happier.

Gus joined him, smiling ear to ear.

Oliver put a grateful arm around the man's shoulders and thanked him profusely. "We could not have done this without you. We all owe this success to you."

Gus shrugged, modest to the core. "We have all played a vital part in this week's success. I am honored to have helped."

"You should know, my Chief-Inspector may offer you a job. I hope you would consider it."

Gus chuckled, his eyes lighting up behind his round spectacles. "I will. I have work to do here first, though. There are people living in the underground who are ready to leave the shadows. I imagine the Cadre's supply of Vampirical Aid will make plenty of options available for those who choose it. We will all be held to the same code of law, and perhaps some of this darkness will pass away."

Oliver nodded and clapped him on the back. "Again, friend, thank you."

"I should think you've every right to swoop into the fray and take her away." Gus nodded to Emmeline with a twinkle of pride in his eye.

Oliver smiled. "I can wait. This is one time I shouldn't pull her out of the crowd."

Emme said something to Isla, who nodded and looked around. Isla spied Oliver and Gus and then whispered back to Emme, whose head whipped up. She followed Isla's pointing hand and locked eyes with Oliver. With a quick murmur to Isla, she shoved a pen and some paper in her cousin's hands and limped her way through the crowd to Oliver.

He met her at the edge of the throng and pulled her gently into his arms, clasping her to him and spinning her slowly in a circle. Her arms squeezed tightly around his neck, and he heard her breath catch.

"Oliver. I love you." She lifted her head, and he still held her close at eye level. "I love you." Her tears fell freely. "I thought you were dead. And then I thought *I* was dead. And all I could think was that you had died not knowing I love you. I never said it, and I am so sorry." She held his face in her hands and kissed him through her tears, heedless of the crowd around them. Her actions drew a few whistles and cheers, and she laughed and kissed him again.

"I have a confession," he told her. "I knew you loved me.

In fact, I believe you have loved me for months. Long before I became your bodyguard."

She rubbed her nose against his. "Hmm. I will admit to finding you moderately attractive, even when you were my worst enemy. Of course, I told myself you were hideous, but there are some things one eventually cannot deny."

He smiled. "I have another confession."

She raised one brow. "Oh?"

"Yes. The very first moment I saw you, refusing to exit a PSRC carriage, I thought you were the most stunning woman I had ever seen."

"Truly? I find that highly unlikely."

"No, it is a fact. Prettiest by far. And then the loudest." He grinned as she put her hands in his hair and lightly pulled.

As the revelry continued around them, he walked a short distance to a bench near the archway and set her down gently, then sat next to her.

"I swore that when I found you, I would never let you go again. So I don't care that we aren't in a quiet spot, all alone and romantic." He wrapped his arms around her, and she put hers around his neck.

"Oh!" She straightened and unfastened a glass heart pin attached to her bodice. "I entrust to you, Detective-Inspector, my heart." Her eyes filmed again, and she laughed, tipping her head as though feeling self-conscious. Her lip trembled, and she bit it impatiently, a light frown creasing her brow. "My own heart of glass, gifted from our dear friend, and now from me to you. I've never been anything but transparent with you, Oliver, and I hope you see in my heart the admiration and adoration I hold there for you." She paused and sniffled, then whispered, "This heart is quite fragile, you see, and I want you to realize how incredibly vulnerable I feel in handing you possession of it. But truly," she continued, her voice unsteady, "I believe it was only ever meant to be yours." She gently fastened the pin to his dusty, tattered lapel.

He clasped her hand and pressed it gently to the spun-glass heart, which rested against his chest. "And you must know by now that I am meant to be yours—mind, body, and soul. It has only ever been you, Emmeline." He thumbed away a tear from her cheek. "It is fitting," he continued, "that I ask you this in a crowd full of people celebrating the advancement of shifter rights, considering we first met at a similar event."

She tipped her head, a smile glinting in her eyes. "Oh? And what are you going to ask me? Here in this crowd of people."

"Emmeline, will you marry me?" He cleared his throat past the lump that had suddenly formed.

"Absolutely, I will." Her eyes were soft and bright. "I love you. I will love you forever."

"Then marry me tonight."

She blinked. "Tonight?"

"Now."

"Now?" She paused, eyes wide. "*Right* now?"

"We almost died today. Multiple times. In fact, over the last several days, we have repeatedly faced death. If this trend continues, we'll be gone by morning, and I want at least a few hours as your husband."

"Do not even tempt fate!" She frowned. "You do have a point, though. But we cannot just get married on the spot."

"Certainly, we can. We'll go to Gretna Green; it's not far at all. Or, we are surrounded by dignitaries and more than a few heads of state, all of whom are enamored of you and would likely be delighted to perform the ceremony." He paused, aware of the role reversal. He was rarely, if ever, impetuous. "If you would rather a more formal engagement, I will impatiently wait until we return home."

She laughed. "When have I ever been enamored of formality? My friends and family are already here, but the only one I care to have in attendance is you." She looked at him, stilled, and took a quiet breath. She released it slowly and leaned forward to place a soft kiss on his lips. "Lysette told me you were dead. I was so afraid. I think I shall be afraid of the dark forever."

He'd wondered how long it would be before she would tell him what had happened after Lysette took her from the lodge. They hadn't had a chance to talk, and while he prided himself on being a patient, rational sort, he wanted to wring Lysette's neck with his bare hands. "Shall we go somewhere quiet? You can tell me what happened."

She shook her head with a sigh. "We've time enough for that, I suppose. And if nothing else, I've discovered who wrote the Bad Letter."

"Lysette."

"You knew?"

"Lawrence told me. We might have guessed. Conley has her in custody—she has much to answer for. She and Sir Ronald will be transferred to jail cells in London soon." He paused. "You may be called upon to testify."

Her lips firmed. "I will do it gladly. Oliver, the things they have done . . ."

He nodded. "They will pay."

She wrinkled her brow. "Have you heard from Madeline?"

He shook his head, and she bit her lip.

A trio of teenaged boys scrambled past, bumping into them, and Emme sucked in her breath. "Stupid foot," she muttered. She lifted her hem and showed him her bare feet.

He pulled her shoe from his coat pocket. "I found this one."

She laughed softly and took it from him. "It may be some time before it fits. I am afraid I will require new bandaging. The manacle ruined my cast."

"Manacle?" He closed his eyes and cupped her head, kissing her forehead. "I really am going to kill her."

Shc pulled back and scowled. "I am going to become equally violent if you persist on kissing my forehead. Or pat my hand."

"It is because I am feeling tender," he said, surprised.

"That is all well and good, but a kiss on the forehead falls short of the mark. Or, rather, misses the mark."

The corner of his mouth ticked upward. "I thought we had determined you are not an exhibitionist."

She rolled her eyes. "I've already kissed you several times in the last few minutes. I suppose one of us must be the forward-thinker. We are at the dawn of a new age, after all, and—"

He cupped her head again, this time bringing her lips to his in a kiss that lasted long enough to draw the attention of the crowd, who again applauded and laughed. They broke contact, and Emme pulled back, smiling and laughing, her cheeks red.

"Never call my bluff, Miss O'Shea." He smiled, smug.

"Oh, I fear I must. If I don't, you might become complacent. Bored with me."

He chuckled and shook his head, arms tightening around her. "If I knew nothing else from the first moment we met, it was that life with you would never, ever, be dull."

"And you love me for it," she murmured in his ear, her tone almost a question.

He took her hand again and pressed it against the glass heart she had given him. "I love you for it. I love you for you. Forever, Emmeline."

She sighed. "Forever."

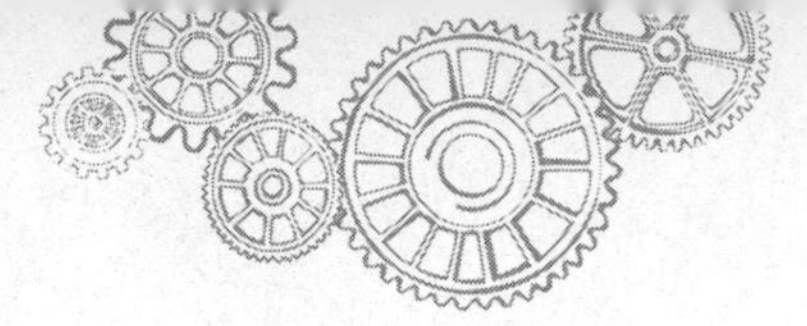

Acknowledgments

This book was so much fun to write, and while I am usually relieved at the end of the process, I was reluctant to let Emme and Oliver go. While they were keeping me company, though, my family held down the fort and, as always, my love and thanks to them: Mark, Nina, Anna, Gunder, Shayla, Thor, and Snooki. Our little home is a castle for me because they are in it.

Many thanks to the Shadow Mountain team: Lisa Mangum, Heidi Taylor Gordon, Callie Hansen, Troy Butcher, and Chris Schoebinger for sharing these stories with the world. I am forever grateful. A bonus thank-you to Parrish Gordon and Spencer Hyde for their creative suggestions for this book's title. I'm certain they would have helped the book sell like hotcakes, but many thanks to Callie for coming up with final version, which is truly lovely.

To Bob Diforio and Pam Howell, you are both so supportive and helpful, and I am so grateful for the two of you. Thank you, as always.

A bajillion thank-yous to my writer friends. The Bear

Lake Monsters (Cory Anderson, Marion Jensen, Suzy G, Krista Jensen, Becki Clayson, Annette Lyon, Sarah Eden, Margot Hovley, Chris Todd Miller, Evelyn Hornbarger, Robison Wells, Josi Kilpack, and Jennifer Moore) have and continue to be not only writing support but friends. And to new friends from the Hidden Springs Writers Retreat, what a joy it is to become acquainted with you all.

To Josi Kilpack and Jennifer Moore, I could not do this without you (or if I tried, it would take a million years and would be lonely and sad). You are sisters of my heart, and I love you.

To my readers, you are the most wonderful support. I cannot tell you sincerely enough how much it means to me when I get alerts that someone has tagged me on Instagram and has wonderful things to say about my books. This is a subjective business, and sometimes book reviews really sting. That you take the time to tell me when you like my stuff is a gift for which I am constantly grateful.

Discussion Questions

1. *Brass Carriages and Glass Hearts* is a steampunk retelling of "Cinderella." What elements of the fairy tale are present in both stories? Where do the two stories diverge?
2. Emme is passionate about speaking out about rights for the shifter community. What issues are you passionate about? What are some ways you are helping your community be more united?
3. Emme's stubbornness often gets her into trouble—but it also means she never gives up, even when things are hard. What are some qualities others may view as negative that might also have a positive application?
4. Oliver was a captain in the military, and later, a well-respected police detective who reveres law and order. Emme is his opposite in many ways. Do those opposite qualities help or hinder their developing relationship?
5. Gus is a nonviolent vampire who simply wishes to live in peace. He and others like him wear a glass heart to symbolize their unity. If you could design a badge or a pin to

symbolize what matters most to you, what would it look like?

6. Both Oliver and Emme are stubborn when it comes to recognizing their feelings for each other. What kinds of things are you stubborn about that have made seeing the truth difficult?
7. The world of Victorian steampunk is all about inventions and innovations. What innovations have you found the most interesting? What would you invent for this world?

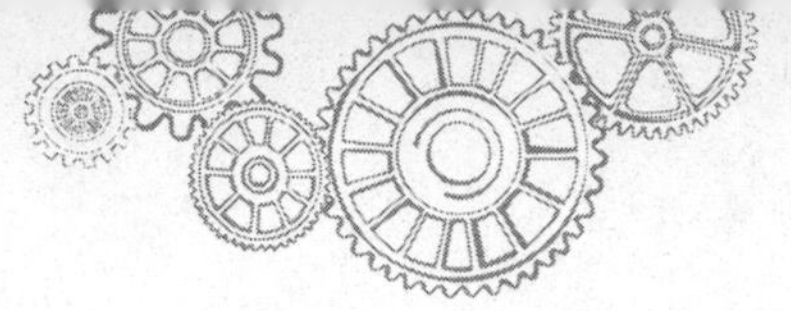

About the Author

Nancy Campbell Allen is the author of seventeen published novels and numerous novellas, that span genres from contemporary romantic suspense to historical fiction. In 2005, her work won the Utah Best of State award, and she received a Whitney Award for *My Fair Gentleman*. She has presented at numerous writing conferences and events since her first book was released in 1999. Nancy received a Bachelor of Science in elementary education from Weber State University. She loves to read, write, travel, and research, and enjoys spending time laughing with family and friends. She is married and the mother of three children.

Visit her at nancycampbellallen.com
on Instagram @authornancycampbellallen
on Facebook at nancycampbellallen
or on Twitter @necallen

FALL IN LOVE WITH A

PROPER ROMANCE

BY

NANCY CAMPBELL ALLEN

Available wherever books are sold